A Flight of Golden Wings

Beryl Matthews

Allison & Busby Limited
12 Fitzroy Mews
London W1T 6DW
allisonandbusby.com

First published in 2007.
This paperback edition published by Allison & Busby in 2016.

A CIP catalogue record for this book is available from
the British Library.

10 9 8 7 6 5 4 3 2 1

ISBN 978-0-7490-1808-5

Typeset in 10.55/15.55 pt Sabon by
Allison & Busby Ltd.

The paper used for this Allison & Busby publication
has been produced from trees that have been legally sourced
from well-managed and credibly certified forests.

Printed and bound by
CPI Group (UK) Ltd, Croydon, CR0 4YY

Aetheris Avidi – Eager for the Air
Motto of the Air Transport Auxiliary

Chapter One

September, 1938

There wasn't a cloud in the sky. It was the kind of day Ruth Aspinall's brother had loved. The pain of loss gripped her as it always did when she thought about Robert. He'd had such a zest for life, not knowing the meaning of caution or fear in his search for any new experience, the more dangerous the better. Six months ago his racing car had overturned and he had been killed instantly.

Ruth sighed. What a waste of a young life, and how she missed her big brother. Her parents were inconsolable at losing their adored son – the son who should have taken over as head of the Aspinall family law firm when they'd gone. Now they only had a daughter left. Oh, Ruth knew she had always come second in their affections, but she didn't mind. They loved her in their own way, and she them, but Robert had been their pride and joy.

The grief pervading their home had been too much for Ruth. Even with twenty rooms in the house she hadn't been able to escape it, so she had driven to Yorkshire. Here, in the tranquillity of the Dales, she had finally been able to allow her own grief to surface, and after six days she had found a measure of comfort.

A movement in the air caught Ruth's attention and she shaded her eyes. There was a large bird soaring above her. Some bird of prey, she guessed, but didn't know what it was. It was so beautiful though. She watched in fascination as it dived and swooped, revelling in the freedom. Then it became motionless, hovering on the wind.

Her brother had learnt to fly, and she smiled, remembering his excitement. 'Was that how you felt, Robert?' she called. 'Did you love the freedom as much as that bird does?' She could almost hear her brother's voice telling her how wonderful it was, and urging her to try it.

She continued to watch as the bird climbed and disappeared from sight, wishing she could be up there with it. The longing almost made her cry out as she turned and ran to her car. She would learn to fly.

The drive back to London took three days. She had taken it slowly for a reason: Ruth was not in the habit of making hasty decisions, and she wanted time to be sure this was what she really wanted. Her emotions had been at a very high pitch and she wanted to be sure that learning to fly wasn't just a reaction to losing her brother – a desire to emulate him in some way. That wouldn't be right; her character was more cautious, and she had often tried to instil that trait into Robert as he had set out on one dangerous adventure after another. But he had only laughed at her in his teasing way.

By the time Ruth reached London there was not the slightest doubt in her mind. It was now a burning ambition, and there was only one person to see. Simon Trent was a friend of the family and had been her brother's instructor. He was highly regarded as a pilot. She would see him before returning to her home in Virginia Water.

It was another beautiful day as Ruth drove through the gates of Heston Airfield and stopped outside the office of the flying school. She got out of her car and gazed around in surprise. The place was alive with activity. She had often come here with her brother, but it had never been this busy. A loud shout caught her attention and she couldn't help smiling. A young man had just tumbled out of a plane, waving his arms around excitedly. He had obviously just flown solo for the first time. Ruth felt the buzz and excitement around the place and her smile broadened. Oh yes, she was going to do this.

'Hello, Ruth,' a quiet voice behind her said.

She spun around, still smiling. 'Simon! I wasn't sure if I'd be able to see you. It's so busy I thought you'd be in the air with a pupil.'

'I've got an hour before my next appointment.'

'Oh, good. I've come at the right time then.' Another plane was preparing for take-off and one more was waiting its turn. 'Why are you so busy?'

'The government is encouraging young men to learn to fly.' Simon sighed deeply. 'There's a war coming, Ruth, and we're going to need all the pilots we can get.'

She had heard the speculation, of course, but Simon sounded so sure. 'It might not happen . . .'

'No, it might not, but we have to be prepared. What's going on in Germany is worrying, to say the least.' He studied Ruth intently, his bright blue eyes curious. 'How are you, and what brings you here today?'

'I've just come back from Yorkshire after a few days on my own. I needed to get away and try to come to terms with Robert's death.'

'And it looks as if you've made your peace with the tragedy.'

'I've finally accepted it. The quiet and solitude helped enormously. Now I feel I can get on with my life. That's what Robert would have wanted. He always said that every moment of life was precious and should be lived to the full. I do wonder if he had a premonition that he would die young.' Ruth sighed. The sadness was still with her and always would be, but at last the pain was easing.

'He had a reckless streak, Ruth.' Simon's expression was thoughtful as he studied her. 'So what are you going to do now? You're an intelligent girl and could get yourself a good job.'

'I've broached the subject several times, but Father says it isn't necessary. The Aspinall law firm is very successful and I don't need to earn a living.' Ruth grimaced. 'I've always gone along with him for a quiet life, but Robert's death has shaken me up. I'm twenty and tired of wasting my life. It's time to make changes. The first thing I'm going to do is learn to fly.'

'And what do your parents think of that?' Simon asked gently, not showing any surprise.

'I honestly don't think they'll mind. You've been flying

for many years without mishap, Simon, and my parents trusted you with Robert. I'm sure they'll do the same with me.' She smiled wryly at the man in front of her. He was around five foot ten and she only had to tilt her head slightly to meet his eyes – eyes that didn't miss a thing, assessing everything and everyone in his quiet way. But under the quietness there was an aura of strength. At twenty-eight he was a most attractive man, but she had always regarded him as one of the family; more like a cousin. However, if he did ever decide to marry, Ruth had no doubt that he would make a wonderful husband for some lucky girl.

'Robert turned out to be an excellent pilot and was a lot more careful in the air than on the ground.' Simon shoved his hands in his pockets and grinned. 'We had some almighty rows at first, but I eventually managed to instil some caution into him.'

'And my parents know that.' Ruth's expression saddened. 'This has been very distressing for them. When they had a son they were overjoyed and wanted another. They waited eight years before I came along. A daughter was not what they had hoped for, and to their disappointment they never had any more children. They've always loved me and I've never minded that Robert was their favourite . . . But to get back to flying.' Ruth gave a chuckle. 'They'll think I've gone crazy, but it wasn't flying that killed Robert. My parents respect and trust you, Simon, so I don't think they'll complain too much if they know you are to be my instructor.'

Simon lit a cigarette, smoking it in silence as he weighed up the situation. He was halfway through the cigarette and still hadn't spoken.

Ruth became anxious. Was he going to turn her down? She didn't want anyone else to teach her. 'Teach me to fly,' she pleaded, her golden brown eyes gleaming with excitement. 'I really want to do this.'

He blew smoke into the air and regarded her thoughtfully. Then he tossed the cigarette end down and ground it out with the toe of his shoe. 'Well, you're wearing slacks, so come with me.'

Excitement welled up in Ruth and she hurried after Simon as he made for a plane. She knew it was an Avro Cadet, the same as her brother had flown. She almost cried out with joy. He hadn't said no.

He hoisted her up and then climbed in himself, making sure her harness was securely fastened.

'That's tight,' she muttered, trying to control her nerves. She had thought they would just make a booking now. She hadn't expected him to dump her in a plane straight away, but she knew him well enough to guess what he was doing. He was going to see if she was really serious about this. Well, she would show him that she was!

Simon was busy taxiing the aircraft and merely ignored her remark, but she was sure she saw his mouth twitch in amusement. Under that quiet exterior there was a wicked sense of humour, and her insides clenched when she wondered what the hell she had let herself in for.

As they left the ground, Ruth gasped, and much to her shame, closed her eyes tight. Simon's deep chuckle made her open them wide. She was glad he was in the instructor's seat and couldn't see her face. 'Well, I've never been in a plane before! Robert wanted to take me up, but I refused.'

'He was a good pilot, Ruth. In fact, he was one of the best pupils I've ever had.'

'He was good at everything he did.' The familiar pain of loss welled up in her. Robert had always been urging her to try flying, enthusiastically trying to convince her that it was a truly wonderful feeling to soar in the air as free as a bird.

Ruth's mouth set in a determined line. She was going to be a good pilot as well.

Apprehension drained from her as she watched the ease with which Simon handled the plane. She began to look around her. What she saw took her breath away. There were a few small clouds, which looked like puffs of cotton wool, and the ground was laid out below them in a patchwork of many shades of green, with patches of gold from the ripe corn.

'Oh, it's beautiful!' she whispered in awe.

'Nothing better on a day like this,' Simon agreed. 'Now, let's see if you're really serious about learning to fly, shall we? And if you've got the stomach for it.'

The little plane banked, slipped sideways and then dropped, making her gasp. When she was sure they were going to hit the ground, Simon climbed again.

The next few minutes were incredible as Simon put the plane through a series of manoeuvres. My God, she thought, he's doing part of his air show routine! She had watched him perform many times, wondering what it must feel like to be tossed about like that. Now she knew.

She experienced an overwhelming sense of exhilaration as they spun around in the air. If Simon was endeavouring to make her change her mind, then he hadn't succeeded. In fact he had done just the opposite. She tipped her head back and laughed with glee.

Much too soon for her they were landing. She would have to get back up there as soon as possible.

Simon taxied back to the office, jumped out and helped Ruth down. She was glad of the help as her legs were shaking rather, but she was determined not to let him see it. It was only excitement, not fear.

'Nice show, Simon,' another pilot called as he walked past with a pupil.

Simon just raised his hand in greeting.

Ruth stood with her hands on her hips waiting for Simon to turn his attention back to her. When he did she tilted her head to one side. 'Were you trying to frighten me, Simon?'

'Hmm. I don't think I succeeded, did I?'

'Ah, you guessed that, did you?' she teased.

'I knew it the moment you shouted at me to do that again.' He was laughing and shaking his head.

Her eyes opened wide. 'I never did!'

'I assure you that's exactly what you did.' He was obviously amused, but his expression showed only respect.

'I don't remember shouting out.' She'd known she had loved every minute of the flight, but was quite unaware that she had acted in such an unrestrained manner. It wasn't like her at all. 'I loved it. You're going to have to teach me, Simon.'

He nodded and urged her towards the hut they used as an office. 'The first thing we'll have to do is curb all the excitement once you're in the air. A good pilot is a safe pilot, one who remains focussed, calm and in control whatever the situation.'

'I understand.' She watched him flick through the appointment book, feeling more light-hearted than she'd done for some time. She was going to learn to fly. That was a start. The next thing would be to find some kind of a job. She'd had enough of wasting her life, and now she wanted to do something useful and fulfilling. Robert's death had been a brutal wake-up call.

That evening Ruth watched her parents with affection as they read the papers after dinner. It was a lovely evening and the doors were wide open, allowing the soothing sound of birds and the perfume of roses to filter into the sitting room. They had been so pleased to see her and she had felt relieved to find them looking more composed than when she left. Terrible as the tragedy had been, it had happened, and nothing could bring Robert back. It was time they all got on with their lives, as her brother would have expected of them. Nothing was going to be the same again, and that fact had to be accepted.

Ruth gazed out at the garden, drinking in the beauty. It was only early September so there was still a profusion of colour. Her mother loved gardening and Ruth knew it had given her some solace as she'd tried to cope with the loss of her much-loved son. Her thoughts drifted back to her flight with Simon and a smile touched her mouth. She had her first lesson in two days' time and couldn't wait. Simon had drilled into her just how much work it was going to be to gain her private pilot licence. He had insisted that she would have to learn how to maintain the aircraft – which would entail getting her hands dirty, he told her dryly. Navigation was another requisite. It was no good messing about in the air if you didn't know where you were going.

Ruth's chuckle at the memory of Simon's lecture had her parents glancing up.

'What's amusing you, my dear?' her father asked, a smile lighting up his tired face.

'I called in to see Simon on my way home—'

'Oh, how is he? Why didn't you bring him home?' Her mother's affection for Simon showed. 'We haven't seen him for weeks.'

'He was busy with pupils. The airfield was a hive of activity, but I managed to catch him when he had an hour to spare. He said the government was encouraging men to learn to fly.'

Her father nodded, his eyes troubled once again. 'The feeling is that there could be a war and we had better be prepared. Pilots will be needed. Poor devils, these young men don't know what they might be letting themselves in for.'

'Do you really think we'll go to war with Germany again, Father? Surely Hitler won't take the risk?'

'Who knows?' Her father shrugged. 'He's a fanatic, and fanatics are notoriously unpredictable.'

A deep sigh came from her mother. 'If it does come I hope Simon keeps out of it.'

'He won't be able to, my dear, and I doubt he would want to.' George Aspinall laid aside his newspaper and turned to his daughter. 'Let's hope it's all talk, shall we?'

Ruth was relieved the subject had been closed. Now was the time to talk seriously to them about her future. 'I'm sure you're right, Father. It's the immediate future I've been thinking about. I want to find a job.'

'You can help me with my charity work,' her mother suggested. 'We're always grateful for willing hands.'

'Thank you, Mother, but I want to earn my own living. I've relied on you and Father for far too long.'

'You know you don't have to worry about that, Ruth.'

'But I do. Couldn't you find me something to do in your offices? I don't care what it is.' Ruth's eyes gleamed as she teased, 'Don't you need a tea girl, or a filing clerk?'

A look of horror crossed her father's face. 'I'm not having my daughter running around at everyone's beck and call! Why don't you go back to university and study law?'

Ruth grimaced and stifled a sigh of exasperation. This subject had come up before, but quite honestly she had no interest in law, as she'd quickly discovered during her time at university. 'I don't want to go back to school. I'll ask Simon if I can work at the flying school while he's teaching me to fly.'

There was a stunned silence as her parents studied their daughter in horror.

'Pardon?' her father growled. 'Did I hear you correctly?'

Ruth cursed herself for dropping that news so carelessly. It wasn't what she had planned at all, but she had spoken without thinking. 'I've asked Simon to teach me to fly and he's agreed.' She leant forward, her expression pleading for understanding. 'I'm wasting my life, and I just can't go on like this.'

'But what use will flying be to you, darling?' Alice Aspinall looked thoroughly confused.

'I don't know, but it's something I really want to do.'

Her father cleared his throat, the first one to recover. 'You say Simon's going to be your instructor?'

She nodded. 'I start in two days' time.'

George looked steadily at his wife. 'Simon's a good pilot, my dear – one of the best. Ruth won't come to any harm with him. We ought to give her our blessing in this endeavour.'

'Of course, you're right, my dear.' Alice straightened her shoulders. 'We always gave Robert full rein to follow his dreams, and we shouldn't stop our daughter doing the same.'

Ruth leapt to her feet with joy, rushing over to hug them both. She had always known they were kind, loving people, but this showed what immense, unselfish courage they had.

'Oh, thank you!' she said gratefully. 'I promise I'll be careful. I'll be the safest pilot there is in the air.'

Chapter Two

As Ruth walked towards the plane for her first lesson she felt excited, but there was also an absolute certainty that this was what she was meant to do. It was a strange feeling, but she had always followed her instinct. Robert had teased her about it constantly. A smile touched her lips as she thought, I'll show you, Robert. One day this will prove to be the best thing I've ever done.

Simon had just spent half an hour outlining what lay ahead of her. If he considered she was going to make a good pilot they would work towards her 'A' licence. Then she would have to log 100 hours solo before trying for the 'B' licence. He had said firmly that if she were serious about this then he expected her to do the thing properly. He was clearly expecting much of her, but that had only increased her determination to succeed. She knew some women flew at air shows and took passengers on paying fun trips, so the prospect was exciting.

However, that was all speculation at the moment, she reminded herself, climbing into the plane. Simon had just been opening the possibilities to her. Everything depended upon her ability as a pilot.

Once in the air Simon ran through the controls again, then told her to take over. 'Stay below the clouds, Ruth, and fly straight and level.'

She followed his instruction, revelling in the thrill of being given a chance so soon. Her concentration was total, listening to the quiet voice of her instructor when she needed to make adjustments to keep straight. It was comforting to know that he would take over in a second if she did something wrong. That knowledge increased her confidence.

The first lesson was only thirty minutes, and when they landed they went straight to the flying school office.

Ruth waited patiently while Simon filled in details of her first flight. When he looked up, she asked eagerly, 'How did I do?'

'Too early to say.' Simon sat back and regarded her thoughtfully. 'But you were calm, obeyed instructions and made necessary adjustments without hesitation. You seemed to have a good feel for the controls, but only time will tell.'

She blew out a breath of relief. Simon's assessment was encouraging, and she knew he didn't waste unnecessary words by saying things he didn't mean. 'Thank you.'

His expression was serious. 'I want you to try and go solo by the end of the month. If you can do that then we'll consider taking the next step. But bear this in mind, Ruth: if you do want to progress to the 'B' private pilot licence, then you'll be doing it during the winter months. It won't be easy, but I'll help you all I can.'

'I know that, but I promise I'll give it all I've got.'

He got to his feet. 'I can't ask for more than that.'

'Simon, is there any work I can do in the office or around the airfield?'

'I know this is going to be expensive, so do you need to earn money to help with the costs?' His expression was understanding. 'I realise that you won't want to ask your parents for help.'

'Oh, no, it's nothing like that. They would help, but I don't need to ask them for financial help. I'm in the fortunate position of being able to pay my own way. It's just that I would like something useful to do between lessons. I'm tired of being a lady of leisure.'

'Do you mind what you do?'

'No, I'll take anything. I offered to be a tea girl in my father's law firm, but he refused.'

Simon tipped his head back and laughed. 'I'll bet he did. Well, I'm snowed under with paperwork and I'd appreciate your help for a couple of days a week. I'll pay you, of course.'

'That's marvellous, thank you, Simon.'

Over the next four weeks, Simon watched Ruth carefully. It was clear she was enjoying the lessons, and her eagerness to get in the air increased with every flight. He'd had serious doubts about Robert's little sister learning to fly. She had always appeared to be a dedicated socialite with nothing to do but enjoy herself, but he was fast revising that opinion;

he now suspected that that was no more than a facade. He knew whenever she had voiced the desire to do something useful, her parents had just waved it away, telling her to go out and have some fun. Robert's death had obviously shaken her and made her take stock of her life. There was a new Ruth Aspinall emerging. She was happy to help in any way she could around the office, and Simon was happy to pay her for that. Paperwork was not his favourite job, and she was a skilled organiser. But more importantly, she was showing a real feel for flying, revelling in each new manoeuvre she mastered, and showing none of her brother's reckless nature.

He sat back away from the controls and said quietly, 'All right, Ruth, take her in.'

With a quick smile she turned for the approach. Her height and speed were all good, but the thing he was most impressed with was her concentration. It was total. He wished some of the boys he was teaching had the same ability. She was going to make a damned good pilot.

The plane touched down with a smoothness even he would have been proud of. At that moment he made up his mind. Jumping out as soon as they had stopped he shut the door, tapped it twice with his hand, and nodded to her. It was time for her to go solo.

'Now's your chance, Ruth, show me what you can do.' Then he walked away from the plane, leaving her on her own for the first time.

When Simon reached the flying school hut, he turned. She was already taxiing into position. Phil, another instructor, joined him. 'Is she ready, Simon? Many of the eager boys don't go solo this quickly.'

'She's ready.' Simon spoke with confidence. 'She's a family friend. I wouldn't dare let her do this if I had the slightest doubt.'

The men watched in silence as Ruth took off, circled the airfield a couple of times and then made a good landing. 'Impressive,' Phil said.

Simon's smile spread. 'Oh, she's more than that, Phil. Ruth Aspinall was meant to fly and is a first-class pilot in the making.'

As Ruth taxied the plane back to where Simon was standing she was surprised at how calm she had been. He hadn't given any indication that he was about to let her go solo, so there hadn't been time to get worked up about it. Over the last four weeks she had often wondered what it would be like to be alone in the air. Now she knew. It was wonderful! The sheer beauty and feeling of freedom had been breathtaking, and much to her astonishment she hadn't been frightened.

Switching off the engine, she clambered out, determined to be dignified about this and not go mad with excitement. But as she walked towards Simon and saw his smiling face, she knew she had done well, and couldn't help laughing out loud in glee.

'How did I do?' she asked when she reached him.

'Not bad.'

'What do you mean, "not bad"? That was pretty nigh on perfect.'

'No, it wasn't –' Simon held out a bottle of champagne he'd been hiding behind his back '– it was flawless.'

Phil shook her hand. 'Well done, Ruth. We'll have you at

the air shows in no time at all. Wish I could stay and enjoy the drink with you, but I've got a lesson now.'

As Phil walked away, Simon draped an arm around Ruth's shoulder. 'Two of my students have cancelled so I've got some free time. What say we go and break the good news to your parents? We could crack open the champagne with them.'

It was a fine Saturday afternoon and they found George and Alice Aspinall in the garden. Ruth was grateful for Simon's presence to help her with this news. Her parents had been very supportive of her desire to fly, but she knew they worried, even though they tried hard to hide it.

'Simon, how lovely to see you!' Ruth's mother greeted him with obvious affection, for he had been a regular visitor to their home when Robert was alive.

'Hello, Mrs Aspinall.' Simon kissed her cheek and then shook hands with George. 'How are you, sir?'

'Fine, fine.' George studied his daughter's flushed face and saw the bottle of champagne. 'It looks as if we have something to celebrate.'

'We have!' Ruth's excitement bubbled over. 'I've just flown solo for the first time.'

'Oh, that's wonderful, darling!' Alice stood up. 'We must indeed drink to such an achievement. I'll go and get some glasses.'

'Well done, my dear.' Her father smiled proudly. 'And you've done it so quickly.'

'Ah, well, Simon's the best instructor anyone could have.'

'He certainly is.' George winked at Simon. 'A good student then, is she?'

24

'Very good.' Simon popped the cork when Alice returned with the glasses and then poured the champagne. He held up his glass. 'To Ruth. That was an excellent solo flight. From what I've seen so far, I believe you have the makings of a very good pilot.'

'Thank you.' This was high praise from a man who didn't waste words. To be told that she could reach such lofty heights in his eyes was more than she had dared to hope for.

'Sit down,' George urged, then turned to his daughter. 'Tell us all about it. Were you nervous?'

'No, Simon didn't give me the chance. He just jumped out of the plane after we'd landed and told me to show him what I could do.'

'And she did.' Simon refilled their glasses, but left his own. He had only taken a couple of sips for the toast. 'No more for me. I have three more lessons today.'

'What comes next, Simon?' Alice squeezed her daughter's hand to show her how pleased she was for her.

'Ruth is good enough to go for her "A" licence. I will now take her through everything necessary to pass the tests. Once that's done she will be able to do cross-country flights to log up 100 hours solo so she can apply for the "B" licence.' Simon faced her, his expression serious. 'All this will take a great deal of study and practise, but if you approach it with the same dedication and enthusiasm you have shown so far, you will be able to do it.'

'I won't let you down, Simon.' That he had such trust in her ability was overwhelming, and she would work hard over the next few months. She wanted to succeed in this more than she had ever wanted anything in her life.

'I know you won't, Ruth. If I had any doubts I wouldn't be pushing you like this.'

'I suppose you'll want me to buy you a plane, Ruth?' George gave a mock sigh, but his mouth twitched. 'As long as you promise not to land on our lawn.'

That made everyone laugh. The Aspinalls' garden was a picture, and the lawn perfection in emerald.

'I wouldn't dare, Father.'

Ruth's mother looked at Simon with concern in her eyes. 'Things are getting nasty in Germany and there's much speculation about war. What do you think will happen, Simon?'

'I really don't know. The signs aren't good, but we'll just have to wait and see how things work out. I don't think anyone knows which way Hitler will jump next.'

'Oh, it might not come to anything.' Ruth didn't like to see her mother so concerned, but she knew Alice followed the news avidly and was no fool. She was clearly digesting each development and weighing up the situation.

'Still, it's something we need to watch. If the worst happens I suppose you'll go in the RAF, Simon? They'll be crying out for pilots with your experience and skill.'

'I expect they will, and it would be an obvious choice for me.' Simon glanced at his watch. 'I won't make a decision until I have to. See you tomorrow, Ruth. You must get in as much flying as possible while the weather's good.'

'I'll be there at nine,' Ruth told him.

After saying goodbye, they watched Simon walk away, and Alice frowned. 'He's being kept busy teaching, isn't he?

The government must think that war with Germany is a possibility and they want as many pilots as possible.'

'Just a precaution, my dear; it's sensible to be prepared.' George drained his glass and smiled at his daughter. 'But enough of this gloomy talk or we'll spoil Ruth's special day.'

'Of course.' Alice's expression cleared. 'I've always been such a worrier, but I'm very proud of our daughter, the pilot!'

Simon had been right when he'd said that the next few months would need complete dedication. As the autumn turned to winter the flying became more and more difficult, and many days Ruth prowled the airfield begging the clouds to lift, rain to stop, or strong winds to drop. She spent almost every day waiting for the weather to clear enough for her to take off. Simon did his best to keep her busy studying navigation, learning about the engines and, in her spare time, helping him around the office.

Ruth was overjoyed when she was given her 'A' licence early in December. But it wasn't until the end of May 1939 that she finally succeeded in earning her 'B' private pilot licence. The required night flight had been tough, and although Simon had flown with her along the route a few times, she had still been terrified that she would get lost. But she hadn't, and her sense of achievement had been enormous. Her parents had thrown a large party in her honour, and now appeared to be quite happy that she had chosen to fly. Any misgivings they might have were carefully hidden and she loved them for that. Knowing what had happened to their son must make them anxious that their daughter was now pursuing such a dangerous pastime. One thing she knew they were happy about was the fact that her instructor was Simon. They trusted him as a pilot and knew he wouldn't allow her to take unnecessary risks.

However, there was a blot on her happiness. They were living in troubled times and speculation about war was growing. Ruth couldn't help wondering if all her effort might turn out to have been wasted. If the country did go to war then pilots like her would be grounded. The men could fly for the RAF, of course, but there wouldn't be anything for women with a private licence.

With this in mind, Ruth spent as much time flying as possible, logging up hours while she had the chance. In the summer months she went with Simon to a couple of air shows and enjoyed them very much.

But everyone was edgy, wondering what the future held.

On the 3rd of September they found out. Britain was at war with Germany.

Chapter Three

Nothing was happening! When war had been declared there had been a flurry of activity as the RAF had taken over the airfield and they'd had to move the flying-school planes. Ruth had helped Simon and Phil to fly them to a base in Cornwall where they would stay for the time being. After that, many pilots like Ruth had been grounded, and the happy days of flying wherever they pleased were over.

She gazed around the garden. It was a riot of colour as flowers of every kind burst into bloom and lifted their faces to the sunshine. Christmas had come and gone, and the New Year of 1940 had arrived to an uncertain future. Now it was spring and such a lovely day. Tipping her head back Ruth studied the clear blue sky. The longing to be up there again was like a physical pain.

'They're calling this the phoney war.' Alice joined her daughter in the garden and smiled as she enjoyed the lovely sight of so much colour.

Ruth jumped. She had been lost in thought and hadn't heard her mother come out. 'Yes, but I don't suppose it feels like that to the boys in France. Things aren't going well, are they?'

'No, it's worrying. Your father thinks this is the calm before the storm here, and things could get very nasty soon. I hope he's wrong.'

'Hmm.' Ruth watched the birds and sighed deeply. 'I thought I might join the WAAF, Mother. I can't hang around doing nothing. It's driving me mad.'

'They don't fly, darling,' Alice pointed out gently, 'and I know that's what you want to do. What about this Air Transport Auxiliary you were telling us about? They've taken on some women, haven't they?'

'Only eight, and they are all instructors with a lot more flying hours than I've logged.'

'Why don't you try them before you make a decision? I don't believe you would be happy in the WAAF.'

'They've got my name on their list, but I don't hold out much hope. There are strong objections to women flying planes in wartime.' She gave a dry laugh. 'At least if I join the WAAF I'll be near planes and be able to weep all over them.'

'Bad as that, is it?' Alice slipped her hand through her daughter's arm.

'It's terrible. I feel bereft and lost. Simon must have felt like this when he failed his physical for the RAF.'

Alice shook her head. 'I think it's ridiculous to fail someone with Simon's flying experience and ability just because his eyesight isn't perfect. I know he does wear glasses for close work, and what difference is being colour-blind going to make? And he didn't even know he had that problem.'

'No, it's never bothered him. But at least the ATA have snapped him up.'

'I know you've explained it to me, Ruth, but what exactly do they hope to achieve?'

'The idea is to utilise pilots with private licences, and that includes some airline pilots, I believe. They are to be used in case of emergency for communication, delivering medical supplies or patients to hospitals, and generally being useful in any kind of an emergency. Planes also need to be ferried from manufacturers to airfields all over the country.' Ruth shrugged. 'There are plenty of women who could do that, as well.'

'Is it a part of the military?'

'No, they are all civilians who have signed a contract to do this work.' Ruth looked at her mother and smiled. 'So what do you really think about me joining the WAAF?'

'That's up to you, darling. You must do what you feel is right for you, but I would urge you not to make a hasty decision.'

At that moment they heard the sound of footsteps on the gravel path and saw Simon walking towards them, looking very smart in his dark blue uniform with gold wings embroidered on the jacket. He also had dark circles of exhaustion around his eyes.

'Simon!' Alice smiled. 'We were just talking about you. Were your ears burning?'

He grinned and held out an envelope to Ruth. 'I've been asked to deliver this to you in person.' She frowned. 'What is it?'

'Open it and see.'

'I'll go and make some tea. Come inside and sit down.' Alice patted Ruth's arm and then walked back in to the house.

31

'Well, don't you want to know what's in the letter?' Simon asked when they were settled in the living room.

The envelope was neatly typed and rather official looking, but there was nothing on it to indicate who it was from. Puzzled, Ruth glanced at Simon. 'What is this, and why have you delivered it by hand?'

Simon sat back, his eyes gleaming in amusement at her hesitation. 'Stop fussing, Ruth. Read it and then all your questions will be answered.'

Without further delay, she slit open the envelope and removed a single sheet of paper. She had to read it twice before she could actually believe what she was seeing. She didn't know whether to laugh or cry.

Alice returned with the tea, and when she noticed her daughter's stunned expression, asked, 'What is it, darling? I hope it isn't bad news.'

It took a while for Ruth to find her voice, so great was her excitement. She spoke in a breathless rush. 'It's the ATA! They've asked to see me. They're going to take on more women pilots!'

This astounding news was too much for Ruth and she was on her feet, reading the letter again – just to make sure. 'Oh, Simon, tell me this is true. Tell me I'm not dreaming!'

'It's true.' Simon leant forward. 'They've decided that women pilots can ferry the trainers and release the men for other types of aircraft.'

'We could fly anything,' Ruth declared with confidence.

'I know that, but don't rush things. Get in first and see how things develop after that.'

She nodded. Simon was sensible, as always. She waved

the letter. 'They're asking me to go for an interview next week at Hatfield. Do you know how many more they are taking, Simon?'

'I'm not sure, but I think it's only five or six at the moment.'

Ruth grimaced. 'What do you think my chances are?'

'I can't answer that,' he told her. 'But you have a number of things in your favour. You have a 'B' licence and have taken a navigation course. You've also done quite a bit of cross-country flying, so that will help. Don't forget to take your log books.'

'I won't.'

'Don't look so worried. I believe you're just the kind of pilot they're looking for, and I've told them so.'

'Oh, thank you!' Ruth's doubt faded as excitement took over. 'I'm sure your recommendation will help enormously.'

'You'd have got in eventually.' Simon rubbed a hand over his eyes. 'Things are not going well in France, as you know, Ruth. A lot of RAF boys have been doing ferry work, but they are now needed as operational pilots. If the signs are correct, then the ATA are going to need all the pilots they can find, male and female.'

'That is good news.' Alice smiled at her daughter. 'I told you to wait before joining the WAAF. You'll be much happier if you're flying, won't she, Simon?'

'Absolutely. You'd have found the WAAF very frustrating, Ruth.'

'How are your parents, Simon?' Alice handed him a cup of tea. 'I haven't seen them for a while.'

'They're fine. Dad's rushed off his feet with the practice. He's just lost his junior doctor to the army.'

'Oh dear. Is he still cross with you for not going to medical school?'

'No, I think he's come to terms with the disappointment, and is even showing some interest in my flying now.' He stood up. 'I must get back. Don't worry, Ruth. Fly in your usual calm and efficient way and you'll sail through the tests.'

With Simon's advice fixed in her mind, Ruth made her way to Hatfield on the appointed day, determined to become a member of the ATA.

She was early and stood by a window watching the planes landing and taking off. It was very busy and there was an air of urgency about the place. No one believed they were being told the whole truth about the situation in France, but it was clear that the Germans were advancing. Ten days earlier on 10th May Winston Churchill had become prime minister and the Germans had invaded Holland, Belgium and Luxembourg.

Ruth's mouth firmed. She had skill as a pilot and was going to damned well use it, she thought. A Magister landed and the pilot stepped out carrying a parachute and headed for the building. The door swung open and a diminutive girl walked in, tossed her parachute on a chair, and then grinned at Ruth.

'Hello, my name's Tricia.' They shook hands. 'God, I'm gasping for a cup of tea.'

'I'm not sure if there's any around. I'm waiting to be interviewed for the ATA.'

'Ah, good, we need more women pilots.'

The door opened again and another woman looked in. 'Tricia, can you take that Magister you've just brought in up to Lee-on-Solent? It's urgent and you're the only one back so far. There's a Tiger Moth waiting there for you to bring back.'

'Oh, and there I thought you were going to ask me to collect a Spitfire!' Both women laughed at the joke. 'I'll just go and check with the Met to see what the weather's doing, then I'll be on my way.' Tricia was already grabbing her parachute and taking some papers from the other woman.

'Don't take any chances with the weather, Tricia. Keep below the clouds.'

The girl nodded in agreement and headed for the door, where she paused and looked at Ruth. 'Good luck. I'll see you around soon, I expect.'

'I really hope so.'

Then she was gone and Ruth was alone again. As the Magister took off and disappeared from sight, she shook her head. Tricia hadn't managed to grab a cup of tea before she'd left. Ruth fidgeted. She wanted to be a part of this so much it hurt.

There was no more time for thought as Ruth was called in for the interview and then taken on a short flight to assess her handling of a plane. She felt she had acquitted herself well, but couldn't help feeling a pang of disappointment when told that she must go to White Waltham for a final test in a few days' time. She had been hoping to get everything settled today, but she was well aware they had to be sure they were going to get a competent and reliable pilot. The women especially were under scrutiny, because some people still believed that women shouldn't be doing such work. Ruth didn't know how many women they had asked to see, but it was certain that she wasn't the only one.

On her way home, Ruth mulled over Tricia's joke about delivering a fighter plane when they were only allowed to fly the trainers. The women must be finding that frustrating, knowing that many of them were more experienced pilots than a lot of the young men now taking to the air . . .

Before Ruth's test at White Waltham, Calais had fallen and the evacuation of Dunkirk was under way. Britain was now in a desperate situation as they tried to rescue the army from the beaches. She hadn't seen or heard from Simon and guessed that he was busy trying to keep the RAF supplied with planes. Her desire to do something to help was increasing with every piece of news she received.

'Do stop pacing, darling,' Ruth's mother urged. 'Your test is tomorrow, then you'll soon be flying again.'

'Sorry I'm so restless, Mother.' Ruth grimaced. 'I hate standing around doing nothing.'

'I know you do, and you've always been the same. Even as a little girl we could never keep you still, but I think we'll all have plenty to do soon.'

Ruth sat down, frowning fiercely. 'What's going to happen to us now? Will Hitler just continue his advance and come straight across the Channel?'

'He'd be a fool not to.' George Aspinall entered. 'But we all know he's unpredictable, and the Channel won't be that easy to cross. My guess is he'll attack by air first.'

For the rest of the day Ruth helped her mother in the garden. This wasn't her favourite activity, but she would do anything to pass the time before her test. And the beauty of the garden helped to ease the worry about the future.

She spent a restless night praying that the weather would be good enough to take the test, and was relieved when morning dawned clear and bright. She was keyed up and had no intention of failing.

When she arrived at the airfield, the examiner wasted no time in taking her up. He said very little except to give her instructions to carry out certain manoeuvres. The only indication he gave after she'd landed was a brief smile and to tell her that she handled a plane well.

Then it was back home to wait again.

The evacuation of Dunkirk ended on the 4th of June, and by some miracle hundreds of thousands of British, Commonwealth, French and Belgian troops had been rescued. To snatch so many from the beaches was an astonishing achievement, but everyone was conscious that the Germans were on the other side of a narrow strip of water.

During the next two weeks, Ruth waited impatiently for the post to arrive. She was sure she had done well in the tests, but didn't dare hope too much, for she knew that if she received a rejection the disappointment would be crushing. She had also been told that the ATA were expanding the women's section and were examining quite a few applicants. She was up against quite a lot of competition and they would be careful about making the right selection.

At last the letter arrived and she couldn't help giving a little jig of delight. She had been accepted and had to report to Hatfield in three days' time.

After telling her parents the good news, Ruth began to pack a small bag, taking only the essentials and two decent dresses, just in case they had time for a social life.

'Didn't you say you had three days before you needed to report?' Ruth's mother came in and frowned at the case on the bed.

'I'm going straight away to see if I can get digs near the airfield.' Ruth smiled to soften the news. Her parents were going to miss having her around, but so many families were facing the same situation. 'I want to get settled first.'

'Of course you do, and that's very sensible,' Alice agreed. 'I'm sure if Robert were still alive he would already be in the RAF.'

Ruth gave an affectionate laugh as she remembered her brother. 'And he'd be right in the thick of things as a fighter pilot.'

'Be careful, darling.' Alice couldn't hide her worry.

'I will, and please try not to worry too much.'

'You know you're asking the impossible of your mother.' Her father joined them. 'Are you taking your car?'

'No, I haven't got enough petrol so I'll leave it here. I'll go by train.'

'Stay and have lunch with us and I'll take you to the station.' George picked up her case. 'I'll put this in my car.'

Ruth agreed to stay for lunch, although she was eager to be on her way – eager to become a part of the war effort and get back in the air again.

Chapter Four

After a rather lengthy lunch, Ruth arrived at her destination later than expected, so she booked a room for the night in the local pub. She dumped her case and went straight downstairs to see if she could get a meal, and while she was enquiring, Tricia came into the bar with another girl.

'Ruth, isn't it?' Tricia smiled broadly when Ruth nodded. 'Nice to see you again. This is Ellen.' Tricia introduced her friend, then said, 'I'm guessing that you've been accepted for the ATA?'

'Yes, I start in three days' time, but thought I'd come early and find somewhere to stay near the airfield.'

'You can share with us, if you like,' Ellen offered without hesitation. 'We rent a cottage just down the road.'

'Oh, thank you!' Ruth was delighted, called the landlord over and cancelled her room right away. He then rustled them up a meal of homemade vegetable soup with hunks of bread.

All conversation stopped while they enjoyed the meal.

'Oh, that's better,' Ellen moaned as she mopped up the last of her soup. 'I haven't had anything but a quick sandwich since breakfast. I've done three deliveries today and a lot of hanging around.'

Tricia laughed. 'The longer the daylight hours the more we can fly, and the way things are going we'll get even busier.'

Ellen nodded, then turned to Ruth. 'We need more pilots, so you are very welcome, but you don't know what you're letting yourself in for.'

'I don't care. I just want to fly.'

'Same as all of us, and we love every minute of it. We are now going to be allowed to ferry all types of non-operational aircraft, like Tigers, Oxfords and Masters.' Tricia gave a satisfied nod at Ruth. 'You've come in at the right time because we can now go to the RAF Central Flying School at Upavon for conversion courses.'

Ruth's eyes opened wide at this news. 'I didn't know that. What are the chances of getting on the course?'

'Ah, another eager one. Just what we want,' Ellen said. 'I expect most of us will eventually do the course because they want to take the men off the trainers so there will be more of them to ferry the operational planes.'

'It's a step in the right direction.' Tricia stood up. 'Come on, Ruth, collect your bag and we'll get you settled in.'

The cottage was small, with two bedrooms and a bathroom upstairs, a tiny kitchen and lounge downstairs. There were two single beds crammed in each upstairs room, and a put-you-up in the lounge. Just outside the back door were four bicycles – for anyone's use, she was told. The whole place had a disorganised but homely feel about it, but the garden was another matter. It was a riot of beautiful flower beds and a lawn her mother would have been proud of.

'My goodness!' Ruth gasped. 'Who's the gardener?'

'Not us.' Tricia held up her hands in horror. 'If I dare touch a plant it withers and dies. Our next-door neighbour, Jim, looks after it for us between his Home Guard duties. He takes a fatherly interest in his flying girls.'

They went back to the kitchen and Tricia put the kettle on to make a pot of tea. 'Take any bed you like, Ruth, while I make some tea.'

The front door slammed and a girl walked in. After tossing her bag on to a chair, she said, 'Oh, good, you're making tea – I'm gasping. Can I bunk here tonight?'

'Of course you can.' Ellen found enough cups and put them on the table. 'Gussie, this is Ruth. She'll be joining us soon.'

'Great to meet you.'

Ruth tried hard not to wince as they shook hands. Tricia and Ellen were not quite as tall as her five feet six, but Gussie was a tall, strong girl with pale blonde hair, and blue eyes that gleamed as if everything was a big joke.

With cups of tea in their hands they trailed into the lounge and settled down. The rest of the evening was hilarious and Ruth couldn't remember when she had laughed so much. She heard tales of getting lost in bad weather, dodging barrage balloons – the pilots weren't allowed to mark such defensive positions on their maps for fear they'd fall into enemy hands – not being allowed to stay at operational airfields because there weren't any facilities for women, and the astonishment of the ground crew when they saw a woman climbing out of a plane that had just landed. But underneath the laughter, Ruth could detect the determination of the women to prove they were capable of the job – and more, if they were allowed the chance. They flew with care to get the planes to their destinations without damage. They had to prove they were as good as the men, if not better. As she listened, Ruth was proud she was about to become a member of this extraordinary group of women.

The next two days were an education for Ruth. Tricia and Ellen disappeared, but there was a steady trickle of women coming and going. It seemed that this was an open house for any female pilot stranded for the night.

On her first day, Ruth reported early and after having assured those in charge that she had digested the standing orders – she would stay within sight of the ground at all times and not fly when the weather was bad or go above the clouds – she joined the rest of the girls to await instructions for the day's work. She didn't have a uniform yet, but she was wearing a pair of navy blue slacks and a light blue blouse.

Everyone was just hanging around, talking, reading, and a couple were even knitting away as fast as they could. After staying at the house, Ruth now knew a few of the women. There was a tall, red-haired woman standing on her own with her hands in her pockets and gazing up at the sky. Ruth walked over to her and smiled. 'Looks like good flying weather today.'

'Yes, it does.' The girl tore her gaze away from the sky and turned to face Ruth. 'I'm Harriet. Have you been with the ATA for long?'

'My name's Ruth and this is my first day. How about you?'

Harriet rubbed her hands together in anticipation. 'Mine as well, and I can't wait to get going.'

They grinned at each other, understanding the eagerness.

Suddenly there was activity as the chits were handed out. Ruth had to collect a Tiger Moth from the manufacturers and deliver it to Luton.

A Fairchild had just landed and when it came to a halt they all piled in. These were being used as taxies to take the pilots to the pick-up points, and would, hopefully, bring them back here at the end of the day's work. But there was no guarantee of this. Many things could happen. If the weather closed in at any time they might have to land at the nearest airfield and stay overnight, continuing their journey when flying conditions improved. On the advice of the more experienced women, Ruth had packed a few essentials in a small bag – just in case.

One of the senior women was flying the taxi and they were soon at de Havilland's – the manufacturers – as it was quite close to Hatfield. After dealing with the necessary paperwork, they collected their aircraft and set off. Ruth couldn't resist a yell of delight once she was airborne, not just because she was flying again, but because she was also doing something to help in this war.

The next three weeks raced by, and Ruth couldn't remember when she had been so happy. At first they had given her the shorter trips, but now she was delivering all over the country. It often entailed nights away and the necessity of finding lodgings, but she didn't care: it was all part of the job. On one occasion she'd even had to get back to Hatfield by train. And she had been chosen to go on the conversion course at Upavon. After that she would be able to fly more types of planes.

Ruth frowned and peered through the windscreen of the Magister. Where had that front come from? The weather ahead looked wild and the rain was already pattering down. Mindful of the directive that they must never 'go over the top' of the clouds, Ruth had no option but to turn back. The damned front followed her, being driven by a strong wind, and by the time she reached Cosford, her nearest airfield, the plane was being buffeted about. It was going to be a tricky landing, but the only sensible thing was to get down. The weather had closed in all around her now and she was losing height all the time in an effort to stay below the clouds.

Finally the airfield came into view and she breathed a sigh of relief. She could easily have missed it in this weather. Landing in some farmer's field was not something she fancied attempting.

Using every ounce of her skill, she made a fairly good landing and silently thanked Simon for his excellent teaching.

She taxied towards the buildings. The rain was coming down in sheets by now.

An aircraft engineer yanked her door open as soon as she had come to a stop. He muttered something under his breath when he was confronted with a woman, then said out loud, 'Blimey, miss, this ain't no weather to be flying in! Not even the birds are leaving the ground!' He laughed at his own joke.

She smiled politely, and then they both ran for the building. Just inside the door the man peered at the golden wings on her newly-issued uniform.

'Ah, you're one of them ATAs. We got another one stranded here as well.'

After shaking the rain out of her hair, Ruth looked up to see Simon walking towards her. 'Simon! You're stuck here as well, then. This weather came up so suddenly . . .'

'I'm afraid so. You handled that tricky landing well.'

'Look who taught me.' She was pleased to see him. 'Where were you going before the weather closed in?'

'Back to White Waltham. And you?'

'Shawbury. Hope the weather clears enough so I can finish the journey tomorrow.'

'Hmm, the forecast isn't good. You'll certainly be stuck here for the night.'

She pulled a face. 'I don't suppose they have any facilities here for women?'

Simon shook his head. 'You'll have to look for digs.'

''Scuse me, miss.' The man who had met her plane approached them. 'My mum will give you a bed for the night. I'll take you in my truck, if you like.'

'Oh, thank you very much.' She was pleased she wouldn't have to trail around in the rain trying to find somewhere to stay.

'I'll just go and get the—' He stopped and tipped his head to one side, listening intently. 'Blimey, there's someone else up there, and that plane don't sound none too healthy.'

They all rushed to the window and scanned the sky.

'Another trainer,' Simon remarked, knowing the sound

of just about every engine. 'Do you know of anyone else coming this way today, Ruth?'

'Several, I think. The manufacturers wanted to clear the planes as quickly as possible. It's a busy day, but I don't know who it might be.' She clenched her fists. Someone was in trouble up there. It was only three o'clock, but very gloomy.

'Get some lights out there,' an officer shouted. 'And the fire truck.'

Ruth watched the men running to obey orders, knowing just how difficult it would be to make out the airfield in this weather. She had been lucky and beaten the worst of the storm. If it was a trainer, as Simon said, then it was more than likely to have a woman pilot, possibly one of their group from Hatfield. But who?

'There it is!' Simon pointed to a speck in the gloom, very low and obviously going to try a landing at the airfield.

'Thank God!' Ruth ran to the door with Simon right behind her. 'Finding this place in such terrible weather is like looking for a needle in a haystack.'

The station commander had a pair of binoculars to his eyes, watching the approach. 'There's smoke pouring out of the engine.'

Ruth was sure her heart stopped beating for a moment. She knew just how dangerous the situation was, but all the women were excellent pilots and hand-picked for their skill, so if it was a woman in that stricken plane, then she'd have a damned good try at landing it.

'Here she comes,' Simon murmured. 'The controls are giving trouble by the look of it.'

They watched in silence as the plane hit the field,

skidded along sideways and ended up on its side.

The men were swarming all over it as soon as it came to a halt and were pulling the pilot out. Ruth recognised the blonde hair at once and sighed in relief. 'It's Gussie, and she appears to be all right. Don't shake hands with her, Simon, she's very strong.'

The tall woman reached them and grinned at Ruth. 'Wow, what a ride! The weather was bad enough, but the poor little darling decided it had had enough. Wouldn't do anything I asked. Couldn't gain enough height to bail out.' Gussie studied the crumpled plane with concern. 'I'm sorry I broke it, though. Where are we, by the way?'

'You don't know?' Ruth noticed a group of men listening intently to their conversation.

'Not a clue, Ruthie. I saw lights and headed for them.'

'This is Cosford.'

Gussie looked at Ruth in astonishment. 'Good Lord! I was a bit off course – I was heading for Luton.'

'Gussie!' Ruth burst out laughing, feeling the tension leave her. 'Stop teasing or the men will believe you. You knew exactly where you were.'

The only answer was an amused chuckle as Gussie studied the man standing next to Ruth. 'I don't believe we've met.'

Simon held out his hand and introduced himself. He didn't even wince when Gussie shook his hand. 'I'm pleased to see you've come out of the crash unscathed.'

'In five years of flying that's the only mishap I've had. Are you the Simon who taught Ruthie to fly?'

Simon nodded and flexed his hand, giving a slow smile. 'Ruth warned me you were strong.'

'Sorry, I keep forgetting that I've got a grip like a vice. Good job I have, though, because I had to fight that plane all the way down. She just wanted to nosedive on me, but I told her I wasn't having that.'

A young man brought two mugs and held them out to Ruth and Gussie. 'The commander said to give you both some hot, sweet tea.'

'Oh, thanks, we're gasping.' Ruth drank gratefully and noticed that Gussie's hands were not quite as steady as usual, but the trembling was quickly brought under control. She was more shaken by the crash than she was allowing the others to see.

The young man was still there, eyeing the golden wings on their uniforms. When Gussie smiled at him, he said quickly, 'I want to fly, and I've asked to be trained. Have you all been flying for long?'

Ruth then explained that Simon was an instructor and had taught her to fly, making the lad turn his attention to Simon. 'Are you staying here tonight, sir?'

'Yes, they've found me a bed.'

'Could I come and talk to you later, when I'm off duty?'

'Of course,' Simon agreed.

The young airman pumped his hand with pleasure. 'Gosh, thanks, sir. I'll see you in the Mess later.' He took the empty mugs and began to walk away, then stopped and turned his head to look at Ruth and Gussie. 'I think you're both very brave. There's Germans up there and they could shoot you down. They wouldn't care that you were unarmed aircraft.'

'We do try to keep out of their way, don't we, Ruthie?'

'Most certainly, but if they're around they usually have Hurricanes and Spitfires on their tails.'

After giving a brief nod, he went on his way, apparently impressed by their attitude.

Ruth glanced around. 'Simon, do you know the man's name who was going to find me lodgings with his mother? I can't see him anywhere and I'm wondering if she will take Gussie as well.'

'He's Sergeant Stan Walker.'

'That's me,' a voice said from behind them. 'I've brought the truck up to the door. Mother will be pleased as punch to put you both up for the night. She loves a bit of company.'

Gussie nodded gratefully. 'That's very kind of her.'

'No, trouble, miss. If you'd like to come with me she'll settle you in and then cook you a bit of supper.'

'Oh, we can't take her rations.' Ruth shook her head. 'Is there a pub nearby?'

'No need for that.' Stan gave them a sly wink. 'I've got a bit of extra food in the truck.'

Gussie had rescued her bag from the stricken plane and she picked it up, eager to be on her way. 'I need to get out of these clothes. They stink of burning oil.'

'I'll be leaving at first light if the weather's all right.' Simon helped Ruth with her bag and followed them out to the truck. 'Get back here early and I'll give you a lift to White Waltham, Gussie. You'll probably be able to cadge another lift from there, or pick up a ferry job.'

'Thanks, that would be great. I'll be here at dawn.'

'Me too.' Ruth smiled. 'Night, Simon.'

He nodded. 'Sleep well.'

'I will.'

As Simon watched the truck drive away, the station commander came and stood beside him.

'I'm surprised those two girls weren't killed. What the hell are we doing allowing them to fly all over the country like this? The ATA are flying without radios or arms. It's dangerous enough for the men, but we shouldn't be asking the women to take the same risks.'

Simon glanced at the officer, irritated by his attitude. 'They have all fought to get into the ATA, and are well aware of the dangers. And they're more experienced and probably better pilots than the young men you're sending into battle with only a few flying hours to their credit. It took real skill and nerve for both of them to find this airfield and get down.'

'I'm not disputing that, but couldn't the ATA recruit more men?'

Simon spoke firmly. 'We are trying, but there's a limited amount of men with private licences. Most of the airline pilots have had to leave, and the RAF have withdrawn most of their pilots from ferrying duties. The manufacturers want the planes cleared as soon as possible in case of attack; planes have to go to and from the maintenance units and the RAF have to be supplied with planes. These women are excellent pilots and we need them.'

'I suppose you're right.' The man gave Simon an apologetic smile. 'Sorry, I was brought up to believe that a woman's place is in the home, but the war has changed everything, hasn't it?'

'Yes, it has, and we have to accept that. We need all the help we can get.'

'Again, you're right.' The officer glanced at his watch. 'You'll join me for dinner, Simon?'

'Thank you.'

During the night the storm blew itself out and, eager to be on his way, Simon was pleased to see Ruth and Gussie arrive at first light.

'What were your digs like?' he asked.

'Lovely. Mrs Walker made a real fuss of us,' Ruth told him. 'Mind you, I've had so much to eat my poor plane might have difficulty leaving the ground!'

The girls were in high spirits, laughing and joking together. It was obvious to Simon that they had put yesterday's troubles behind them. That was the past, and this was a new day. He was proud of them. The ATA had chosen their pilots not only for their skill, but also for their temperament.

Ruth checked over her plane with meticulous care, as always, and was quickly on her way. Simon watched until she was out of sight and then headed back to White Waltham with Gussie as a lively passenger.

Chapter Five

North Dakota. August, 1940

'Lucy, will you wing walk for me at tomorrow's circus?'

Lucy Nelson watched her brother stride into the room. 'Why? And where have you been for the last three days? We've got a show tomorrow and you disappear without telling any of us!'

'I've been to New York.' He shrugged out of his jacket and tossed it on a chair.

What was he up to? Lucy knew her brother well and could sense a change in him. There was an air of quiet determination about him – and yes, he was hiding something. But getting information out of Jack Nelson was just about impossible. He would only tell you things when it was all settled. He could be infuriating at times. When he stood in front of her he was a good head and shoulders taller than her five feet five. Then the usual gleam of mirth came into his eyes.

'Well, will you do it?'

She shook her head. 'I've got a better idea, Jack. You go on the wing and I'll fly the plane.'

'Can't do that. The crowd like to see a pretty girl on the wing.'

'Flattery won't work with me, big brother. Where's Sue, anyway?'

'She's having a baby and can't do it any more.' Jack gave his most beguiling smile. 'Come on, do this for me. It'll be the only time because this is my last show.'

Lucy was surprised by this news. Her brother was an ace pilot and lived to fly. 'You're giving up barnstorming?'

'Yep.' He sat down and stretched out his long legs.

Once again, Lucy wondered why she hadn't been born with his elegance. Oh, she was pretty enough with her corn-coloured hair and hazel eyes, but there was something extra special about her brother. While Lucy was mulling this over, their mother came in from the yard carrying a load of clothes that had been drying in the stiff breeze.

'I never thought I'd hear you say you weren't going to fly again.'

'Hi, Ma.' Jack stood up and relieved his mother of her burden. 'Where'd you want these?'

'Just leave them on the table.' Bet studied her son with curiosity. 'So, where have you been, and why are you going on about not flying?'

'I'll still be flying, but not here. I've been to New York to see a man who's recruiting men to fly in the ATA. Next week I'm off to Montreal to take a flying test and conversion course, and then I'm going to England.'

There was a stunned silence as Bet and Lucy tried to absorb that news.

'You're doing *what*?' Lucy gasped, when her mind started to function again.

'I'm going to England.'

'Whoa! Hold on a minute!' Bet sat on the nearest chair as if her legs would no longer hold her. 'You can't go over there! They're at war and the Germans are going to invade any minute now.'

'If they do, then I promise I'll take the nearest plane and fly right back here.' Jack's expression became grim. 'They're fighting for their lives, Ma, and need all the help they can get.'

'I know that.' Bet had recovered somewhat from the shock. 'But they don't stand a chance – everyone says so.'

'I believe everyone's underestimating them. They won't be so easy to defeat.'

'I hope you're right.' Bet gave her son a pleading look. 'But it isn't our war, son.'

'I know that's what some feel, and I understand it seems to be a long way from us, but what do you think will happen if the Nazis gain control of all of Europe? Britain is the only country standing in Hitler's way. He's got to be stopped and I'm going to help.'

From the determined look on her brother's face, Lucy knew that his mind was made up and nothing on this earth would make him change it. That he was going off to another country frightened her, but she was also intrigued. Jack must have been planning this for a while, but had said nothing about it. She wanted to know more.

'Did you say you are joining their air f—?'

Bet interrupted her daughter. 'Please don't do that, Jack. And what's this ATA? I've never heard of it.'

He reached out and patted his mother's arm. 'Don't look so worried, Ma. ATA is short for the Air Transport Auxiliary.'

'But America is neutral: you can't go and fight for the Allies!'

'The ATA is a civilian organisation of pilots with private licenses, not military, so it's OK.'

Now Lucy was more than interested. 'What do they do?'

'They collect new planes from the manufacturers and deliver them to wherever they're needed.'

Bet gave an audible sigh of relief. 'So you won't be in their military?'

'No, I won't, Ma. None of the planes are armed. It's purely a delivery service, but a vital job if the RAF are to be kept supplied with aircraft.'

Lucy went and sat beside her brother. 'Are they only taking men?'

'Lucy!' Bet almost growled. 'Not you as well! Anyway, they won't let women fly in wartime.'

Jack pursed his lips as he surveyed his sister's animated expression. 'There are women in the ATA. In fact, there are women doing all kinds of jobs over there. They are drawing on every resource they have, but they are only asking for men from overseas, at the moment.'

'How did you hear about this?' Lucy was disappointed to discover that only men were being recruited, but things might change later. She must keep a close eye on this organisation. 'And why didn't you tell us?'

'Some of the pilots were talking about it at the last show. A couple are already in Montreal and should be leaving for England any time now.' He paused. 'And I didn't tell you because I knew you'd want to do this as well . . . and you're not going, even if they do start to take American women.'

Lucy bristled. 'Hey, when did you decide to tell me what I can or can't do?'

'Stop it, you two!' Bet hollered. 'You're working up to a fight.'

Brother and sister glared at each other, and then grimaced. They adored each other, but boy, could they erupt at times, both having strong personalities. Their arguments were legendary.

'That's better. Now let's get one thing straight. When your pa died fifteen years ago I was left to bring you up on my own. And I don't think I've done a bad job.' Bet looked smug.

'You're a great mom.' Lucy went to her mother and gave her a hug. 'We've been a lot to handle, haven't we?'

'I can't argue with that, but I'm not complaining, and I've never tried to stop you doing what you wanted. Have I ever objected that the two of you spend your time tossing about in the air?'

Jack and Lucy shook their heads.

Bet grunted in satisfaction at their response. 'Well, I don't like that any more than I like the idea of Jack jumping into the middle of a war – *someone else's war*,' she added pointedly. 'But you're grown now and must make your own decisions, but I'm relieved that Lucy can't go as well – because I know she would.'

The disappointment showed on Lucy's face as she sat down again. Mom was right; she would be right on Jack's tail if at all possible.

'Now, don't look like that, my girl. You've followed your brother around since you could crawl, but you've got to let him go, just as I've got to do the same, damned fool that he is.'

'I know, Mom, but I'll go if I can.'

'I don't doubt it.' Bet glared at them, trying to hide her worry.

Jack gave his sister an understanding smile. 'I can see you're determined so I'll see what the situation is when I get there and I'll let you know if they start taking women from here.'

'Promise?' Lucy swallowed her concern. Again Mom was right: she had been her brother's shadow for as long as she could remember, and it hurt to realise that he was going overseas without her. She had never been separated from him, and it would be hard to take.

'How did I ever raise such crazy kids?' Bet stood up. 'Now, I've got a heap of ironing to do.'

'This needs to be tighter.'

Lucy winced as Jack adjusted the harness, desperately regretting that she'd given in. But he'd won, as usual. Being strapped on top of the wing was not a whole lot of fun as far as she was concerned. She liked to be in control, and that was the last thing she'd be, stuck up here.

'That's better,' Jack grunted with satisfaction. 'You're a little taller than Sue.'

'I don't know how you talked me into this, but I wouldn't do it for anyone else.' Lucy took a deep breath, longing for this ordeal to be over.

'I know that, and I appreciate it.' He climbed off the wing, jumped to the ground and grinned up at her. 'I'll buy you a huge steak after the show.'

'Don't mention food,' she groaned as her stomach did an uncomfortable lurch. 'Let's get this stunt over with. And no fancy stuff, Jack, or I'll kill you when we get down.'

'You'll have a nice smooth ride, I promise.' After a final check that everything was in order, he got in the cockpit and was soon thundering along the field to reach take-off speed.

Lucy closed her eyes and gritted her teeth. She hadn't eaten a thing today and was glad her stomach was empty. Like her brother, she was a good aerobatic pilot, and as they left the ground, she wished she had her hands on the controls. Stuck up here at the mercy of the wind and pilot was no fun, but she trusted Jack, and that was the only reason she was doing this.

The plane banked and turned to make a low-level sweep over the crowd. She knew the routine and managed a wave as if she was enjoying the ride. It was a good job they couldn't hear her cussing.

When they landed Lucy's relief was immense, but when her brother climbed on to the wing to release her from the harness, she swore under her breath. 'You'll have to help me down. I don't think my legs are going to work properly.'

'You did great, and the crowd loved it.' He placed an arm around her waist and guided her down to the ground. He gave her cheek a peck. 'Thanks, I know how you hated doing that.'

Her stomach growled. 'You can show your gratitude by getting me a strong coffee and a couple of doughnuts. I've got my routine to do in half an hour.'

Jack laughed. 'Hey, you're feeling better already.'

'Yep.' Her grin spread, happy now the ordeal was over. 'All I've got to do now is make my legs work.'

The day of Jack's departure came all too quickly. Lucy and Bet smiled brightly as they waved him on his way, knowing full well that they were going to have a good cry once he'd gone. They were still having a job to understand why he had decided to do this, but it was clear that he considered it very important. Lucy did wonder if it was for a new challenge, but when she'd mentioned this to him, he'd just shaken his head, but hadn't explained his motives – he never did. He'd just said it was something he had to do.

The tears came, were mopped up, and mother and daughter tried to ease their loss with coffee and freshly-baked cookies.

Bet managed a watery smile. 'Jack never could stand anyone being bullied or treated unjustly, could he? Do you remember how he would always wade in and sort out any arguments at school or in the neighbourhood? He must feel the same about this war and just had to do something about it.'

'Of course! I've been trying to work out why he was doing this, but I'd forgotten that. He never could stand by and do nothing, could he, Mom.'

'That's Jack all over.' Bet poured them another cup of coffee. 'He said he'd try and come home before he's shipped to England.'

'He'll do his best,' Lucy agreed, feeling a little better now. They'd see him again soon.

'What are you going to do now, Lucy?'

She shrugged. 'Still fly in the shows, I suppose, but it won't be the same without Jack. And he's not the only one leaving. Two more of the regular pilots are joining our air force in case we enter the war.'

'This damned war in Europe is reaching out and touching us whether we like it or not, isn't it?'

'It sure is, but only on a personal level. If Jack hadn't decided to get involved, I doubt we'd have realised this. Do you think America will stay out of it?'

'I think the President would like us to become involved, but he knows the majority of Americans are against being dragged into a war they feel has nothing to do with them.'

Lucy helped herself to another cookie, her thoughts sombre.

'We are helping, though,' Bet said quietly. 'We're sending food and arms to them.'

'And Jack,' Lucy murmured.

Bet spoke with a catch in her voice. 'And Jack.'

Chapter Six

There were ships as far as the eye could see. Jack shielded his cigarette to light it, then drew in deeply and blew out the smoke, watching it being snatched away on the wind. It was only the middle of October, but out at sea the weather was cold. They had set sail from Halifax three days ago. The journey to Liverpool would take around sixteen days in all. Jack leant on the rail, his gaze sweeping the ocean. What a sight! He'd been told that there were more than sixty ships in the convoy, and he couldn't help wondering how many would reach England. It would be a massacre if the U-boats found them.

His thoughts drifted back over the last few weeks. After arriving in Montreal he'd gone on to Ottowa to be checked out on Harvards, then to Toronto for twin-engine planes. It had been a busy time, but he'd got through it all easily, much to his relief. He'd made up his mind to go to England and would have been upset if they'd turned him down. He was a good pilot, though, and his newly-acquired instructor's licence had been helpful. He was glad he'd taken that six months ago. He'd never visited this beleaguered country before, but he'd always felt drawn towards it, and as soon as he'd heard about the struggle they were having, he wanted to help in any way he could. He knew a lot of people back home thought he was crazy, but that didn't bother him.

He hadn't managed to get home before they'd sailed because they had been on standby, waiting for the convoy to assemble. He was sorry about that, but perhaps it was for the best. The first parting had been hard enough, but this one would have been worse.

'Did you manage to get any sleep?'

Jack turned as another American pilot joined him. They were the only two on this convoy, but others were waiting to come. 'Not much, Don.' He held out the packet of cigarettes. 'How about you?'

Don took a cigarette and lit it. 'Wide awake all night. Men were snoring all around me, but I kept waiting for a bloody torpedo to come through the bulkhead.'

'I know what you mean. Wish we could have flown over.'

'Yeah. Safer and more comfortable.' Don leant on the rail next to Jack, scanning the ocean. 'These merchant seamen are brave men. I'm on edge making one trip, but they go back and forth the whole time knowing that each journey might be their last.'

'The fighter pilots in England know they could die at any time but, like the seamen, they keep fighting. And what about London with bombs raining down night after night? How are the people coping?'

'I can't imagine.' Don rubbed a hand over his eyes. 'What do you think we'll find when we get there? Providing we make it, of course.'

'We'll make it. There's a couple of destroyers guarding us.'

Don gave his companion an incredulous look. 'Ever the optimist, Jack. It's a nasty thought that there might be U-boats gathering for the kill.'

'Nah.' Jack slapped Don on the back and grinned. 'There's a storm brewing, I'm told, and that will make attack difficult. We'll get there. That poor bloody country needs all the help it can get. Now, let's get some food. I'm starving.'

Don tossed his cigarette into the sea. 'Well, in that case, we'd better eat before the storm hits. And you're right: we're both here because we can't stand by and watch the Nazis gain even more power. They've got to be stopped, and Britain's the prize they want now. That maniac is after world domination.'

'He won't get it.' Jack spoke confidently. 'He hasn't been able to knock out the RAF, and without that he can't invade.'

'True.' Don rubbed his hands together and smiled for the first time. 'I can't wait to get over there. It should be exciting. I wonder if we'll get to fly Spitfires?'

'Sure we will.'

The entire convoy had made it. Jack and Don watched the activity as they docked in Liverpool. It was early morning, but the place was buzzing with noise as the men shouted instruction, smiles on their faces to see the ships arriving safely. No time was being wasted in securing the ships and getting them unloaded. There were others waiting to come in for unloading as soon as there was room.

'My God!' Don breathed out a breath of amazement. 'They look pleased to see us, but I'll bet they're not as relieved as I am to see land again.'

Jack felt excitement race through him. They were here at last. 'This is an island, don't forget, and these ships are their life blood.'

Don nodded grimly. 'And Hitler knows that.'

They fell silent as they drank in their first encounter with a nation at war. The sense of urgency was palpable, and they were both eager to get off the ship that had been their home for the last sixteen days.

'They said someone would meet us,' Don muttered, scanning the people on the dock for likely candidates. As the gangplank was lowered two men walked towards it. 'There! That might be them, Jack.'

Before Jack could answer, an officer came up to them. 'You can go ashore now, and good luck.'

They shook hands, and Jack said, 'Thanks for getting us here safely.'

'Our pleasure. The U-boats didn't find us this time.'

Don looked as if he couldn't quite believe the officer's casual tone. 'How could they possibly miss such a huge convoy?'

'Oh, it happens sometimes – not often – but the ocean is a large place. Now, I believe your escort has arrived.'

As the officer walked away, Jack and Don hoisted their

bags on to their shoulders and made their way off the ship. They stepped on to the dockside with relief, for neither of them had enjoyed the journey.

There was no doubt that the two men were waiting for them. They were wearing dark blue uniforms with the distinctive gold wings on their jackets. The Americans had been told about the infamous English reserve, but the polite, formal greeting still took them by surprise, especially as Jack was sure he'd met one of them before. He couldn't place him at the moment, though.

After introductions were made, they were asked if they'd had a good journey. Neither American knew what to say, and they merely shrugged and said, 'Yeah, sure.'

'Good.' The man who had introduced himself as Captain Johnson ushered them towards a car.

'Where are we going?' Don fell into step beside him.

'London first, then on to Maidenhead.'

On reaching the car and stowing their bags in the trunk – or boot, as the English called it – Don got in the front with Captain Johnson, who was driving, and Jack sat in the back with the other man – Captain Simon Trent. He studied the man beside him carefully. Not only was the name familiar, but also the face. They had met before, but where? He frowned as a wide smile appeared on Simon's face.

'Placed me yet?'

After searching his memory, Jack clicked his fingers. 'Berlin, 1936. We were there for an air display.'

'That's right. I recognised your name and volunteered to come and meet you.'

'It's great to see you.' Jack was elated to find someone he already knew, albeit a very brief acquaintance.

There wasn't time to talk, as they were soon pulling up outside a railway station.

Captain Johnson turned in his seat. 'Let's hope there are still trains running to London. They took another pasting last night. Better check, Simon, before I leave you.'

'Right.'

Jack watched Simon until he went through the door, and then turned to Captain Johnson. 'Why are we going to London? I thought we were to be stationed at a place called White Waltham.'

'Oh, you are,' the captain said briskly. 'But that will have to be your first stop, and Simon will see if he can get transport from there for you. If not, it will have to be another train, I'm afraid. The timetable can be rather erratic.'

'We're in luck.' Simon came back to the car and held open the door. 'There's a train expected in about half an hour.'

'Good. I'll leave you to look after our guests.'

Jack and Don exchanged amused glances at being referred to as guests, and as soon as they had their bags, the car sped off, obviously in a hurry.

The station was crowded, and it looked as if some people had been there for a long time. It was a sea of uniforms. Some were sitting on the platform, eyes closed, others were reading; some were in circles with playing cards in their hands as they gambled away the time, and their money. The new recruits followed Simon as he weaved his way towards a kiosk with the letters 'WVS' painted on it.

'How many trains are they expecting?' Don muttered, as they pushed through the throng.

Simon heard and looked back, giving an apologetic shrug. 'Just one. It will be an uncomfortable journey, and we'll probably have to stand all the way . . . Three strong teas,' Simon said when they reached the kiosk.

'Righty-ho.' The woman peered at Simon's uniform and frowned. 'Why you got gold wings for?'

'It's the Air Transport Auxiliary.'

'Ah, you're a pilot then.' She nodded approval and set about pouring the tea. 'You peckish? We've got some sandwiches.'

'Lovely, thanks.' Simon turned to Jack and Don. 'Hungry?'

'Starving,' they answered in unison.

The WVS woman looked them over doubtfully. 'You ain't military.'

'You can give them refreshments.' Simon's tone was amused. 'They're pilots as well, just arrived from America.'

'What?' An elderly face appeared from the back of the kiosk. 'Don't tell me they've come into the war and no one told me?'

'I'm afraid not, ma'am.' Jack beamed, thoroughly enjoying the encounter. 'But some of us want to help.'

The woman let out a huge laugh. 'Hark at that! I ain't never been called ma'am before. Makes me feel like the bloody queen! You're welcome, lads.'

The head disappeared, and the next minute all three men had steaming mugs of tea and chunky sandwiches. There wasn't much filling in them, but Jack and Don were too hungry to bother about that. However, Don was examining his mug with an expression of distaste on his face, and glanced up when he heard Simon chuckle.

'Sorry, but we don't have any coffee. You'll get used to it. The British run on endless cups of tea.'

Jack took a cautious sip of the dark brown liquid and found it quite refreshing. 'And you aren't doing too badly on it, from what we've heard.'

Simon's only reply was a brief nod as someone caught his attention. It was an RAF pilot with a string of coloured tapes under his wings.

Jack and Don stepped back slightly, not wanting to intrude on Simon's conversation, and studied the young man with interest.

'He's only a kid,' Don muttered under his breath to Jack.

'Yeah, until you look into his eyes. He's seen and done things we can only imagine.'

Don looked excited. 'We've only been here a short time, but it's already dawning on me what the people of this country are doing. Look around, Jack. Nearly everyone's in a uniform of some kind.'

'And if they're not, then they're working in factories or on the land.'

They had been so lost in thought that Simon's voice startled them. The young pilot was now joking with the WVS woman as he took his tea and bun.

'Hey, Peter!' Simon called. 'They never offered us one of those.'

The pilot winked. 'You're wearing the wrong coloured wings.' He stopped briefly in front of Jack and Don. 'Good of you to offer to help us. Just keep the Spits coming. We have a habit of breaking them.'

Don was grinning as the pilot wandered off, eating and drinking as he weaved his way through the crowd. 'Gee, I just love the accent. Where's he going?'

'London, to let off a bit of steam.' Simon drew in a quiet breath. 'He was one of my pupils and is a damned good pilot. That's why he's still alive.'

'Isn't London a dangerous place to go and have fun?' Don asked.

'I don't know what you're expecting, but life goes on in spite of the bombing.' Simon finished his tea and returned all their mugs to the kiosk. 'There's still plenty of dances or concerts going on. A few bombs won't bother Peter and his friends too much.'

Jack thought back to the gloomy reports being broadcast in America, and pursed his lips. 'You know, if you listen to some of the news in our country, then you'd get the impression that this country doesn't stand a chance.'

'And do you believe that?' Simon asked.

'We wouldn't be here if we did.'

Simon nodded approval at the reply. 'We've had, and still are having, a tough time, but the threat of invasion has receded for the time being. The Germans couldn't break the RAF, and now Hitler has unleashed his fury against the civilians. He's just making us bloody angry, and that is a big mistake on his part.'

At that moment there was the sound of a train approaching, and the station erupted into activity.

Simon urged them towards the front of the platform. 'Push on anywhere, even if it looks full.'

'All these people will never get on. It's already full.' Jack was looking at a sea of people already on the train as it pulled to a halt.

'Want to bet?' Simon grabbed the nearest door and swung it open, dragging Jack and Don with him. 'Good, it's a corridor train. That will be the best place to stand.'

It was an experience for the two Americans, but they stuck to Simon, who was clearly used to travelling like this. Nobody seemed to mind as they pushed their way through to reach the corridor. It was standing room only, and when the train started to move, the platform was miraculously empty.

Jack shook his head in disbelief. 'I'm glad I didn't take you up on that bet, Simon. How long will we be in London?'

'Depends. The man in charge wants to meet you, and he'll explain about the work we're doing. Then we'll go to Maidenhead as soon as possible.' Simon gave them an enquiring look. 'Unless you want to do a bit of sightseeing, of course?'

'I wouldn't mind having a look round, see for myself just what's really happening over here.' Jack noticed that Don was nodding eagerly. He turned back to Simon. 'That's if we can spare the time, of course.'

'No problem. You're not expected to report until the day after next, so we'll stay in London overnight.'

It wasn't easy to conduct a conversation when they were all packed tightly into the train, but Jack was far too interested in the passing countryside to be aware of the discomfort of the journey. As they left the industrial areas and came to open country, he felt something tighten in his chest. After sixteen days of seeing only grey seas and grey ships, the colour green almost hurt his eyes as they passed fields with sheep and cattle grazing. The tranquil scenes were hard to equate with a country fighting for its existence, and yet he only had to glance at the mass of uniforms around him for that fact to be abundantly clear.

At that moment Jack Nelson fell in love with the country he had just arrived in, a country and people he had chosen to help in their struggle against the sweeping tide of Nazism. His contribution would be small, but he was glad he'd come. He hadn't quite been able to work out Don's reasons for coming here. He expressed concern about the Nazis, but Jack had a feeling that he was after excitement. They had met for the first time on the conversion course and he'd found out that Don flew cargo – anything and anywhere. The man seemed to crave adventure and he must have thought he could find it here. But whatever his friend's motive, Jack was sure of his own, and it was desire to help in any way he could. There was no way he could have remained in his comfortable world. The dire reports he had listened to on the wireless had driven him to come here.

Feeling quite shaken by the emotions running through him, Jack fished in his pocket for a pack of cigarettes and held it out to Simon. The quiet man had said very little, and Jack didn't expect him to in this crush. He was very aware of the notices plastered everywhere – *Careless Talk Costs Lives*. When Simon took a cigarette Jack held his lighter for him, then lit one for himself. Don was busy trying to get to know a couple of girls in army uniform, but Jack had no need to while away the time in that way. He would get to know people soon enough, but for the moment he wanted to be quiet. His gaze returned to the window. Soon he would be flying over scencs like this, and he couldn't wait.

Jack wasn't aware of time passing, but suddenly the beauty was no longer there. The train was now rumbling slowly through bombed and smoking ruins.

'My God!' Don now had his face pressed to the window next to Jack. 'What a mess!'

'Welcome to London,' Simon said with a grimace. 'They took another battering last night.'

There were murmurs running through the crowd as everyone studied the devastation.

'The bastards!' a young sailor exploded. 'I told my missus to get out, but she won't go. Says she's safe down the Tube stations at night, and they ain't chasing her out of our home.'

There were nods all round at this declaration, and Jack guessed that many of the men and women going on leave were in a similar situation. They must never know what they were going to find, or if their homes would still be standing. He tried to imagine how it would be if his ma and sister were living here, but they weren't; they were safe in America, and he was having a hard time getting his head around this. But he knew one thing: he would be as mad and concerned as the people around him. And the angrier they became the harder they would fight. Hitler had made serious blunders in his assessment of this country's determination. He should have invaded immediately on the heels of Dunkirk, but he hadn't, and his hesitation had lost him the advantage. The man was a fool, and that would eventually lead to his defeat.

The train finally eased into the station and the passengers disgorged, all anxious to get to their various destinations. There weren't any station names up as far as Jack could see, so he had no idea where they were. It was just the same outside the station. All the road signs had been removed.

Don scratched his head, looking round. 'How do you find out where you want to go?'

Simon guided them down a road. 'We didn't want the Germans to know where they were if they landed. If you come up on your own any time you can always ask a policeman or Air Raid Warden.'

'Yeah, right.' Don grinned at Jack. 'That should be quite an adventure.'

Their momentary amusement didn't last long as they made their way past one bombsite after another.

'That's recent.' Jack pointed to a shell of a building still on fire, and as they watched, a wall came crashing down, filling the air with dust and smoke. Rescuers were still digging in one ruin, looking for survivors. It was a sight that would always be vivid in his memory. 'One report I heard said that London was ablaze night after night. Now I believe it.'

Simon nodded grimly. 'And if we stay tonight, you'll see for yourself.'

Chapter Seven

'What a day! The visibility was terrible.' Ruth sat at the kitchen table and rested her head in her hands. 'Thank heaven for railways lines! And if the weather hadn't cleared enough for me to get a lift back, I'd have been stuck up north for the night.'

'Get lost, did you?' Tricia plonked a mug in front of Ruth. 'Drink that and you'll soon feel better.'

Ruth's nose twitched as the aroma caught her attention. She took a sip to make sure her senses weren't deceiving her. 'Coffee! Real coffee! Where did you get this?'

Gussie, who now lived with them permanently, rubbed her hands together in glee. 'The weather was so bad that I got lost as well. I was almost flying on empty when out of the gloom I spied an airfield. It was White Waltham. After I'd landed, Simon introduced me to a couple of Americans who arrived two weeks ago. One of them had packets of American coffee in his bag and he gave me one.'

The look of pure innocence on Gussie's face made Ruth suspicious. She had a lively and unpredictable nature, and a habit of involving them in all sorts of crazy schemes. There was more to this than a generous gift, and when Ruth saw Tricia smirking as well, she was sure of it. She narrowed her eyes and asked, 'What have we got to do for it?'

'Nothing!' Gussie declared forcefully, then shrieked with laughter. 'Oh, you ought to see your face, Ruthie! Now would I get you into any kind of trouble?'

'Yes!' Ruth and Tricia declared together.

'I just turned on the charm and . . . I had to make a *tiny* promise – but not one you'll object to,' she added hastily.

'How tiny?' Ruth was having difficulty maintaining a stern expression. Gussie was incorrigible, but very easy to forgive.

'They're all going to a dance tonight in Maidenhead, and I promised the three of us would go.'

'Just a minute, Gussie, you said there were two Americans, but there are three of us – four if Ellen gets back.'

'Ellen's had to go back home because her mother's very ill,' Tricia told her. 'I doubt if we'll see her again.'

'Oh, that's a shame. Let's hope her mother soon recovers. Anyway, that still leaves three of us.'

'Simon's going as well.' Tricia was busy inspecting her nails, then she looked up and winked. 'I'll look after him.'

Ruth was intrigued. 'Oh, I didn't know you had your eyes on him.'

'Don't get me wrong, Ruth, it's nothing romantic, but I like him and he's a good dancer.'

'And I'll keep Don company.' Gussie picked up Ruth's empty cup and poured her another cup of fragrant coffee.

'Jack Nelson's yours. Just wait until you see him.'

'I dread to think what he'll be like,' Ruth muttered. This second cup of coffee looked very much like a bribe. 'How are we going to get there and back?'

'Don said he'd come and collect us.'

'What in? A bomber?'

Gussie roared. 'I wouldn't put that past him!'

Ruth couldn't believe this. 'It's quite a way, you know, and we've got to get back in time to report for duty in the morning.'

Gussie pulled Ruth out of the chair. 'Oh, you are a worryguts, Ruthie. I don't know what they're going to arrange, but Simon will be there and he'll make sure we get back all right. Now, go and sort out your best frock. We've all been working hard, so let's have some fun tonight.'

With a resigned shrug, Ruth stood up, pushing away her tiredness. There was never any point arguing with Gussie when she was in the mood for a night out. And anyway, she was right: they were due for a break.

'Don't pinch all the hot water!' Tricia called as Ruth made her way up the stairs.

'First one to the bathroom gets a bath!' Ruth shrieked as she heard a stampede behind her. The stairs were so narrow she knew they couldn't get past her. Scrambling up the last few steps she shot into the bathroom and slammed the door, locking it securely behind her as her friends threatened dire action if they were left with cold water. Her desire to do nothing for the evening had disappeared. They would have a good time tonight, regardless of whatever unattractive man they had dumped on her for the evening.

* * *

They were ready and waiting by seven o'clock, wondering how they were going to get to Maidenhead if their promised lift didn't arrive. Now she was dressed up Ruth was looking forward to the evening. She wished she had her car. Perhaps she'd bring it next time she went home. The petrol ration was meagre, but it could be saved for occasions like this.

The time passed and it was nearly eight when Tricia looked at the clock again. 'Are you sure they're coming for us, Gussie?'

She nodded firmly. 'Don told me he'd fix it. These Americans are very enterprising.'

'I'll bet they are,' Ruth muttered under her breath, but the girls heard anyway.

'Don't you like them?' Tricia asked.

'I like the ones I've met very much. It's just the one Gussie has set me up with I'm suspicious about.'

Gussie looked up at the ceiling in mock despair. 'He's gorgeous, you dope. Do you think I'd lumber you with someone obnoxious?'

'Yes, and if he's so wonderful, why haven't you grabbed him for yourself?'

'Because Don is lively and fun. Jack's quieter. The steady type, I'd say, and much more suited to you, Ruthie.'

Tricia grinned at the expression on Ruth's face. 'I don't think you're doing a very good job of convincing her, Gussie.'

'She isn't, but at least he's a pilot, so he must have some brains.'

'Oh, he's got more than that.' Gussie's wink was wicked, and then she got up and peered out of the window. 'How about if we commandeer one of the taxi planes for tonight?'

'Oh no you don't!' Ruth and Tricia pulled Gussie away from the window and made her sit down. 'You are *not* going to get us in trouble tonight.'

'We've all done our night-flying tests, and the conversion course for Masters and Oxfords—'

'*No!*' Tricia raised her voice to emphasise the refusal. 'You'll get us chucked out of the ATA with a stunt like that.'

'If they don't come within the next half an hour, then we could all go to the pub,' Ruth suggested.

'That's a good idea.' Gussie nodded approval. 'There's a nice RAF pilot who goes in there regularly.'

Ruth and Tricia groaned.

'How can one person have so much energy?' Tricia asked Ruth.

'It's a complete mystery to me,' Ruth replied.

'What's that?' Gussie shot to her feet and rushed to the window. 'He's here and he's got his hands on an RAF truck!'

They all crowded to have a look as the vehicle stopped outside the cottage. A man jumped down, followed by another.

'Simon's come with Don.' Gussie rushed to open the front door with Tricia right on her heels.

When the men came in, Ruth studied the American. He was of average height, with dark hair and pale blue eyes that shone with devilment. Attractive enough, Ruth admitted, but Gussie was right: he looked just the type for their exuberant friend. The other one hadn't bothered to come, so she'd have to wait a bit longer before she met him.

After being introduced, Ruth smiled at Simon. 'How did you get hold of the truck?'

'Borrowing the truck was easy enough, but filling it

with petrol was quite another thing. That was down to our American friends. They promised the RAF boys plenty of partners for the dance if they could have the "gas", as they call it, so they've been out scouring Maidenhead for girls.'

'And have they done that?'

Simon's shoulders shook in silent amusement. 'I'd say so. I counted twenty being helped out of the truck before we came for you.'

Don urged everyone out of the door, eager to get going. When he tried to climb into the driver's seat, Simon stopped him. 'I'm not risking the girls' lives with your driving; they're too valuable. You were on the wrong side of the road nearly all the way here.'

'I kept forgetting you drive on the other side.' Don gave way easily with only a smirk on his face. 'I'll go in the back with the girls.'

They soon sorted themselves out with Simon and Tricia in the front and the rest of them in the back. Ruth made herself as comfortable as possible in the bouncing truck. Simon was obviously in charge of this little expedition and keeping a rein on the flamboyant natures of Gussie and Don.

The dance was in full swing when they arrived, and as soon as Ruth heard the sound of the band her feet started tapping. She loved dancing, and if the American Gussie had lumbered her with didn't dance, there were plenty of other partners. The men outnumbered the girls. It looked as if everyone was off duty tonight. She scanned the faces, waving now and again to people she knew. The ATA were out in force.

They started to push their way through the crowd when

someone crashed into Ruth. The man next to her had been holding a full pint of beer, and as she fell against him the glass shot in the air and liquid covered the front of her frock. Ruth was horrified. Gussie had urged her to put on her best frock, and she'd done just that. Now it was ruined.

'Gee, honey, I'm sorry.'

The dancer who'd caused the disaster had produced a white handkerchief from his pocket and was busy trying to mop up the mess. Furious, she pushed his hand away. 'Stop it! You'll make it worse. And don't call me honey.'

'I'm real sorry, ma'am. That's delicate material. I'll buy you a new one if it can't be cleaned.'

Ruth glared at him in disbelief. 'This is pure silk and bought in Paris just before the war. It can't be replaced.'

He reached out again to dab at the spoilt frock.

'I said leave it!' With a growl of fury she turned away and made her way over to the bar where the rest of her friends were busy trying to get drinks.

'Ruth!' Tricia gasped when she joined them. 'What's happened to your beautiful frock?'

'Some idiot Canadian bumped into me and a man nearby poured his drink all over me. Just look at it! It's ruined!'

'What are you having, Ruth?' Simon had managed to get to the front of the queue.

'Something strong, and a glass of hemlock for that tall clumsy oaf with the fair hair.'

Gussie followed Ruth's furious gaze. 'Oh dear, you don't mean the man making his way towards us, do you?'

'Yes! And if he dares to come anywhere near me again . . .' She noticed Gussie's expression. 'Do you know him?'

'Er . . . yes, actually, that's Jack Nelson, the American I told you about.'

'Well, one meeting with him is enough. Don't let him anywhere near me, Gussie. The blasted man's dangerous!' She watched as her friend waylaid Jack and talked to him earnestly.

'It doesn't look as if you've taken a liking to Jack.'

With a drink in her hands Ruth told Simon what had happened.

He sipped his beer and then said quietly, 'It's only a frock, Ruth, and I'm sure you have plenty more.'

'You're saying I'm overreacting?'

'Well, aren't you?'

'Oh, damn, Simon, why do you always have to be so sensible? But you're right, what does one frock matter – even if it is special. However, if that's the man Gussie has tried to fix me up with, then I'm not interested.'

'That's a shame. He's a good man, Ruth.'

'I'll take your word for that, Simon, but I would rather not have anything to do with him. What's he doing here, anyway? America started conscription at the end of October, and Roosevelt has been elected for another term as President. Why isn't he in his own country?'

'All that happened just after he arrived here, and if you're suggesting that he might have signed up for the ATA to avoid his responsibilities at home, then you're quite wrong.' Simon's voice was reproachful. 'It isn't like you to be so judgemental, Ruth.'

She suddenly felt ashamed. 'Oh, I'm sorry. You're quite right. I shouldn't have snapped at him. It *was* an accident.'

'And one I'm sure he regrets.' Simon finished his beer and

put down the glass. 'Let me tell you about Jack Nelson. We met some time ago at an air show. He's a damned good pilot and a likeable man. I was delighted when I knew he was coming to sign up for the ATA. He's a qualified instructor, and just the type we are crying out for. I met him and Don at Liverpool and took them to London. There was a bad raid that night, and a building near us was flattened. We were in a cellar, and as soon as the dust had settled, Jack was out there digging in the ruins to help find those trapped. He never stopped until everyone was out. The raid was still going on, but he never thought of taking cover again. He cares, Ruth, and that's why he's here.'

She groaned. 'Now you're making me feel even worse. I'll apologise during the evening.'

'Good enough.' Simon nodded, and then wandered off just as Gussie and Tricia joined Ruth with more drinks in their hands.

Gussie handed her another beer. 'Jack's really upset about the accident, Ruth. Won't you reconsider and let me introduce you to him? He wants to meet you very much.'

'Why?'

'Because, apart from being a stunning-looking girl, you're a bloody good pilot and, if the truth be told, one of the best we've got in the women's section.'

'Where on earth did you get that idea?' Ruth was stunned.

'It didn't take us long to recognise your skill. Most of us climb in a plane and just fly it, but you don't. You have a special feel and seem to become a part of the aircraft.'

Ruth's eyes narrowed as she studied Gussie. 'How many drinks have you had?'

'She's right, Ruth,' Tricia said. 'Everyone says the same

thing. Pretty soon they'll *have* to let us fly operational aircraft, and you will be chosen to be one of our pathfinders.'

The three girls were now in a huddle, the dance forgotten as they discussed the subject close to their hearts – the right to fly Spitfires and Hurricanes. There was talk about this radical step, but those in authority were still resisting the idea. The women's section of the ATA was determined to break down this barrier.

'And once we do that there will be no stopping us.' Gussie's face was glowing. 'I can't wait to get my hands on a Spitfire.' They all nodded in agreement.

'We can fly anything!' Tricia declared. 'And the sooner the men realise that, the better.'

'Bet we could even manage the big four-engine planes, as well.'

'That's a bit optimistic, Gussie.' Ruth smiled at her friend's excitement. 'That's something the men will never let us do.'

Gussie's mouth set in a determined line. 'That day will come, you'll see. And you'll be one of the first to be given the chance, so don't you break anything, or they'll think again. There will be a huge responsibility on the first girls.'

'I agree, but you're wrong about me. There are plenty who are more experienced pilots.'

'More experienced, yes –' Tricia nodded, '– but not many are better pilots. Simon says so, and he's very proud of you—'

Their conversation was brought to an abrupt halt when Don draped his arms around Ruth's and Gussie's shoulders. 'Hey, what's all this? You all look so serious. I thought we'd come to dance and have fun?'

Ruth turned and found herself face to face with Jack Nelson. It felt as if a jolt of electricity had shot through her. She hadn't really looked at him before; she had been too upset. He had hair the colour of wet sand and his eyes were a startling navy blue. She tore her gaze away from him as Don introduced another man.

'This is Rob. He was one of the first of us to come here, and is an old flying buddy of Jack's. He's an instructor for the ATA.'

They all shook hands, and Ruth liked him instantly. He was older – in his early forties, she guessed. His dark hair was peppered with grey at the temples, and he had the same quiet air about him as Simon. An ideal temperament for an instructor.

'How did that happen?' he asked Ruth, noting her wet, stained dress.

Jack held up his hands. 'My fault, I'm afraid, and I don't think she will ever forgive me. But I can understand that. If I'd ruined one of my sister's frocks, she would have my hide.'

Rob gave a deep, rumbling laugh. 'She sure would. Jack and Lucy fly like angels and fight like demons.'

'Your sister's a pilot?' Gussie asked.

'Yeah, we were in a flying circus together. She's good, but likes to be in control.' Jack then told them about the time he'd persuaded her to wing walk for him, and had them all laughing at his vivid description.

'Even I wouldn't do that.' Gussie actually shuddered.

While they were all discussing the horrors of performing such a stunt, Ruth noticed that Jack had his gaze fixed on her. She spoke softly, for his ears only. 'I'm sorry I was rude. It *was* an accident.'

He inclined his head. 'Thanks, and I'm real sorry. I promise you that when this war is over I'll take you to Paris and buy you another dress.'

She was pleased by the flamboyant offer. 'I'll hold you to that.'

'That's a date, then.'

Her attention was caught by Rob. 'Will you dance with me, Ruth?'

'I'd love to, but I smell like a brewery.'

'My favourite perfume.' He held out his hand and led her on to the dance floor.

From then on the evening flew by. She danced with Jack twice and found that they got on well together, although there was a certain tension between them. She put this down to their unfortunate first meeting. Which was a shame, Ruth thought, for he seemed a pleasant man, but the fact that she had to spend the entire evening in a ruined dress made it hard to forget the incident. As the pale cream silk dried, the stain from shoulder to hem was even more visible. But the damage was done, so she ignored it and settled down to enjoy the evening. Jack had claimed the last dance and asked her if she would write to his sister. She had taken the address and promised she would.

Chapter Eight

'There are two letters from Jack,' Lucy called to her mother as she rushed into the house. 'One for each of us.'

Mother and daughter eagerly ripped open the envelopes and sat in silence as they read.

'Well—' Bet looked up '—he seems to be enjoying himself.'

'Yeah,' Lucy agreed. Hers was a chatty letter, which didn't say much about the work he was doing, but perhaps they weren't allowed to. She shuffled through the rest of the mail and stopped when she came across another letter addressed to her bearing an English stamp.

'What's that?' Bet peered over her daughter's shoulder. 'That isn't Jack's writing.'

'No.' Lucy opened it and began to read, her excitement mounting. Then she screamed with laughter.

'What is it? Who's it from?'

'A girl by the name of Ruth. She's one of the ATA pilots and Jack has asked her to write to me.' She picked up her brother's letter and kissed it. 'Thank you, big brother.'

'That's nice, but what's making you laugh so much?'

Lucy then explained about Ruth's first meeting with Jack. 'Ruth says she gave him a hard time.'

'Good on her.' Bet nodded approval. 'I like the sound of her.'

'Me too, and if she put Jack in his place when she met him, then she's got guts.'

'She must have forgiven him if she has written to you.'

Lucy gurgled. 'Have you ever known anyone stay mad at Jack for long? He must have liked her, though, if he asked her to write to me.'

'Perhaps she reminds him of you.'

'If she gave him a hard time then she probably does.' Lucy found paper and pen, and then settled at the table. 'Gosh, it was kind of her to write. I must answer straight away.'

Bet sat beside her daughter and watched her excitement with a touch of sadness in her eyes. 'You want to go, don't you?'

Lucy glanced up, put down her pen and nodded, her expression wistful. 'I want to go so much it hurts. I want to join the women who are doing such a vital job. And with Jack not here I feel as if part of me is missing.'

Leaning forward, Bet patted her daughter's hand. 'Then you'd better find out if you can go to England.'

'Oh, Mom!' Lucy's eyes were moist. Their mother was the most unselfish person she knew. 'If I do that you'll be on your own.'

'Hey, I'm not in my dotage, and I've got lots of friends.' Bet stood up. 'Go to it, my girl. Ask Ruth; she'll know what your chances are. And, from the sound of it, your brother needs someone to keep an eye on him, though this girl Ruth seems as if she's quite up to the job.' She started to walk away, then turned back. 'Christmas is only four weeks away. Hope Jack won't be spending it on his own. We'd better see about sending him a food parcel. If we do it straight away, it might get there in time.'

'Good idea, Mom. I'll send Ruth one as well. And don't worry about Jack; he'll have lots of people to celebrate with. He isn't the only American there.'

'I know, but it won't be like family, will it?'

Lucy watched her mother leave the room. This was hard on her – on both of them – but there would be thousands without their families around them this festive season. Knowing she was going to miss her brother like mad this year, Lucy settled down to write a long letter to him, and another to Ruth.

'Haven't you finished yet?' Bet asked, making Lucy jump.

Glancing at the clock Lucy was surprised to see that she had been writing for nearly two hours. The bulky letters had to be folded carefully to make them fit in the envelopes. 'I'll go and post these. Have you got any?'

'Yes, I'll come with you and we'll go to the market to find things we can send to England.'

The day was clear and cold, perfect for flying. Jack whistled softly, always content when he was in the air. But he had to remain vigilant because he was delivering an unarmed Hurricane to Henlow, and he didn't want to bump into any stray Germans. That had happened to him once, but there had been plenty of cloud cover for him to hide in that day.

Not today, though. After he delivered this plane he had to get back to the factory airfield near Hatfield and collect a Spitfire. Boy, would he like to see what they could do, but they had strict instructions not to indulge in aerobatics. Their job was to fly straight and see that the planes were delivered without damage. He often watched the RAF pilots toss their planes around in the air, and longed to be up there with them, but they were doing their job – and a damned good one – and he was doing his, and loving it. He yearned for home at times – that was only natural – but he was so pleased he'd come to England. He was doing something worthwhile, and he couldn't remember when he'd been so happy.

After landing at Henlow and checking in, Jack was given another chitty with instructions to take a Hurricane to Luton. This was how it went most of the time. There were a lot of planes to be shifted, and the workload increased when the weather was good. When the weather turned nasty, flying was out of the question and the planes piled up. The manufacturers didn't like this and wanted everything moved as quickly as possible in case of raids.

When he arrived at Luton, Jack was pleased to see Simon there with the Anson.

'Hello, Jack. Where are you off to next?'

'The factory airfield at Hatfield. Any chance of a lift?'

'I'm taking pilots back to White Waltham, but I can go there after I've dropped them off. There are three here now, and another two to collect at Brooklands.'

'That's great. It will save me time. I've got to collect a Spitfire for delivery to Prestwick and I'd like to complete the delivery today.'

Simon glanced at his watch. 'How long since you've had anything to eat?'

'Nothing since breakfast at six this morning.' The mention of food made Jack realise just how hungry he was.

Simon shook his head. 'I know we're hellishly busy, Jack, but you must eat. Let's go and see what they've got in the Mess for lunch.'

The other pilots were already eating when they got there, so they collected their meals and sat with them. Jack knew one, Stan, but he'd never met the others. One was English, Charles, and the other a Canadian by the name of Ed. After the introductions, Jack started on his meal. It was a pie made mostly with vegetables, but he was too hungry to bother what it was. Rationing was tough and you were grateful for a hot meal at any time.

'How are you adapting to the food here?' Simon asked.

'OK. It isn't very interesting, but I get so hungry it doesn't worry me.' Jack sighed, his mind going back to his mother's laden table. 'I must admit that I'd love a large steak sometimes.'

'Wouldn't we all!' Ed cleared his plate and sat back. 'But you must admit that the cooks do a bloody good job with what they've got.'

Everyone nodded in agreement.

Simon drank the last of his tea and stood up. 'We'd better get going. Jack wants to get on his way to Prestwick.'

The Anson was refuelled and ready for them, and they were soon in the air again. Jack was content to relax and watch Simon at the controls. They used the most reliable pilots for the taxi work. The last thing they wanted was an accident with a plane filled with experienced pilots. As soon as they landed at Brooklands and drew to a halt, two pilots clambered in, and they were on their way once again. Jack never ceased to marvel at the efficiency of the organisation. The number of aircraft being shifted was phenomenal. The setting up of the Air Transport Auxiliary, using civilians with private pilot licences, had been a stroke of genius. As fast as the factories built the planes, they were collected and delivered to operational units all over the country. They were all so busy that it was clear that more pilots were needed.

The weather was still holding fair when they reached White Waltham. This was Jack's home base, but with the next delivery he might not be back tonight. Everything depended on the weather. He hoped he could get a lift back and wouldn't have to endure the discomfort of a train journey.

'Let's grab a cup of tea first, Jack.' Simon was striding towards the hut. 'Then I'll take you to your pick-up point.'

Jack suppressed a grin of amusement. There was always tea available wherever they went, and to tell the truth, he was getting as bad as the English. He was developing quite a taste for the stuff. Don still needed his coffee and had taken to drinking Camp Coffee in desperation. It was a brown liquid from a bottle, and Jack had tried it once. That had been enough! He would rather have tea.

Simon handed him a mug of steaming brew, and he asked, 'Have you seen Ruth lately?'

'Not since the dance. I saw Tricia the other day, and they are as busy as us, but I expect we'll bump into them some time.'

Jack grimaced. 'Don't use that word, Simon. I wonder if she managed to clean the dress.'

'No idea, but they'll do something with it. We all try not to waste anything, knowing most of our supplies have to come by sea. The motto is "make do and mend". Now, we'd better get a move on.'

Once at the factory airfield, Jack collected the delivery chitty and the plane. Wasting no time, he took off. With luck he could get there before nightfall.

With a following wind he was making good time and got as far as Speke before an ominous clunk from the engine forced him to land. He was given a bed for the night in the officers' quarters and retired early, determined to continue his journey at first light. Knowing the mechanics would be working on the plane to get it repaired by morning, he slept as soon as his head touched the pillow.

'Sir, wake up!'

Jack opened his eyes and saw a sergeant standing beside the bed with a mug in his hand. He took the tea and drank thirstily. The blackout shutters were still in place and the room was lit with only a low wattage bulb. 'What time is it? Have I overslept?'

'It's six o'clock, sir. There's a phone call for you.'

'Who the hell's phoning at this hour? It isn't even light yet!'

'It's your HQ, and they said it was urgent that they contact you before you left this morning.'

He was immediately out of bed and pulling on his clothes.

It must be something out of the ordinary for them to call him so early. The sergeant took him to an operations room where he was handed a phone. 'Nelson,' he said briskly.

'Jack . . .' Rob hesitated. 'Sorry about the early call but

I wanted to tell you this myself, and I knew you'd be on your way at dawn. There's been an accident. Late yesterday afternoon Don took off from Weston-super-Mare when his engine caught fire. An eyewitness said he was too low to bail out and it looked as if he was heading out to sea. The RAF Sea Rescue searched while there was still enough light and then gave up. They'll try again this morning.'

Jack took a deep breath. 'Thanks for letting me know, Rob.'

'Phone me when you reach Prestwick and I'll let you know if he's been found.'

'Right, I'll do that. Oh, and Rob, when we were on the ship coming over, Don told me he couldn't swim.'

'Damn!' was Rob's only comment before he put down the phone.

'Bad news, sir?' The sergeant was studying him with curiosity.

Jack nodded. 'There's been an accident and the man I came over here with is missing.'

'Is he in the drink, sir?'

'What?'

'Ain't you never heard that expression before? I don't suppose you would have, you being Canadian. It means has he gone down in the sea?'

'Oh, yes, they think he might have.' The corners of Jack's mouth turned up in a wry smile. He was always being taken for a Canadian. 'And I'm American.'

'Really?' The sergeant frowned. 'That's right. I did hear that some of you had come over.'

'There are quite a few of us now. We have private pilot licenses and the ATA need all the help they can get, so here we are.'

'And right good of you too, sir.' The sergeant surveyed him with respect. 'You're all doing a necessary job. I've seen a few women climbing in and out of planes, as well. Came as a bit of a shock at first, I can tell you.'

'Wait until you see them flying Spitfires.' Jack couldn't resist the tease.

'Oh, never, sir! They can't do that!' He was shaking his head in denial. 'Those little girls can't fly fighters. How you finding things over here, then?'

'I'm enjoying the work. The camaraderie is terrific and we've been welcomed by everyone in the ATA.' Jack was happy to chat, pushing away his worry about Don. Losing family and friends was part of everyday life in this war. He'd only been here a short time, but he'd seen many people stoically deal with their grief and carry on. They were determined to win, and it was the only way. He'd chosen to join in their struggle, and he also had a job to do.

'There's only one problem. We're supposed to have a common language but, as you've just seen, I find some of the expressions difficult to understand, and it's easy to get into trouble if we say the wrong thing – like calling someone a bum.'

The sergeant smirked. 'Ah, well, you would. Not the thing at all. Sorry about your mate, but they'll do their best to find him.'

This man was being kind and understanding and Jack appreciated that. 'If I know Don, I expect he came down in the shallow end.'

'That's right, sir. Now, how about I rustle you up some breakfast and then you can make an early start? The weather's holding good, according to the Met boys.'

* * *

As soon as Jack landed at Prestwick, he checked in and then phoned Rob.

'Good news, Jack. The Home Guard found Don on the beach last night, unconscious, but he's alive. He's safely tucked up in hospital now. They didn't know who he was because he wasn't wearing his jacket and he had no identification on him. He seems to have lost everything in his struggle to get out of the plane. He's regained consciousness now and has been able to tell them who he is.'

'Thank God!'

'Yeah.' There was an amused rumble from Rob. 'He told them that he didn't have enough height to jump so he thought the sea might be softer. He could see the shore, and although he can't swim, he managed to doggy-paddle ashore. He was exhausted and crawled to a sheltered spot before passing out. The Home Guard found him soon after he reached the shore, thank God, or he would have died of cold.'

Jack let out a ragged sigh of relief. If Don was telling the tale then he was all right. 'The stupid bastard. Still, he's alive and I'll buy him a pint when I get back.'

'How are you going to get back?' Rob asked.

'Don't know yet. I'll see if I can pick up another delivery.'

'See you when you get back then.'

Jack put down the phone and, as he went to get tea and see about another plane, there was a spring in his step.

Chapter Nine

'We've all got a couple of days off for Christmas, so what are you going to do, Gussie?' Ruth asked, as they sat around the kitchen table after a long day's work.

'I'm taking Don home with me. I thought a real family Christmas would do him good after the crash.'

Tricia looked up after checking the toast under the grill. 'I don't know how he survived that. The sea's no place to end up in at this time of year.'

'He said he doesn't remember much after he reached the shore. But the Home Guard arrested him thinking he might be a German. One was standing by his bed when he came round and wouldn't leave until everyone was satisfied he was an ATA pilot. He'd had a terrible struggle to get out of the plane before it disappeared under the waves. But he got off lightly. All he had were a few cuts and bruises, and after a few days in hospital he was back to normal.'

'Or as normal as he'll ever be. He's got a wild streak to

him,' Ruth remarked, making everyone nod in agreement. 'What are you doing, Tricia?'

'I've invited Rob for Christmas. Our American friends will be a long way from home this year and feeling lonely. We've got quite a few different nationalities in the ATA now, and everyone off duty is taking someone under their wing for the holiday period. It's a shame we can't do the same for all of them, but feeding more than one extra would be difficult.'

Gussie stared pointedly at Ruth. 'That leaves Jack on his own.'

Before Ruth could digest that remark, there was a knock on the front door, and she went to see who it was.

Their neighbour was standing on the doorstep with a huge parcel in his hands. 'This came for you today and I took it in for you. It's from America.' He winked. 'Lucky you, it's heavy and there might be some tasty treats in there for you. Still, you girls deserve to be spoilt.'

Ruth thanked him and watched him walk back down the path in his Home Guard uniform. He took a great interest in them and she knew he boasted about knowing them when he was in the pub at night. The parcel was indeed heavy and she had to kick the door shut with her foot before staggering back to the kitchen.

'What've you got there?' Tricia made room on the table.

'Wow! It's from America. Open it quick.' Gussie couldn't contain her excitement.

Ruth was just as eager and tore it open. As she brought out each item they all groaned in bliss. There were tins of ham, salmon, fruit, cream, coffee, biscuits and even a Christmas cake fully iced with a snowman on the top. 'Oh, my!' was all she could say, as she read the card included with the goodies.

'Who's it from?' Tricia couldn't take her eyes off the array of luxuries.

'Jack's sister and mother.' Ruth began to sort the food into three piles, being as fair as she could with the items. 'I'm going to keep the Christmas cake, if you don't mind. My mother will go into raptures about that.'

Gussie and Tricia gave her a puzzled look.

'Now, I think there's a bit of everything in each pile. You each take which one you want.'

'But, Ruthie, this was sent to you. You can't give it away!' Gussie protested.

'I can't keep it all. It would be greedy. And anyway,' she gave her friends a stern look, 'you're each taking home an American for Christmas, so go on, take it and I'll write and tell Lucy and her mother that we shared it.'

'Well, if you're sure . . .' Tricia pointed to the selection nearest to her. 'Can I have those?'

'Of course.' After the girls had each chosen, Ruth had the rest, and they all did a jig of delight.

When they'd calmed down, Tricia said, 'Invite Jack, Ruth. We can't leave him on his own. He's bound to miss his family like mad.'

'I'll ask him as soon as I see him.'

It was nearly a week before Ruth came across Jack. The weather was dreadful, but Ruth had a 'priority' Master to deliver to the flying school at Ternhill. That meant it was urgent and she had to stay with it and not take another delivery if it wasn't ready. It was always up to ATA pilots to make their own decisions whether to fly or not. She had the Met report and it wasn't encouraging. She scanned the sky, anxious to be on her way.

'What you going to do, miss?' the man in charge asked. 'Shall I fill her up?'

There was a little break in the clouds just appearing and her decision was made. 'Yes, I'll have a go.'

She was on her way at once, but soon realised she had made the wrong decision. However, knowing the delivery was urgent, she pressed on. By the time she reached the Midlands visibility was so bad she was finding it hard to make out the landmarks. It even looked as if it could snow. Reluctantly, Ruth turned back. She hated doing this, but there was nothing else for it: she couldn't risk the plane, or her own life. By the time she reached Little Rissington, the threatened snow had caught her up. It was only wet stuff and not settling, but it made flying conditions dicey. She was relieved to land.

'Nasty weather you've brought with you, miss.' An RAF corporal had jumped up immediately to help her out. 'Where was you going?'

'Ternhill. This is a priority delivery.'

He pursed his lips. 'Well, you ain't going to make it today. There's another one of your pilots been forced down here as well. He brought in that Spitfire over there.'

She climbed out, hoping it was someone she knew and could spend the evening with. There would be a long wait until she could resume her journey. She'd check in first, and then phone Hatfield to let them know where she was.

As soon as she put the phone down and looked up at the man standing beside her, she knew that all hopes of pleasant company had disappeared. He was glowering at her.

'What the hell do you think you're doing, flying in this

weather?' Jack Nelson growled in exasperation.

'Nice to see you too, Jack,' she said haughtily as she stalked past him in search of a cup of tea and a sandwich.

Jack followed. 'You haven't answered my damned question.'

His attitude infuriated her and she turned, eyes blazing. 'It's none of your bloody business! We each have the right to make our own decisions, remember? And the fact that you're stranded here as well is a bit like the pot calling the kettle black, isn't it?'

He tipped his head back and sighed deeply. When he looked back at her there was amusement in his eyes. 'I'll need an interpreter for that.'

The corporal appeared beside them carrying a tray holding two steaming mugs of tea and a pile of sandwiches. He was grinning wickedly after hearing their argument. 'What she means is that you ain't got no cause to tell her off, seeing as you was up there too.'

'And if you dare say it's all right for you because you're a man, I'll thump you.' Ruth stood with hands on hips, not prepared to take any nonsense from this man.

'Yeah, right.' Jack took the tray and placed it on a table near them. Then he held up his hands. 'Sorry, honey—'

'Don't call me that!'

He grimaced. 'I seem to say the wrong thing every time we meet. Truce?'

He held a chair for her and they sat at the table. Before answering, she took one of the mugs and sipped the tea, making him wait, and then she nodded. 'Don't take me for a fool, Jack. I know what I'm doing, and aware of the risks we take every day.'

'You don't need to increase those risks by taking unnecessary—'

'Jack!' she stopped him sharply. 'You're doing it again.'

'Sorry, sorry!' He lifted his hands in a gesture she was becoming familiar with, making her annoyance drain away.

'Do you carry on like this with your sister?'

'Yeah, she hates it too. Boy, do we fight!' He gave an amused chuckle as he remembered.

'Well, pack it in, because I don't want to fight with you every time we meet. It would spoil my parents' Christmas.'

He looked completely puzzled. 'How could I spoil your folks' Christmas?'

Now Ruth was enjoying herself. Confusing him was much more fun that arguing with him. 'Because you're spending the holiday with us.'

There was a protracted silence as he studied her intently. Then he said, 'I am?'

'Yep, and you'd better behave yourself, fly boy.' Her American accent was terrible and had them both grinning.

'That's extremely kind of you, Miss Aspinall. I would like that very much.' Jack's effort at an English accent was quite polished.

'You've been practising.'

'I'm surrounded by it every day. I'd rather like to learn some cockney rhyming slang, but I haven't found a cockney yet.'

Ruth bit into a sandwich and swallowed before she spoke, struggling to keep a straight face. 'An American sounding like a cockney is too awful to contemplate. Promise me you won't try?'

'OK.' He examined the contents of his sandwich, shrugged, and then devoured it with obvious enjoyment.

She hadn't seen this side of Jack before, and had to admit

that he was rather appealing. 'I've had a letter from your sister. She sounds nice.'

Jack nodded. 'She's the best.'

'Lucy and your mother also sent me a huge food parcel. I shared it with Tricia and Gussie.'

'Hey!' He looked offended. 'They haven't sent me one!'

'Perhaps it's still in the post. Anyway, I've written to thank them and explained what I've done. They've made three hungry pilots very happy.'

'They'll like that, thanks.'

With the plate now empty, Ruth stood up. 'It's getting dark so I'd better go and find myself digs for the night, and hope this shocking weather clears by morning.'

'I'll come with you.' Jack was also on his feet.

'There's no need. They'll give you a bed here for the night, but there aren't any facilities for women.' She turned to the corporal who had just arrived to clear their plates. 'Do you know where I can stay tonight?'

'Try the King's Head, miss. They usually have a room. It's just outside the gates, about twenty yards to the left.'

'Thanks.' Ruth noted that Jack already had his coat on. 'Don't come out in the dreadful weather. This is routine for us female pilots.'

'Hey, my ma brought me up to be a gentleman. I'll see you safely to the King's Head. And it's no use you arguing.'

Ruth rolled her eyes at the RAF man, and then gave a dramatic sigh. 'Now he's gone all polite and masterful.'

'You bet.' Jack took her arm and they walked out into the sleet.

* * *

By seven o'clock the next morning, Ruth was back at the airfield, after spending a comfortable night in the pub. It was now dry, but the cloud base was still low. She'd already checked with the Met and they'd told her that there was a chance the weather might brighten by mid-morning, but she was anxious to get going.

Jack came and stood beside her, also surveying the sky. 'Sleep well?'

'Yes, thanks. Did you?'

'Not bad.' He shoved his hands in his pockets, still gazing upwards. 'I'm on my way back to White Waltham, and the weather's improving in that direction, I'm told.'

'Oh, well, you can go then.'

He nodded. 'Soon as I've had something to eat. You're going in the opposite direction and that doesn't look too good.'

From the tone of his voice she guessed that he was about to start giving her orders again. 'It's borderline, and I'm going to give it a try.'

'Hmm.' He digested this news for a moment. 'I could take a look-see for you.'

She smothered an inward sigh. 'You'll be wasting petrol. Seamen are risking their lives to bring in the stuff.'

'Leave it for a couple of hours, Ruth. It might be clearer by then.'

'Jack!' Ruth was getting exasperated, but she couldn't be angry because he was only showing concern for her safety, and she could understand how he was feeling. The men had lost a very experienced pilot last week. 'I have a priority delivery, and I've already lost time. I want to get to Ternhill today.'

He glanced down at her. 'You'll turn back if it's too bad?'

'Caution is my middle name, Jack.'

'I'd be happier if it was your first name.'

'Jack, pack it in.' She gave him an exasperated glance. 'I've had breakfast at the pub, but I'll have a cup of tea with you while you eat.'

That would keep her on the ground for a while longer, he thought with satisfaction as they made their way to the Mess.

Jack watched while Ruth took off, and then headed for the Spitfire. He didn't know why he had shouted at her yesterday. She seemed to have a sensible head on her shoulders, and she'd been doing this job longer than he had. If anyone knew the dangers and risks, it was her.

After carefully checking over the plane, he climbed in and took off, experiencing the same thrill he felt every time he flew one of these wonderful planes. He talked himself out of worrying about Ruth. Simon was full of praise for her skill as a pilot, and she was well used to the vagaries of the English weather. He'd exploded at her because of frustration at being grounded by the weather, he thought. Yes, that was it. After all, why should he get in such a stew about someone he seemed to upset every time they met?

Ahead he glimpsed a patch of blue sky. He whistled softly as he zoomed towards it, doing a little wiggle of the wings. And what about that invitation to her folks' home for Christmas? Gee, that was great. Perhaps they could spend some time together without arguing . . .

Chapter Ten

Don had only been in hospital for a week and then went straight back to flying, seeming none the worse for his accident. He'd gone home with Gussie, whose family would, no doubt, make a huge fuss of him. Jack was also looking forward to Christmas. They had from Christmas Eve and wouldn't have to return to duty for three days. The trains weren't heated, and it had been a cold journey, but they'd both travelled in their warm flying boots.

'Here we are.' Ruth stopped by a gap in a high wall. 'They took our wrought iron gates for the war effort.'

Jack stopped and stared. To his mind this was everything an English country house should be. The two-storey building was old and elegant. There were large black timbers set in the structure that reached up to the roof. It was the kind of place he'd only seen in magazines.

'Jack,' Ruth called as he lingered.

He caught her up. 'Your house is absolutely stunning.'

'It is nice, isn't it? It's been in our family for five generations. Come on, let's get out of the cold.'

Inside it was warm and homely, the sort of place you could relax in and be comfortable. He had wondered briefly if it would be a show place, but that wasn't the case. Oh, he was going to enjoy spending Christmas in this gorgeous house.

'Mum, Dad, this is Jack Nelson,' Ruth introduced their guest.

Her father was the first to step up, pleasure on his face. 'Welcome, Jack, we're pleased you could come.'

'It was good of you to invite me, sir.'

Ruth's mother clasped his hand. 'You come and sit by the fire. You must be frozen. I'll make some tea and show you to your room afterwards.' She hesitated. 'Or would you prefer coffee? Your mother and sister very kindly sent some to Ruth.'

'Tea will be just fine, ma'am.' He grinned at Ruth. 'I don't know how we'd fly without it.'

Watching her parents fuss over Jack with undisguised pleasure made Ruth realise that he was around the same age Robert would have been. Robert would always be missed, especially at this time of year, but having Jack here would help to fill that gap in some way. And her family would help to ease the fact that Jack's family were a long way away.

'Sit down,' her father urged, as his wife hurried off to make the tea. Then he turned to his daughter. 'How long have you got, Ruth?'

'We have to go back on Boxing Day.'

'Splendid. Let's hope the Luftwaffe leaves poor old

London alone over the holiday! Did you know, Ruth, that our law chambers had all the windows blown out the other night?'

'No! Was anyone hurt?'

'The place was empty, thank goodness. Ah, here comes the tea. Ruth and Jack don't have to go back until Boxing Day, my dear.'

'How lovely. That means you'll be able to have a nice rest.'

Jack stood up and took the tray from Ruth's mother, then placed it on the table before the fire. 'Yes, we managed to get more time off than we'd expected.'

Ruth helped her mother pour the tea and hand it round. 'I'll take my car back with me, Dad. I've been saving my petrol ration.'

'Good idea. Trains will probably be scarce when you have to return. After we've had tea I'll check it over and take it to the garage for the petrol.'

Jack seemed completely at ease with Ruth's parents, and they were obviously impressed. His manners were impeccable without being forced or insincere. Ruth relaxed. They had clashed a couple of times and she'd been doubtful about bringing him home with her, but her fears had been groundless. They had seen each other infrequently – more like passing ships in the night – but she was beginning to realise that he really was a charming, intelligent man. Don had an air of brashness about him, but that was completely absent in Jack Nelson, and she wondered why she had never noticed it before.

When her father stood up and said that he was going to

see to her car, Jack also got to his feet. 'I'll come with you, sir, if that's all right.'

Her father's pleasure couldn't have been more evident. 'Of course, and call me George. Get your coat. I wouldn't be surprised if we had snow soon.'

When the men had left the room, Ruth put another log on the fire, then settled down to enjoy a quiet time with her mother.

'That's a nice young man, dear. Thank you for bringing him home.' She gazed at her daughter thoughtfully. 'Do you see much of him?'

'Now, Mum,' Ruth scolded gently. 'I know that look. He's just a colleague.'

'Oh, I hoped he might be special to you, seeing as you've brought him home.'

'We have a few different nationalities in the ATA, and we've tried to see that they all have company over Christmas. I write to Jack's sister, so he was the natural choice to come with me.'

'I see.'

'I doubt that!' Ruth shook her head. Knowing her mother's romantic nature, she changed the subject. 'Tell me what you've been up to lately.'

They had been talking for quite a while when Ruth's mother glanced at the clock. 'Whatever is keeping them? I'll be serving lunch in half an hour.'

'I'll see if they're in the garage.' Ruth slipped on her coat, and as she stepped outside a blast of icy wind almost took her breath away. Their garage was no warmer, but the two men inside seemed oblivious to the cold. She closed the door quietly behind her and watched, a lump in her throat. She had seen her father and brother like this so many times. Jack had his head under the bonnet of her car, and her father was in the driver's seat.

'Try it now, George,' Jack called.

The engine roared into life and Jack cocked his head to one side as he listened, then stood back with a grunt of satisfaction. 'That sounds healthier.'

'It certainly does.' George turned off the engine and climbed out of the MG. 'You know what you're doing with engines, don't you?'

Jack nodded as he snapped the bonnet back into place and began trying to clean the worst of the grease from his hands with an old rag. 'I've always serviced my own plane – didn't trust anyone else.'

At that moment, Ruth's father spotted her. 'Did you hear that, darling? Your little car has never sounded so sweet.'

'Lovely, Dad, and thank you, Jack.' She tried to look stern, but couldn't manage it. How her father must miss moments like this now Robert was gone. 'Mother is wondering where you've got to. Lunch will be ready any moment.'

'Oh, gracious, is that the time? We'd better get cleaned up, Jack. Alice will be cross if we're late.' George rubbed his cold hands together. 'You've got just over half a tank of petrol, Ruth. That should get you back to base with a little to spare.'

'That's good. At least we won't have a cold train journey back.' She ushered them towards the door. 'I'll show you to your room, Jack.'

'I'll do that, darling. You go and help your mother with the lunch.'

*   *   *

Christmas had been a huge success. Ruth's parents had taken to Jack from the moment he'd stepped through the door. He had come away with an open invitation to visit them any time he had a break from flying. He would always be welcome, they had told him sincerely. Ruth hadn't seen them so happy for some time, and it did her heart good to watch their animated faces as they talked and laughed with him. She hoped he would keep his promise and go and see them as often as he could. Her respect for him had also grown over the holiday.

One of the first things she did when she returned to Hatfield was write to Jack's sister and mother, knowing they would be comforted to know that Jack hadn't spent Christmas alone.

1941 swept in with icy conditions, making flying difficult. At times a blanket of snow covered the ground, obscuring familiar landmarks that were the only means of navigation. The ATA always carried maps, but they weren't a lot of good in such conditions.

'Bloody hell!' Gussie stomped into the Mess, wearing a balaclava, scarf, two pairs of trousers and two jackets. In this weather the girls all squeezed into as much clothing as they could. Some of the trainers had open cockpits, and it was perishing. This was one job the men were quite happy to leave to the women.

'I missed a barrage balloon by a whisker today.' Gussie was standing right in front of the fire in an effort to thaw out. 'And do you know what some sarcastic bloke said after I'd had to go round again before landing?'

She waited until she had everyone's attention. '"Your approach was a bit out, miss"! I pointed out – quite politely – that we have to navigate by sight, and that's difficult when the airfield, and surrounding area, is just a white blanket of snow. I told him that his approach would have been off as well.' Gussie looked smug. 'I studied his uniform devoid of wings and added, "That's if you could fly, of course".'

There were muted giggles. Any man who tried to get the better of Gussie was dicing with danger.

At that moment their head of operations came into the Mess and surveyed the pilots with affection. 'The factories are screaming for planes to be shifted. There are far too many of them standing around, and with the raids we've had lately, they're getting edgy. But –' She held up her hand as the girls began to get up '– the weather's bad, so don't take any chances.'

That was the pattern for the next three months. They flew when they could, and sometimes when they shouldn't. There was also a lot of hanging around, waiting for an improvement in the weather. Ruth saw little of Jack, but heard from her parents that he had spent two days with them at the end of February. They sounded delighted, and she was grateful to him for visiting them. She hadn't been able to get home herself, because she had either been flying or on a course of some kind or another.

They all longed for the spring, but with the return of better weather, the Luftwaffe intensified its attacks, once again pounding the ports, factories and other strategic areas of the South and Midlands. Other parts of the country also suffered.

It was in the spring that the ATA advertised for more pilots. The number of flying hours required was reduced and the grade of Cadet was introduced. With manufacturers working at full capacity and with the lengthening days it wasn't unusual for the pilots to make several deliveries in one day.

There were sad times when an ATA pilot was killed. They lost one woman who had been a very experienced pilot. Ruth hadn't known her well, but they all felt the loss of one of their group.

July was on them before they'd had time to notice the passing months. Ruth, like the rest of the girls, was concentrating on her job. There wasn't any question of them taking much time off: if the weather was good, they flew.

Ruth walked into the Mess one morning, having been brought back by the taxi Anson after her second delivery that day, to an air of suppressed excitement, though everybody was trying to appear casual.

'What's going on?' she asked, tossing down her parachute. 'I saw Captain Anders, the flying technical officer from White Waltham, as I came in. Anyone know what he's doing here?'

Gussie was leaning against the wall, filing her nails and looking totally at ease. 'I'm glad you're back in time because they're going to let some of us have a go at flying that Hurricane he's brought with him.' She then spoilt her casual attitude by grinning wickedly. 'And about time too!'

'Who's been chosen?' Ruth's insides tightened with anticipation.

'Don't know yet, but they'll have to use some of us who are already here.' Tricia gazed longingly out of the window at the Hurricane.

The first one to be called was Sally Westbury. She had been in the ATA from the beginning and now worked mostly on the administration side, but she was one of the most experienced pilots in the group and often flew the Anson.

They all rushed outside to watch this momentous occasion. Everyone was well aware how much depended on this flight. One mistake and the whole idea would be shelved.

No one spoke as Sally took off, completed the required circuit and made a perfect landing.

She climbed out and walked towards the waiting girls. Only they saw the sly wink she gave them. 'Lovely plane to fly, and so easy to handle.'

With those words of encouragement their hopes soared. They'd always been confident that they could fly the operational aircraft, and now they were finally being given the chance.

Ruth was called next and felt Tricia squeeze her hand. They were all maintaining an air of calm, wanting to let the officer see that they were taking this in their stride.

As Ruth took off all her tension disappeared. The speed and roar of the engine was exhilarating, and her concentration was total, as she determined to do as well as Sally. One bad move and this chance would be snatched from them. She couldn't help giving a quiet little yelp of delight when her landing was smooth – the kind of landing no one could criticise.

Tricia and Gussie were next, and they both kept up the

standard. The officer couldn't find fault with the way they'd handled the fighter, and left to make his report.

There was great excitement in the Mess, with those who hadn't been given the chance demanding to know when they could fly one.

The officer in charge of the Hatfield group clapped her hands for quiet. Jane ran the women's section with enthusiasm and efficiency, fighting all the time for them to take on a bigger role in the ATA. She wanted them on an equal footing with the men, and wouldn't stop until she had achieved that for them. 'That was an impressive display of flying. With the excellent *Ferry Pilots' Handling Notes* we now have, you will now be able to fly any plane in this group.'

'What about the four engines?' Gussie asked.

'We've broken down one barrier, the next one I'm still working on, so be patient. Now, I suggest that you go out tonight and celebrate.'

'What shall we wear tonight?' Tricia asked, as they made plans for a night in London. They had arranged to meet more of the girls there, so they could all celebrate together.

'I'm wearing my uniform.' Gussie was examining her lipstick to make sure there was enough left for the evening. Then she looked up at her friends. 'We'll be flying fighters as well from now on, and we've got a right to our golden wings.'

'I agree,' Ruth said. 'Let's all go in uniform for a change, and we can use my car. I've got enough petrol for this one trip.'

An hour later they all squeezed into Ruth's car, in high spirits, and set off for London.

* * *

With flying over for the day, Jack was still in the Mess, listening to the wireless. In April Germany had invaded Yugoslavia and Greece and, having failed in their attempt to bring Britain to her knees and complete his domination of Europe, Hitler had turned his attention to Russia. Was there no end to the man's ambition?

'Still here, Jack?' Simon sat down beside him.

'Yeah. Don's in Scotland, and the rest of them are scattered all over the country. It'll be a bit lonely at the house tonight so I thought I'd stay here for a while.' Jack changed the subject. Most of the time he was too busy to feel homesick, but it had a habit of creeping up on him when he relaxed. He changed the subject. 'The factories are turning out planes as fast as we can shift them. We need more pilots, Simon.'

'We'll have a few more from today. Haven't you heard?'

'What?'

'Four of the women flew a Hurricane today under the watchful eyes of Captain Anders.'

'Wow! Who was it, and how did they do?'

'It was Sally, Ruth, Tricia and Gussie. Anders told me they flew them with ease, and he was particularly pleased with the smooth landings. He sees no reason why they shouldn't all soon be flying the operational planes in this group.'

'Good for them!' Jack slapped his knee in delight. 'Hey, we ought to go and congratulate them.'

'That will have to wait until tomorrow. The last I heard they were all heading for London for a night out.'

Jack was disappointed. He saw very little of Ruth and

would have enjoyed joining in their celebrations. 'They should have told us and we could have gone with them.'

'That wouldn't have been right, Jack. What they did today was a milestone for them, and they'll want to share this moment with each other.'

'Of course they will.' Jack stood up. 'But there's nothing to stop us raising a glass to their success. Come on, Simon, I'll buy you a pint at the pub.'

Chapter Eleven

'Hey, Mom!' Lucy tore into the house waving a letter. 'The girls are flying the fighters now! Jack says there's talk of them taking on some American women pilots, but he doesn't know yet who will be in charge of the recruitment. He suggests I contact the committee he saw. They've got an office in the Waldorf Astoria in New York, and should be able to help me.'

Bet watched her excited daughter with a heavy heart, certain now that both of her children were going to end up in a country at war, and so far from home. Nevertheless, she smiled. It had been inevitable. She'd known that from the moment Jack had dropped his bombshell. 'You'd better write at once then, honey.'

'You sure you don't mind?'

'I mind, but you're not going to be happy unless you do this,' Bet said wistfully. 'I've seen the way you wait for the mail, unable to contain yourself as you search for a letter from Jack or Ruth.'

Lucy hugged her mother. 'You're the best, do you know that?'

'Of course I know it. Isn't that what I've always told you?' Bet asked, making them both chuckle.

'Sure.' Lucy sat at the table, paper and pen at the ready to write her important letter. She couldn't wait to join Jack in England. She missed him terribly, but it was more than that. This was a once in a lifetime opportunity to do something quite unheard of in the flying world – women flying all kinds of operational aircraft! She just had to be a part of it.

'Think carefully about what you're getting into, Lucy.' Bet spoke gently, not wanting to interfere, but desperate that her daughter should realise the full consequences of what she was planning. Jack was a man now, and a sensible one at that, but Lucy was her little girl. 'Pilots are losing their lives in the ATA, and the sea crossing is terribly dangerous. A few pilots have died when their ship was torpedoed.'

Lucy put down the pen and turned to face her mother. She understood her concerns. 'I've thought long and hard about this, Mom. I'm aware of the risks and am prepared to take them. These women are making history and, like Jack, I want to be a part of their struggle to survive. The work they're doing is essential if the RAF are to keep the planes flying.' Lucy gave her mother a wry grimace. 'It's all your fault, you know. You've brought us up to have a social conscience, and to care about anyone suffering injustice.'

'So I did.' Bet patted her daughter's shoulder. 'And I wouldn't have you any other way, so write your letter.'

It only took Lucy about ten minutes and she was running

for the nearest mailbox. As the letter plopped inside, she turned and walked back to the house. All she could do now was wait.

At first they had only been given Hurricanes to deliver, but now Ruth had finally got her hands on a Spitfire. The nose was raised, obstructing the view on take-off and landing, but once in the air it was a dream. This one was straight from the factory and had to be delivered to the maintenance unit to have the guns and radio fitted. She saw the airfield ahead and turned to make her approach, sorry the short flight was over, but there would be many more after this.

Her landing was smooth and she taxied towards a parking place being indicated by an RAF man.

He jumped up almost before she had stopped and leant into the cockpit to release her harness, swore and shot back, looking at her in astonishment. 'Blimey! You're a woman! You can't fly Spits!'

'Really?' She unsnapped the harness and smiled sweetly before climbing out. Then she looked up at the sound of a plane coming in to land. 'Here comes another one. I don't suppose anyone's told her she can't fly it either.'

There were three men now watching the Spitfire execute a perfect landing.

'Bloody hell!' one muttered. 'What are you women going to do next?'

'The bombers are next on our list,' Ruth told them. There was much shaking of heads and knowing looks.

'You'd never be able to control them, ducky. You ain't strong enough.'

Ruth chose to ignore them. It was quite likely that they would never be allowed to fly the big four-engine planes, but she did love to tease the men. Some had readily accepted them for their skill as pilots, but others still had closed minds.

Tricia climbed out and jumped to the ground. 'Gussie's right behind me. The factory's got fighters lined up and are shouting for them to be shifted fast. Sally's coming in the Anson to take us back.'

'We'd better go and report in then.' Ruth hoisted her parachute on to her shoulder and walked beside her friend, leaving the men open-mouthed in utter disbelief.

Just then a fighter screamed low over the airfield, climbed and waggled its wings.

'That's Gussie,' they said in unison.

Ruth pulled a face. 'And I bet she's been throwing that plane all over the sky just for the hell of it. She'll be hauled over the coals if anyone finds out.'

'Hmm.' Tricia sighed wistfully. 'But it would be worth it. Don't tell me you weren't tempted, Ruth.'

'Oh, I was tempted, but we're not in the military and could be sacked. I love flying for the ATA far too much to risk it.' She cast her friend a sideways glance. 'Mind you, I'd wait until I was well out of sight of everyone if I did have some fun with the Spit. Not that I would, of course.'

'No, of course you wouldn't. Neither would I.' Tricia had a look of complete innocence on her face. 'Let's get the tea lined up for our stunt pilot.'

Ten minutes later, Gussie joined them, looking her usual lively self. She grabbed a mug. 'Oh, thanks, I'm gasping. There's two more on their way.'

The men had followed Gussie as if they couldn't quite believe their eyes at the sight of these women nonchalantly carrying parachutes after flying *their* fighters.

'All women?' one croaked. 'Flying Spitfires?'

Gussie took a gulp of tea. 'A couple are in Hurricanes, I believe.'

One man lifted his hands in a gesture of surrender. 'What's the world coming to?'

They were on their second cup of tea when the others arrived, quickly followed by Sally. The taxi service was becoming very efficient and enabled them to save time so they could take on more deliveries.

After everyone had finished their refreshments – for they never knew when they would have time for anything more – they all climbed into the Anson, and were on their way to collect the next delivery.

Dumfries was Ruth's next destination. On arrival she went to see if they had another delivery to go from there.

'We've got something for Hawarden,' the operations officer told her.

That would get her part of the way home, and she might be able to get another ferry job from there. 'Good, I'll take it.'

He gave her a strange look. 'You don't know what it is yet.'

She managed to keep the smile on her face with effort when she saw the plane he was pointing out. She had been lucky up to now and managed to avoid this particular plane. It was an Airacobra. The pilots who had flown it said that at low speeds it vibrated badly, and had a nasty habit of swinging on take-off. These were just two of its many faults, according to reports.

'I'll see to the paperwork,' she stated confidently. There was no way she could refuse this ferry. The girls were all very aware that any adverse report about them could hold them back in the future. Planes had to be shifted, and they never refused, whatever their odd characteristics.

The officer still looked doubtful. 'You've flown it before, have you?'

'No.' She took out the book of *Handling Notes* from her pocket and flipped it open at the Airacobra page. 'I've got everything I need here.'

He took the book out of her hands and turned the pages slowly. Then he sucked in a breath and shook his head. 'Are you telling me that you step into a strange aircraft armed only with these notes?'

'And our maps.' She waited while he continued to study the *Handling Notes* with great interest.

'These are good. First time I've seen them.'

'They're excellent.' He was clearly interested so she explained further for him. 'The aircraft are put into certain classes. Once we've flown one type in each class, we are cleared to fly all the others in that class.'

'Even if you've never seen it before?' He was still having difficulty grasping this.

She nodded. 'But you must have come across this before now. The men use the same system.'

'I've only just been posted here.' The look he cast her was one of respect. 'These notes cover dozens of aircraft. You're expected to fly any of them?'

'If they've got to be shifted, then we fly them.'

'The Airacobra isn't liked by the RAF.'

'It isn't a favourite of the ATA either, but we've never bent one, and I don't intend to be the first. Now, I'd like to get the delivery chit and be on my way.'

'Of course.'

With the necessary papers in her pocket and a phone call to Hatfield to let them know where she was going, Ruth climbed into the plane. After checking the controls against her *Handling Notes,* she patted it and said firmly, 'You just behave yourself and don't disgrace either of us. We've got an audience.'

Giving a confident wave to the group of men who had gathered to watch, she set off, making sure she kept up the revs. It did have a tendency to swing about on take-off, but Ruth got it into the air without any mishap. Now all she had to do was land at Hawarden. At least there was plenty of space there to land a temperamental aircraft.

The airfield was a welcome sight and the landing was accomplished without too much difficulty. She knew that there were one or two pilots who actually liked flying this plane, but after this experience it certainly wasn't top of her list. Some planes were loved and almost flew themselves, others were not so nice; but it was all in a day's work for them.

'Have you got anything that needs to go south?' she asked on checking in.

'No, sorry.'

Oh, blast! she thought. She would have to phone Hatfield and see if there was any chance of being picked up, and if not, then it would be a train journey. That was such a waste of time when she could be making another delivery. She'd try something else first. 'Is there any chance of cadging a lift?'

'Well, there's couple more of your lot here. Why don't you see what they're doing? You'll find them in the Mess, I think.'

Ruth's stomach growled. She hadn't had anything to eat since breakfast, and it was now gone two o'clock. 'Can I get something to eat?'

'They'll rustle you up something.'

'Thanks.' Ruth had been here many times before and knew where to go. When she walked in she picked out the distinctive dark blue ATA uniform immediately, and headed towards the table where the two men were sitting.

They were deep in conversation and leapt to their feet, taken by surprise when she greeted them. It was Don and Jack.

'Ruth!' Don gave her a bear hug, which produced whistles from some of the other men there.

Jack didn't follow his friend's exuberant greeting, but just gave a lazy smile. 'What have you brought in?'

'An Airacobra.'

Pulling a comical face, Don held a chair for her to sit down. 'The first time I flew one of those I thought it was going to shake itself to bits. How did you get on with it?'

'Not bad, but it's not one of the nicest planes I've ever flown.' She glanced at their empty plates. 'I'm starving.'

'I'll get you something.' Jack stood up at once. 'What do you want?'

'Anything.' She watched him stride towards the counter and, not for the first time, couldn't help noticing that he moved with smooth elegance for such a big man.

He soon returned with a plate of spam, chips and a couple of slices of bread and margarine.

'Oh, lovely, thanks.' She tucked in, eating steadily until there wasn't a scrap left. Then she sighed. 'That's better.'

'Have you got another delivery to pick up from here?' Jack asked.

She shook her head, taking a gulp of the tea Don had just given her. 'What are you both doing?'

'Don's on his way to Prestwick, and I've managed to get a lift to Brize Norton in an RAF Hudson. I'm sure they'll take you as well.'

'That would be terrific, Jack. When are they leaving?'

'In around twenty minutes' time.' Jack stood up again. 'Let's go and see the pilot.'

After saying cheerio to Don, they made their way over to the plane. The pilot was doing the pre-flight checks.

'Could you take me as well, please?' Ruth asked.

He merely nodded. 'Hop on board. We'll be leaving in a few minutes.'

Don was already in a Spitfire, and tearing along to gain take-off speed.

'He's enjoying himself,' Ruth remarked, as they watched the plane climb into the air.

'Yeah.' Jack helped her into the plane. 'But aren't we all? The ATA is giving us the chance to fly many different aircraft. It's a rare opportunity, and one we'll probably never get again.'

'You're quite right.' Ruth settled down. 'Who would have believed women would be flying fighters.'

Jack nodded. 'Lucy's dead jealous, and is frantic to get over here and join in.'

'She told me. Do you know if she's heard anything yet?'

'No, and Ma said she practically attacks the mailman every day. She won't let him go until he's proved he hasn't got a delivery for her.'

Ruth could just picture the scene. 'I know exactly how she feels.'

Further conversation was out of the question as the engines roared into life. They both relaxed and closed their eyes, taking this chance to rest until they reached Brize Norton. They might be able to get another delivery from there, or catch the taxi Anson back to base.

On arrival, they found Rob there looking distraught. Ruth was sure there were tears in his eyes. She had soon discovered that the Americans showed their emotions, unashamed, where the English tried to keep them hidden. She liked that about them.

'What's happened, Rob?' Jack was already by his side.

'Tricia's missing.' His voice was husky.

Ruth's heart missed a couple of beats, but she quickly assured herself that there would be a perfectly good reason for them losing track of her. 'She could have landed at any airfield, Rob, and hasn't reported in yet.'

He shook his head miserably, and she realised that there was more to his friendship with Tricia than just spending Christmas with her and her family. This very likeable man was in love with Tricia.

'She was ferrying an Oxford to here, but she's three hours overdue.' Rob ran a hand over his eyes. 'I've been flying the area looking for any sign of her, but there's nothing.'

'That's good, isn't it?' Ruth didn't want to admit that something awful might have happened, but now she had the facts, she was terribly worried.

Jack placed an arm around Rob's shoulders. 'Come and have some tea. There's nothing more you can do at the moment.' He reached out with his other hand and took hold of Ruth's arm. 'You too.'

They didn't get a chance to drink their tea as the phone rang and was handed over to Rob.

Ruth watched in horror as all colour drained from Rob's face as he said, 'And the pilot?'

Jack was close to Ruth, a hand resting on her arm. They were both silent, bracing themselves for whatever news was to come. From Rob's expression, it wasn't good.

Rob replaced the phone carefully, and then lifted his head to face them.

'She's down. They've found the plane in a wooded area.' He drew in a huge breath. 'Tricia's dead.'

Chapter Twelve

Ruth turned slowly, numb with disbelief, and walked outside. She needed some fresh air. The pain of loss was almost too much to bear. Tricia, who had become a treasured friend, would no longer sit around the kitchen table with them, laughing and chatting the evening away. Tricia, with her quiet ways and abundant charm, would no longer be a part of their lives. Ruth shook her head, trying to clear it. Her friend had been a careful and meticulous pilot, checking every detail before deciding to fly. There had been numerous occasions when Ruth would have taken a chance on the weather, and Tricia had stopped her. And she had been absolutely right to do so each time. Whatever had happened to that plane must have been sudden and unexpected.

Ruth felt arms wrap around her from behind and knew it was Jack without looking. She hoped he wasn't going to make a fuss. She couldn't handle that at the moment. Her emotions were too raw. When he remained silent, she leant back and relaxed against his chest, grateful for his quiet strength.

They remained like that for several minutes, then, feeling more in control, she said, 'How's Rob?'

'OK. He's keeping busy talking to the men who found the plane, demanding every detail. There isn't much he doesn't know about aircraft.'

'I didn't realise they were so close. Tricia never said anything.'

'Rob adored her. He said she was the loveliest girl he'd ever known, but he never told her how he felt.'

'That's a shame. I'm sure the age difference wouldn't have bothered Tricia.'

'Rob said he was nearly old enough to be her father. He was content just to have her as a friend.'

Ruth gave a ragged sigh. 'She was special.'

'You all are, honey.' Jack kissed the top of her head, then turned her to face him, his expression concerned. 'She isn't the first to lose her life doing this job, and she won't be the last, but is there one of you who would stop flying?'

'No, emphatically not! I must get back and tell Gussie.'

'I expect she already knows, but we must all get back. Rob came in a Lysander, so I'll fly the three of us home.'

The word 'home' jarred Ruth. Their little cottage had always been like home to them, but it would never be the same again without Tricia. Ruth had waved her off this morning as they'd gone their separate ways, never dreaming that that would be the last time she would see her friend. What a devastating thing to have happened.

They walked back inside and found Rob drinking a mug of tea, looking shaken but composed. Two more mugs appeared and were handed to Jack and Ruth. They took them gratefully.

'Sorry to hear the bad news,' the sergeant told them. 'She came here often and was a lovely girl. Always a bright smile and cheery word for everyone.'

Ruth took a gulp of tea. 'Yes, she was. She'll be a great loss to all of us.'

'Fly us back now, Jack.' Rob drained his mug and put it down with a determined air. 'I must go and see Tricia's parents. And I've managed to get myself assigned to the investigation team.'

'Do you think that's wise?' Jack asked him. 'It will be a damned painful task—'

'I know, but it's something I want to do – I must do.'

They stopped at White Waltham first to drop off Rob, and then flew on to Hatfield. Jack stuck by Ruth's side as they walked into the Mess. A lot of the girls were there. They were subdued, but there was no weeping, just a gritty determination to carry on. Some were even on their way out to collect more planes to deliver. Once again Jack was awed by the fortitude and strength demonstrated by the people of this small island.

His respect grew when Gussie said to Ruth, 'It's a bugger, isn't it? Some kids said they heard a big bang and saw the plane coming straight down.'

'Want some tea, Jack?' Sally asked. 'It's a fresh pot.'

'No thanks, I'm full of the stuff.'

Gussie picked up her parachute, giving Ruth's shoulder a squeeze as she walked past. 'I've got another ferry, but I'll see you tonight. We'll go to the pub and get sloshed, eh?' Ruth nodded in agreement.

'We've got planes to shift.' Captain Jane Preston, the head of operations, was standing in the doorway with a bunch of chits in her hand. She looked grim, but steady.

Jack watched as the girls straightened up and filed over to take the chits. It was business as usual, and the fact that they'd just lost a much-loved friend wasn't going to stop them doing the job. He'd seen this with fighter pilots. Regardless of their losses they still sprinted for their aircraft, ready for another battle. Some reckoned it was sheer bloody-mindedness on their part, but if this was what it took to win the war against Hitler, then they had his respect.

As the girls left, Ruth paused in front of Jack. She touched his arm gently. 'Thanks. You'll see Rob's all right, won't you?'

'Sure.' He bent and kissed her cheek, then watched as she walked out to the waiting Anson.

'They'll be all right.' Jane stood beside him. 'It's best to keep them busy, but they're strong women and know the importance of the work they're doing. It hurts to lose someone close, but we are at war and tragedies are an everyday occurrence. Don't think we're unfeeling, Jack. We'll all grieve quietly in our own way.'

'I wish the folks back home could see this. I know they hear the news reports and are shown pictures of the destruction, but I doubt they understand the courage it takes to deal with the disasters. There's no way you can lose this war.'

Jane Preston cast him an amused glance. 'We've never believed that we would, but we've also known that it's going to be a long, bloody fight. We could do with some help, though.'

He knew she was referring to America coming into the war, but there was still little sign of that happening. He smiled down at her. 'I'm here.'

She laughed. 'So you are. And we're very grateful to have you and your fellow countrymen. Do you know that we are in the process of recruiting some of your female pilots?'

'I'd heard talk about it. Is this now definite? Only my sister's a damned good pilot and desperate to come.'

'Really?' Jane wrote a name and address on a piece of paper and gave it to Jack. 'This is one of your women pilots. She came over to see our operation, and I believe she has plans to start up something similar in America. But she has agreed that a small contingent of women should sign up with us. Tell your sister to contact her.'

'Thanks, I'll write straight away.'

Jane Preston studied him thoughtfully. 'It doesn't sound as if this tragedy has persuaded you to stop your sister from coming.'

'Nope, and it won't stop Lucy, either.'

'Good, she sounds just the type we need. I look forward to meeting her if she makes it through the selection process. Now, I must get back to work.'

Jack watched as she left the room, head high and step sure, and yet he knew she was feeling the loss of one of her pilots. He'd seen the pain in her eyes.

There was nothing more he could do to help. They

were all handling this in their own way. He'd better get back to White Waltham. The ferrying had to go on.

Their little cottage seemed empty without Tricia. Not that she ever made much noise, but her cheerful presence was missed terribly. Ruth and Gussie had completed the last delivery for the day, and they had been glad to have something to keep them occupied. Losing their friend had hit them hard, and they didn't want to stay in tonight. The cottage held so many memories, and they kept expecting Tricia to come in, smiling in her usual way and longing for a cup of tea.

Neither of them felt like eating, but they went through the motions and made some toast. They were about to eat it when there was a knock at the door.

Their neighbour was standing on the doorstep wearing his Home Guard uniform and standing to attention. He thrust a bunch of garden flowers at Ruth. 'I heard the bad news. I'm sorry. She was a nice kid. Let me know when the funeral is.' Then he turned and marched smartly down the path and out of the gate.

This gesture was too much for Ruth and, for the first time, the tears began to fall.

'Oh, hell!' Gussie had come up behind her and took the flowers out of Ruth's hand. She swiped away tears from her own eyes. 'Tricia wouldn't have wanted us to do this. We've got lots of happy memories so let's concentrate on those, shall we? Come on, we must wash our faces and go to the pub. What we need is some lively company.'

*　*　*

The investigation showed that there had been a serious mechanical failure and the plane had broken up in the air, giving the pilot no chance to bail out. The report concluded that it was highly likely that Tricia had been dead before the plane hit the ground. The fact that the end had probably been swift gave a small measure of comfort to her family and friends.

The church was packed for the funeral. Rob stood with Tricia's parents, grim faced as he supported the grieving couple. It brought back vivid memories of her brother's funeral, and Ruth knew just how they were feeling. It was a terrible thing to lose a child in the prime of life. The ATA were there in force, the golden wings on their uniforms glistening in the bright sunshine.

Their neighbour was also there with his entire Home Guard platoon, saluting smartly as the coffin was lowered into the ground. Ruth thought it a fine gesture of respect. As soon as the funeral was over, Jack left her side and went straight over to the family, shaking each hand in turn. He was a very thoughtful and caring man.

There were even more planes to be ferried, and with the increase in the types they were allowed to fly, the women all felt that they were playing a greater part in the ATA. They took pleasure in each new type of plane they added to their list, but Ruth and Gussie missed having Tricia around and were, therefore, delighted when told that they had been included in a group of women going to take over the Hamble Ferry Pool on the 29th of September – two days' time.

Flying that day had been washed out, but Ruth and Gussie hung around the Mess in case they were needed. They were the only two there as everyone else had given up and gone home for the night.

Gussie sat next to Ruth. 'Have you heard from Jack's sister lately?'

'I feel guilty about that.' Ruth grimaced. 'We've been so busy and I haven't written since Tricia was killed. I'll do it today without fail.'

The words were no sooner out of her mouth than Jack strode in.

'You're not flying in this weather, surely?' Ruth said. 'The rain's coming down in stair rods and even the birds are walking.'

'Nope.' He shook his head and folded his long frame on to a chair next to them. 'I came by car. Don's stuck up in Scotland, so I thought I'd take you girls out for a drink.'

'Now there's an offer I can't refuse.' Gussie brightened at once. 'Especially with such a good-looking fellow.'

Jack winked at Ruth. 'After that compliment I might even run to a meal as well.'

'Flattery works every time.' Gussie pulled him to his feet and kissed his cheek. 'You're on, big man. Is it to be the pub or can you afford the Swan Hotel, to celebrate our move to Hamble?'

After patting his breast pocket, he nodded. 'Let's see what the hotel has to offer.'

Now in high spirits, they sprinted for the car, relieved after hanging around most of the day to have the chance of an evening out.

Gussie got in the back, leaving Ruth to sit in the front with Jack. 'Have you heard from your sister lately?' Ruth asked.

'Had a letter today.' The windscreen wipers on the car Jack had borrowed were having trouble coping with the deluge and he had to drive slowly. 'She's survived the selection process and is waiting for a date to go to Canada for the conversion course.'

'Oh, that's wonderful!' Ruth felt even worse now. 'I'm sorry I haven't written for some weeks.'

He glanced across briefly and reached out to cover her hand with his, giving it a gentle squeeze. 'You've had a lot on your mind. Lucy understands. She's longing to meet you.'

'Me too.' Ruth turned slightly to face him. 'Is she as kind as you?'

He laughed. 'You've been taking lessons from Gussie. But I'm sorry, gals, my pockets won't run to champagne as well.'

'Oh damn!' Gussie swore. 'Nice try though, Ruthie.'

And that was how the evening went, with lively talk and a lot of laughter. Jack had taken Ruth's remark as a joke, but she'd meant it. She was becoming far too fond of him.

Chapter Thirteen

Hamble was a delightful village close to Southampton. Ruth and Gussie were lucky enough to find a small house to rent close enough to the airfield for them to be able to cycle there. Ruth saved her petrol ration so they could use the car for trips out now and again. They soon made themselves comfortable and were happy about the move. Tricia would always be missed, and they often talked about her with affection. But this was a new start and just what they needed.

Most of the deliveries taken on by the Hamble pool were of short duration, and there were more than enough planes to keep them all busy. That was just the way they liked it.

The autumn turned to winter and Ruth had hardly seen anything of Jack. Every pilot in the ATA was taking on as many deliveries as they could fit in during the daylight hours. By early December Ruth had decided she must track down Jack. Her parents wanted him to spend Christmas with them again – and so did she. It was disconcerting how often he invaded her thoughts now. She fought against the attraction because he was just passing through this country and would return home one day, but she was fighting a losing battle. She knew her parents were hoping that he was going to be a permanent fixture in all of their lives but, like her, they were realistic. Dakota was a long way away, and that was his home.

It was almost dark when Ruth landed the Spitfire at Hamble. She would take this on to Brize Norton in the morning, weather permitting. There was an excited buzz when she walked into the Mess. 'What's going on?' she asked.

'Haven't you heard?' Sally was clearly moved.

Ruth shook her head. 'I've been in the air most of the day.'

'The Japanese have bombed the American Fleet at Pearl Harbor. They've sunk a lot of their ships.'

'Oh, dear God!' Ruth's first thought was for the Americans working for the ATA. They would be devastated. 'Gussie, we must go and see Jack, Don and Rob.'

Her friend nodded, looking thoughtful. 'I expect we'll be losing our American pilots now. They'll want to get back home.'

The realisation that they might lose Jack sooner than expected was upsetting, making Ruth aware of just how used she had got to him being around. And Lucy would never come now.

It was about seven o'clock when Ruth and Gussie reached White Waltham. As soon as they walked in it was clear that no one had left. The Mess was crowded and noisy.

Simon spotted them first and pushed his way over to them. 'Ah, glad you've come. Gussie, perhaps you can calm Don down. He's fighting mad.'

'I'm not surprised. They were attacked without warning. What a despicable thing to do.' Gussie left them to find Don.

'How are the other Americans taking it, Simon?' Ruth asked.

'Shocked, angry and very vocal on the subject. Some are already packing to return home. We're going to miss them, but we're hoping to persuade some of the instructors to stay. We need them at the flying school.'

An ember of hope flickered inside Ruth. Jack had recently moved to the school and was more involved in teaching than ferrying . . .

'But this isn't the time to bring up the subject. We'll have to discuss it when everyone's got over the shock of the Japanese attack.'

'I can see that. What a terrible thing to have happened, Simon.'

'Yes, I agree, but from a purely selfish point of view, don't you see what this could mean?'

She ran the implication of the Japanese attack through her mind, and then she looked at Simon in surprise. She had been too concerned about Jack and the others to give this much thought. 'You think America will now come into the war with Germany?'

Simon nodded. 'It's a possibility.'

'But it's Japan who did this, not Germany.'

'I know, but you can bet that Churchill and Roosevelt are already talking. However, we'll have to wait and see what develops over the next few days.' Then Simon's mouth thinned with anger. 'In the meantime, our American friends are going to need our help and support. They're reeling at this despicable, cowardly act.'

'Hi, Ruth.'

She spun around to face Jack, and then touched his arm in a gesture of understanding. 'I'm so sorry, Jack.'

'Yeah.' He held tight to her hand for a moment, and then looked down into her face. 'Thanks for coming. Gussie's quietened Don. He's going home on the first available flight he can cadge, so are some of the others. Rob's definitely staying, Simon.'

'I'm pleased to hear that. He's a first-class instructor.' Simon hesitated for a moment. 'If any of you do decide to stay, you'll be more than welcome. You know that, don't you?'

Jack nodded, draping an arm around Ruth's shoulders. 'Don's managed to stockpile a few bottles of whisky from his trips to Scotland. You'll join us in seeing how many we can empty, won't you?'

After that things moved quickly. The attack on Pearl Harbour came on 7th December; on 8th December Britain and her allies declared war on Japan. On 11th December Hitler declared war on the United States, and they responded with a declaration of war against Germany and Italy. In a few short days the whole face of the war had changed, and Britain was no longer alone.

A week later, Ruth arrived home to find Gussie looking far from happy, which was unusual. She checked to see if the tea in the pot was still hot. It was, so she poured herself a cup and sat down. 'Why the long face, Gussie?'

'Don left today. He managed to get a lift in a bomber returning to America.'

'Oh, I'm sorry. You'll miss him, won't you?'

She shrugged. 'He was fun to be with, but not the type to want commitment of any kind, Ruthie. As soon as I heard about Pearl Harbor I knew he'd be leaving. I managed to see him before he left. He couldn't wait to get home. He said he'd keep in touch, but I know I'll never see or hear from him again.'

'That's quite a few who've gone already.' Ruth began to peel potatoes ready for their dinner. 'I know Rob's staying, but Jack hasn't decided yet. I must see him soon. If he's still here at Christmas, I hope he'll spend it with my parents. They like him, and this might be the last chance they'll have to spend some time with him.' She pulled a face. 'The partings you have to face in a war are hard, aren't they?'

'He won't leave without telling you, Ruthie,' Gussie said kindly. 'From what I've seen, you two were made for each other, but this damned war doesn't give anyone a chance to develop a proper relationship. Working for the ATA means we're scattered all over the country and only ever meet in passing.'

'That's true. I didn't like Jack when we first met, but he's grown on me.'

Gussie attacked a carrot. 'They have a habit of doing that, and then they up and leave you. The buggers.'

Ruth hit Gussie on the arm. 'Your language gets worse.'

'Must be the company I've been keeping. Don's language was colourful at times.' Gussie gave an inelegant snort. 'Anyway, why are we fretting over a couple of men? There's a war on and we've got better things to do – like flying all these lovely planes! We're lucky to be doing something we love so much, and should count our blessings, Ruthie.'

'Quite right.' Ruth popped sausages in the pan and watched them sizzle.

'Hey, where did you get all those?'

'There's a rather nice butcher in the village. I happened to be wearing my uniform at the time, and he said he'd heard about us. He was so interested in talking to me that I think he forgot to weigh the sausages.'

'Good move, Ruthie!'

They were both in better spirits as they sat down to enjoy their meal. There were constant changes to their lives now, and they just had to accept it and carry on.

Because Simon had run his own flying school before the war, he was doing more and more administration work at the ATA school. Not that he minded. He was making regular flights in the taxi and at least one delivery a day, so he was still doing plenty of flying.

With work over for the day he was relaxing in the Mess when he saw Jack wander in looking distracted. Ever since Pearl Harbor, Simon had been expecting him to say that he would be returning to America. Quite a few of the others had gone, except Rob, who had no intention of leaving. Simon was hoping Jack would stay as well. He was an excellent instructor and the pupils got on well with him. He was going to be sorely missed if he did leave them.

Jack was standing just inside the doorway, and then he spotted Simon and headed for him.

'Hi, Simon, mind if I talk to you?'

'Sit down, Jack, and tell me what's on your mind.' Simon pushed a mug and the pot towards him. 'The tea's still hot.'

'Thanks.' Jack poured and stirred sugar into the tea. After a pause, he looked up. 'I've always been restless.

That's why I took up flying. I thought barnstorming around the country would help me to find what I was looking for. But it didn't. When I decided to come here I had no idea what to expect. I found death and destruction, beauty and kindness, freezing cold lodgings and terrible food. I found laughter and sadness, and a dogged determination to survive, whatever the cost.'

Simon wondered where this was leading, but he said nothing, allowing Jack to talk freely – something he rarely did.

'I've also found genuine friendship, and I've never been so happy. I love what I'm doing; I love the country and the people. For the first time in my life I feel as if I'm where I should be. I've thought long and hard about what I should do. I can't leave, Simon. I belong here and I've decided to stay.'

'That's good news indeed, Jack. We need you.'

'Thanks.' He sat back and smiled for the first time. 'It's taken a lot of soul-searching, but I know I've made the right decision.'

'And talking of need, could you fly the taxi for me tomorrow?'

'Sure, no problem.'

'Thanks, I'll give you the schedule in the morning.' Simon was delighted Jack was staying. Not only was he a first-class pilot, but also he had become a good friend, and Simon had enormous respect for the tall American.

The girls had collected their delivery chits and were waiting for the taxi, which was coming from White Waltham today. Ruth smothered a laugh as she watched Gussie. Fed up with spending too much time on the ground because of short days and bad weather, and missing Don, her friend had taken up knitting. She was sitting in the corner of the Mess, a deep frown on her face and tongue caught between her teeth. The wool was a tangled heap, as usual, and Ruth knew it wouldn't be long before it was dumped on her to sort out. Gussie had even tried to knit in the taxi, but that only resulted in more dropped stitches. The sooner she found herself another boyfriend, the better, because Gussie didn't appear to have a creative bone in her body.

One of the recent additions to their group at Hamble was Sylvia, a petite, glamorous blonde, but a good pilot. The only problem was that it was sometimes difficult to see her in the cockpit and it was disconcerting to see a fighter flying itself. She was also not known for her patience.

'We'll lose this slot of clear weather if we don't get going soon.' She sighed irritably. 'Where the blazes is that taxi?'

'Just coming in now.' Gussie thrust the knitting at Ruth. 'Do the usual, Ruthie.'

Stuffing it in her bag, Ruth fought back a smile. Perhaps she could lose it during the day.

'Ah, it's the big man himself.' Gussie's frown disappeared as Jack strode in.

'Hi, gals, who wants a lift this morning?'

Sylvia sidled up to Ruth. 'Who's that? I haven't seen him before.'

'Jack Nelson. He's one of our American instructors.'

'Really?' Sylvia hadn't taken her eyes off Jack as he talked with Jane, receiving further instructions for the day. 'I wouldn't mind him instructing me in a few things. American, you say?'

'That's right,' Ruth said. But she was talking to an empty space. Sylvia was already across the room.

'Why didn't you warn her off, Ruthie?'

'He doesn't belong to me, Gussie.'

'No, but that's your fault. You try to pretend that you don't care for him, but you do. Why on earth don't you make a move – just like that bundle of sex appeal is doing right now?'

Jack had his head bent as he listened to something Sylvia was saying, a smile on his face. Ruth turned away, not wanting to acknowledge the stab of jealousy she felt. 'I'm not going to chase after any man. You know the American men aren't slow when it comes to chatting up the girls, but Jack's never shown the slightest interest in me, except as a friend. I'm not going to make a fool of myself!'

Gussie pursed her lips. 'But you are going to invite him home for Christmas?'

'Of course. My parents want him to come.'

'Of course.' Gussie raised her eyes to the ceiling in exasperation. 'And your feelings don't come into it?'

'Certainly not. I admit that I'm attracted to him, but it's up to him to make the first move, if he's interested.'

'Right, gals, lets get this show in the air.' Jack waved across the room to Ruth and Gussie, and then walked out with Sylvia at his side.

'Men are so easily taken in by a pretty face, aren't they?' Gussie muttered as they piled into the Anson. 'Not that yours isn't lovely, Ruthie,' she added hastily.

Ruth laughed. 'Do you know, Gussie, I believe there's a real romantic under your devil-may-care attitude.'

'Course there is. Have you only just discovered that?'

Three of them got out at Cowley; the rest were going on to another factory airfield at Aston Down.

When Jack jumped down to help them out, Ruth took her chance to mention her parents' invitation. There was no telling when she would run into him again. 'My parents would like you to join us for Christmas again – that's if you'll still be here, of course.'

'Tell them thanks, I'd like that.' His smile was one of genuine pleasure. 'I'm not leaving, Ruth. I've decided to stay here.'

'Oh, I'm so glad.' Ruth couldn't hide her relief at Jack's decision to stay, and then tried to cover it by saying, 'Simon and everyone at the flying school will be pleased that both you and Rob are staying.'

'So they've said.' Jack tipped his head on one side, thoughtfully. 'And what about you, honey; are *you* pleased I'm staying?'

'Of course I am,' she admitted. What was the point of denying it? 'And my parents will be over the moon.'

'Jack!' There were calls from the inside of the plane. 'Will you stop gassing? We've got work to do.'

'You'd better get going,' Ruth laughed, 'or they'll take off without you.'

He spun around quickly. 'Whoa, gals, don't worry – I'll get you there in no time at all.'

With a couple of easy moves, Jack was back in the pilot's seat, the banter continuing as he turned for take-off.

Gussie and Ruth were waving and grinning. Sylvia was still standing beside them.

'Erm . . . you seem very friendly with him, Ruth. Would I be treading on your toes by making up to him?'

'Not at all,' she lied. 'He's a good friend, that's all.'

'So you don't mind?'

'Do your best.' Ruth smiled sweetly as the thought ran through her head – *and I'll break your neck if you succeed*.

They went their separate ways. Ruth collected a Spitfire for delivery to Ternhill, and soared into the air, elated. Jack was staying and she'd just admitted to herself that her feelings for him had grown to more than friendship. She was a fool, of course, but with his decision to stay the day of parting had been postponed.

She listened to the sound of the Merlin engine and felt the power of the plane. This aircraft could do so much but, as ferry pilots, they had to fly them straight from one destination to another. She glanced around, up, down and behind, to check that the sky was empty. No one would know.

For ten minutes she indulged in rolls, spins and even a somersault. When she straightened out again she was breathless with sheer joy. The Spitfire certainly lived up to its reputation. What a plane!

Another quick look around showed she was still up there on her own. She'd just broken all the rules, but that was the kind of mood she was in.

'Just you watch out, Jack Nelson,' she shouted. 'You're next, and to hell with the consequences!'

Chapter Fourteen

There was a lot in the mailbox that morning and Lucy shuffled the letters looking for the important ones. There were two from Jack, one for each of them. He could send letters addressed to both of them, but he never did. Their mother always received a separate one from him. He was thoughtful like that, and she knew it meant a lot to their mom.

Lucy's hand shook slightly when she saw the letter she had been waiting anxiously for, but she'd save that for later, knowing her mother would be upset if it was a date for her to go to Canada at last. After the terrible attack by the Japanese, she was praying that the idea of sending female pilots over to England had not been cancelled. Even if Jack came home, she still wanted to go. If the scheme was cancelled then she would make her own way to England. Ruth would help her when she arrived, she was sure.

'Anything from Jack?' Bet was waiting for Lucy. She handed over her mother's letters, and they both sat down to read.

'He's not coming back, Lucy.' Bet's voice was heavy with disappointment. 'I was sure he would now we are at war as well.'

Jack obviously hadn't gone into detail in Bet's letter, but in Lucy's he had spelt out his reasons for staying. It listed the good and bad points and how important he felt the work was. But the unspoken words came through loud and clear: he loved what he was doing and he loved where he was. She read this out to her mother.

There was silence for a moment as Bet digested her son's reasons for staying with the ATA. Then she gave Lucy a tremulous smile. 'He's happy, isn't he?'

'Yes, Mom, I believe he's found something special in England.'

'I'm sure glad about that. He was a restless boy from the moment he was born. And as he grew he was always looking over the horizon to see what was there. I never did know what he was looking for, but I guess he's found it at last.' Bet read further down her own letter. 'He says he's spending Christmas with Ruth's folks again. I wonder if there's a romance between him and Ruth?'

'He's never said.'

'No, well, he wouldn't. You know your brother, Lucy.'

'Sure do. Whatever he feels for her, he'll keep to himself.'

The next letter Lucy opened was from Ruth. She yelped with delight when a photo fell out. 'Wow, look at this, Mom! It's some of the girls sitting on a Spitfire!'

Bet was immediately next to her daughter as they studied the picture. 'Which one's Ruth?'

'She says she's on the wing, third from the left. There,

that's her. Oh, look at the way they're all laughing, and isn't she pretty? And don't they look terrific in their uniforms!'

'They're a fine bunch.' Bet stifled a sigh when she saw her daughter's animated expression. 'Now Jack's staying I suppose you'll still go and join them?'

'I'd have gone even if Jack had come back.'

'Course you would. I raised a couple of brave youngsters, didn't I?' She kissed her daughter's cheek. 'Have you heard anything yet?'

'I think this is news.' Lucy studied the letter in her hands, but made no move to open it.

'Don't keep us in suspense. See what it says.'

Lucy slit open the envelope, her heart thumping, and read slowly.

'Well?'

'I've been asked to go to Canada in six weeks' time to go through various tests.' The excitement and relief suddenly became too much for her and she leapt to her feet, dragging her mother up and dancing her around the room. 'They want me, Mom! They want me!'

'Never doubted it for a minute. You and your brother are the best damned pilots in the whole world.' Bet joined in her daughter's celebration with enthusiasm. 'I'm real proud of both of you.'

Christmas came and went, followed by the New Year. No one knew what 1942 would bring, but one thing was for sure: if Lucy did well in Canada, she would soon be heading for England. And so would a lot of American troops, by the look of things.

Bet had joined up with a group of women and thrown herself into fundraising to help the war effort. She had also gone to work in an engineering factory making parts for tanks. Lucy was relieved to see all this activity. At least her mother wouldn't be sitting at home alone while both of her children were overseas.

The time arrived for Lucy to make her way to Montreal, and she was pleased she'd spent the last few months training for her instructor's rating. She'd seen Jack do this before he'd applied to join the ATA, and she was sure it had helped her in the selection process.

There were twenty-five girls hoping to be chosen, and it was an exciting time. After trying out in Harvards and undergoing lengthy medical and other flying tests, the first ones were selected. Lucy was overjoyed to be chosen as one of the first five to make the journey. The others would follow at intervals. Then it was on a train to Newfoundland to await the convoy to take them to England.

Spring was just around the corner, and Ruth wandered in her mother's garden. It was always referred to in this way because it was entirely Alice's domain. Ruth had two days off and had come home to relax. The Hamble pool had doubled in size since they'd moved there, and the women had progressed, taking on more and more different aircraft. Ruth and Gussie had applied for the Class 4+ rating so they could fly all types of twin-engine planes, but they hadn't heard anything yet.

'Hi, Ruth.'

She spun around, surprised. 'Jack! I didn't know you

were coming. I could have brought you in my car.'

'I didn't know myself until Simon told me to clear off for a couple of days. Only not as politely as that.'

'Why did he do that?' Now she came to look closely at him, he did appear to be rather drawn and tired.

'Jane told me that the first batch of American women are on their way. Lucy's one of them.'

She guessed immediately his concern. 'You're worried about the sea journey.'

'Yeah, it's damned dangerous.'

'You made it all right, Jack, and there's no reason why Lucy shouldn't.' She placed a hand on his arm in a gesture of reassurance.

He clasped her hand. 'I know that, but some haven't.'

She was well aware that some pilots had been lost at sea on the way over when their ships had been torpedoed, but she spoke brightly. 'I'm really going to meet her at last! Do you know when she's arriving?'

'No, Jane couldn't give me that information, but she said she'd let me know as soon as the ship docks.'

'Tea's ready!' Ruth's mother called.

Jack still held Ruth's hand as they walked back to the house. She couldn't help remembering her wild ride in the Spitfire and declaring that he was next on her list. But she hadn't done anything about it. They were closer now and they shared an easy friendship, but he'd only ever kissed her on the cheek, like a brother. She just couldn't fathom what his true feelings for her were, so she kept their meetings light. However, she was pleased he'd come to her when worried about his sister, but he was certainly different from some of the American troops who had arrived at the end of January. From the tales she'd heard, they pursued the girls with enthusiasm, and loved the British pubs. They were determined to make the best of being so far away from home, and no one could blame them for that.

'Why don't you both go to the pictures tonight?' Ruth's mother suggested as she handed round the tea. 'They're showing *Gone with the Wind* again at the Rex cinema. You haven't seen it yet, have you, Ruth?'

She was about to protest that Jack wouldn't want to go, but was stopped.

'What?' Jack looked at Ruth in surprise. 'You haven't seen it yet?'

'I just haven't found the time.'

'We'll have to put that right.' He turned to Alice. 'Do you know what time it's showing?'

'Last house is seven o'clock.'

'Shall we go, Ruth? It'll do us good to relax. It's a great film and I wouldn't mind seeing it again.'

He seemed so enthusiastic that she couldn't refuse. At least it would take his mind off worrying about his sister for a while. She nodded. 'We can take my car. I've got enough petrol for that short journey.'

'Don't worry about that, my dear.' Her father gave her a sly wink. 'I've got a couple of gallons in the garage. I've been saving them for you.'

'Want to drive?' Ruth asked as they were leaving. When Jack nodded, she tossed him the keys.

He seemed more relaxed now and began to talk about his barnstorming days, and some of the crazy things he and

153

Lucy had got up to. 'There was this Austrian pilot who chased Lucy from show to show. She couldn't get rid of him. He was nice enough, but she just wasn't interested. The war in Europe put a stop to it when he had to return home – much to Lucy's relief.'

That reminded Ruth about Sylvia, and she couldn't stop herself from asking, 'Have you seen much of Sylvia?'

There was a slight hesitation, then he said, 'I've tripped over her now and again.'

The way he'd phrased the answer told her that Sylvia had indeed been running after him. She was quite lovely looking and had caused a lot of interest amongst the men. They were queuing up to take her out, and Ruth couldn't imagine that Jack would be immune to her obvious charms. 'She's been interested in you ever since she first saw you. Have you taken her out?'

'Nope. She's not my type – and I like to do the running.' Knowing Jack as she did, that was amusing and she laughed. 'What's so funny?'

'Oh, Jack, if a girl waited for you to make a move, she'd be old and grey by the time you noticed her!'

The car screeched to a stop as he hit the brakes suddenly, making her gasp in surprise. They were on a narrow country road and it was pitch black. He'd even turned off the small amount of lights they were allowed on the car.

'Meaning?'

'You can't stop here. If another car comes along they won't be able to see us.' She scrabbled in her bag for a torch, a necessary requirement in a country completely blacked out from dusk to dawn.

'We're not moving until you explain that last remark.'

'Don't mess about, Jack. We'll miss the picture.' When he didn't speak, she sighed. 'I only meant that you aren't like a lot of your countrymen. Chasing girls seems to be a favourite pastime of theirs.'

'They're a long way from home and lonely, Ruth.'

'I know that, and the English girls like them too.'

'We're a very likable race. Now, back to your last remark. Are you referring to you and me?'

Oh, hell, how did she get herself into this mess? 'Just forget I said it.'

'Not a chance. Your ma and pa have been real good to me, and I wasn't about to throw their hospitality back in their faces by hitting on their daughter, however much I want to. Get out of the car.'

'Pardon?' She found her torch and shone it on his face. The damned man was laughing at her!

'It's my blasted car! You get out!'

She heard the car door open and then footsteps walking around the back. She craned her neck, but it was too dark to see what he was up to. Then her door opened and she was hauled out. He pinned her against the car so she couldn't move.

'Ma brought me up to be a gentleman where women are concerned, but I'm going to forget all about that now.'

When his lips met hers, the intensity of the kiss literally took her breath away. She'd heard that expression, but had never believed it – until now.

When she slipped her arms around him the kiss softened and she responded, pouring out the love she had kept so carefully hidden.

When he stepped back slightly and began to run his hands up and down her arms, she held on to the car for support.

'Ah, hell, honey, I knew that would happen if I ever touched you. As much as I need to carry you into those woods and make love to you, I'm not going to. You can't afford to be distracted at the moment because you've been chosen, along with Gussie, to go to the flying school for your Class 4+ rating.'

That news snapped Ruth back to the here and now. 'How do you know this? We haven't been told yet.'

'Rob told me today. The news will be waiting for you when you get back from leave. We need more pilots cleared to fly all the twin-engine aircraft.'

There was a different kind of excitement running through her now. Being this close to Jack had scrambled her brains for a moment, but now she was focussed again. 'We're making progress, aren't we?'

'You sure are.' He kissed her firmly. 'Now, you forget this ever happened and concentrate on what you have to do. I'll be around, watching and waiting.'

She gaped at him in the dark. She couldn't believe this. He'd kissed her senseless, and now he was saying that this was the end? He couldn't do that. She didn't want him to do that.

He guessed her inner turmoil. 'Look, honey, we can't afford to get heavily involved at this time. There's too much to do, and the job isn't without risk. We must wait.'

'Wait? Suppose I meet someone else while you're *waiting*?'

'If another man gets anywhere near you, then he'll have me to deal with.' He reached past her and opened the door. 'Now get in. We've got a film to see.'

Very aware of the determined tone of his voice, she obeyed. She wasn't very experienced with men, and he had her thoroughly confused. But she was sure of one thing: she loved this unusual American. How very stupid of her, but it wasn't any good fretting; it had happened and that was that. It was something she was going to have to come to terms with.

Ruth was sure it had been a good picture, but she couldn't remember a thing about it. During the long sleepless night her mind cleared, and she knew Jack was right. If she was about to graduate to the twin-engine bombers, then she was going to need all her wits about her.

She smiled when she recalled him saying that any man who came near her would have him to deal with. It showed he cared, and that would have to be enough for the moment. They were in the middle of a war, and while many were rushing into hasty romances, that wasn't Jack's way. Only the future would tell if their relationship was going to be permanent – or merely a fly-past.

Chapter Fifteen

Ruth had worked for twelve days without a break when the news arrived that they would be going to the flying school in a week's time. Now she had a much-needed rest for three days, and wondered where Jack was. She'd hardly seen him since the weekend at her parents' house. He was terribly busy, she knew, just like the rest of them. If a day was washed out by the weather, they had to work extra hard to clear the backlog from the factories. But the work was satisfying and they were all in their element flying so many different planes. And now she was about to add more to the list. Gussie was taking it all in her stride, but Ruth was extra excited about taking this step forward. At times like this she couldn't help thinking of Tricia with sadness. How she would have loved the chance to be a part of this.

She poured herself another cup of tea. She was still in the Mess waiting for Gussie to return. Perhaps they'd go to the pub tonight. The door opened and Jack strolled in.

'Hi, there.' He kissed her firmly. 'What brings you here?'

'Uh-oh.' He placed his fingers under her chin and lifted her face to study it carefully. 'Aren't you pleased to see me?'

'Of course I am.' She pulled a face. 'Sorry, Jack. I'm tired and was just thinking about Tricia.'

He sat beside her. 'I expect she's up there urging you all on. Are you too tired to come to London with me?'

She straightened up. 'No. Where are we going?'

'The Savoy. Lucy's there.'

'What?' Ruth's tiredness was immediately forgotten. 'When did she arrive? What's she doing in the Savoy?'

'They docked yesterday. There's five of them and they've been booked into the hotel for two days before being brought down here.'

'Wow, lucky them! The ATA did that?'

Jack shook his head. 'No, it's being paid for by the American woman in charge. I phoned Lucy and she's got a bottle of champagne waiting for us.'

Ruth was about to ask where they'd got champagne from, but changed her mind. These girls were obviously being treated to a bit of luxury before starting work as ferry pilots. Good luck to them. She leapt to her feet. 'I must change.'

'You're just fine the way you are.'

'You sure?' She glanced down at her slacks. 'I've got a skirt here. It won't take me a minute to freshen up and put that on.'

'OK, but hurry. I told Lucy we'd be there in an hour.'

'We'll never make that. You know how unpredictable the trains are, and I'm nearly out of petrol.'

He looked smug. 'I've borrowed Simon's car, and I won't mention where the gas came from.'

'*Petrol*,' she corrected, giving his arm a sharp tap.

'Whatever.' He shrugged and bent his head to give her another kiss. 'Hurry.'

It was a good job the Mess was empty, Ruth thought, as she hurried to the washroom. He was in an affectionate mood, and obviously relieved that his sister had made it safely. This could be an entertaining evening, in more ways than one.

As soon as they walked into the bar at the Savoy, there was a loud shriek of delight and a girl hurled herself at Jack. He lifted her off the floor and spun her round and round. 'Hiya, big brother.'

'Hi, yourself. Great digs you've got here.' He placed her back on the floor and pulled Ruth forward. 'Ruth, this noisy bundle is my sister.'

There was no time for Ruth to say anything before she was clasped in an enthusiastic hug.

Jack was laughing at the surprise on Ruth's face. 'Lucy, you don't greet the English like that for the first time. You shake hands and say how pleased you are to meet them.'

'Oh, listen to his accent!' his sister exclaimed, dragging him towards her friends. 'This is my big brother.' Then she gave him a saucy glance. 'Anyway, I don't have to be like that with Ruth. We already know each other.' She gave Ruth another hug for good measure. 'I'm sure glad to see you at last, and thanks for all the letters you've sent. We did wonder at times if we were going to make it. Ships kept disappearing from the convoy, and no one would tell us where they'd gone. Come and meet the rest of the gang. This is Edna, Pat, Betty and Sara.'

They took Jack at his word and, laughing, they all shook hands.

'Barman!' Lucy called. 'You got our champagne nice and cold?'

'I have, miss.' He produced a bottle and glasses, and seemed fascinated by the ATA uniform. He spoke quietly to Jack. 'I hope you don't mind me asking, sir, but are you Free French?'

'No, we're Air Transport Auxiliary. I'm American and my friend is English.'

He still looked puzzled. 'Excuse my ignorance, sir, but what do you do?'

'We fly planes from factories and deliver them wherever they're needed.'

'You're both wearing wings, so does the lady do the same?'

'Sure, there are a lot of women in the ATA. They fly anything.'

'And we've come over to join them,' Pat said. 'Don't they look great? I can't wait to get my hands on a Spitfire.'

The barman's mouth dropped open, and he looked as if he wanted to ask more questions, but he had to attend to other customers.

It turned out to be a lively evening and they gathered quite a crowd around them, including several American soldiers who had been attracted by the sound of the American accent. The drink was flowing freely, but Ruth had never been fond of too much alcohol. She noticed that Jack was also making do with one glass, refusing all attempts to buy him more.

'Can you stay the night?' Lucy asked. 'We've got another day in London before we join you. I'm sure they could find you a room – *rooms,*' she corrected quickly.

Jack shook his head. 'I'm flying in the morning.' He glanced at Ruth. 'You stay if you've got the time.'

'I'm going to spend a couple of days with my parents before going on a course.' She really needed a rest, and that wouldn't be possible if she stayed in London with this boisterous crowd of girls. They were obviously determined to have a good time, and she knew she would probably feel the same if she found herself in New York, but gaining her new rating was the only thing on her mind at the moment. The chance to fly twin-engine bombers was an exciting one, and she was determined to pass the tests.

'What course is that?' Pat asked. She was slightly older than the others, and had a direct, intelligent way about her.

Ruth was reluctant to go into details. 'Oh, it's just to upgrade my rating. We all do them from time to time.'

Pat was about to continue with the questions when Jack stood up. 'We must get back, but we'll see you all in a couple of days.'

It took them at least ten minutes to get out of the door. They'd parked the car round the back of the hotel and Jack placed an arm around Ruth as they walked along the Strand for a few yards, and then down a side street.

When they sat in the car, Jack turned to her. 'Overpowering in a group, aren't they? But they're the pick of the bunch.

They're finding it all very exciting at the moment, but they'll settle down once they start ferrying.'

'I liked them.' Ruth touched Jack's arm. 'Lucy's lovely, and I look forward to getting to know her better.'

'They'll be going to Luton first, then to White Waltham to take some tests, and they're going to have to learn to navigate around this country.' Jack started the car and they made their way along the Strand, heading for home.

Ruth relaxed, content to let Jack do the driving, her tiredness returning. She would go to her parents' and sleep for two days.

Simon leant against the wall and watched the American girls in the room. A couple had been quite disgruntled to discover they had to take flying tests before they could start work. His gaze lingered on Jack's sister. The sun was streaming through the window and turning her corn-coloured hair to gold. She was quite lovely and had a good temperament, just like her brother. She had taken all the tests with cheerful good humour, and now they were at White Waltham for more instruction before they could start work.

Captain Anders was about to give them a lecture, and Simon wondered how the girls would take the news of more delays before they could start the job they came here to do.

'You have all passed the flying tests, but no one doubted that. You wouldn't have got this far if you hadn't been competent pilots. I know some of you thought it was a waste of time, but the ATA has its rules.' He paused, glancing at each one in turn, then continued. 'I am now going to give you a list of dos and don'ts. For the most part you will be flying planes coming straight from the factories. They will not be fitted with radios or any navigational aids, so you must at all times keep below the clouds or you will get lost. The weather in this country can be changeable. Always check with the Met. The decision on whether to fly or not will be yours. Don't take chances. We don't look kindly on aircraft getting damaged.' He paused again. 'And we don't like losing pilots, so don't be reckless. We will sack you if we discover that you can't be trusted. And that brings me to another point. Members of the ATA are not part of the military, as you already know, so there is no need to salute anyone. We wear a uniform to identify us because we fly into operational airfields. The task ahead of you now is to learn to navigate around this country. An additional hazard you will encounter is that all the factory sites are well camouflaged. These are not easy to spot from the air unless you know they are there. These are all things you must learn before you can start work.'

Simon managed to keep a straight face with difficulty when there were several groans.

'How long is that going to take?' It was Pat who spoke.

'That will be entirely up to you. Learn fast, ladies, because we need you. The instructors here will give you all the help you need. Listen to them.' With a brief nod, he left the room.

Betty gave a growl of frustration. 'What's with all these delays? We're experienced pilots, and I thought we'd start work straight away.'

'It would help to know where we're going, though,' Lucy pointed out. 'We'd soon get lost if we didn't know the landmarks, especially as some are hard to spot.'

Ah, thought Simon, Jack's sister has his good sense. Now it was his turn. He stepped forward. 'Absolutely right, Miss Nelson. The sooner we start the sooner you'll get to work.'

At the end of the day, Jack was waiting for Simon. 'How are they doing?'

'Fine. Once we got started they soon realised the importance of what we're trying to teach them. There are hazards in this country they have never encountered before. Like our weather, balloons, ground crews who will shoot at them if they fly too high and aren't easy to identify – not to mention marauding Luftwaffe who won't know they are unarmed women flying the planes.'

'I guess they soon got the point.'

'Very quickly.' Simon walked beside Jack as they made their way to the Mess. 'They're a bright bunch, and we'll soon be able to put them to work. Your sister seems the steady sort.'

'Yeah, she's a darling.' Jack grinned. 'Come and have a drink with us tonight. I'm going to introduce Lucy to the English pub.'

'I'd like that. Where are you going?'

'The Stag, just down the road. See you there around eight.'

'I'll get there as soon as I can. I've got some paperwork to deal with first.'

The pub was packed when Simon arrived. He pushed through the sea of uniforms – being close to Portsmouth

165

there were quite a few sailors there. Someone was pounding away on the piano and the singing was enthusiastic. And the evening had only just begun.

Simon found Jack, Rob and Lucy in the other bar where it was marginally quieter.

Lucy waved when she saw him. 'Hi, teacher. Isn't this fun? Come and have a drink.'

When he reached them, Jack already had a pint of bitter on the table for him. He knew Simon's tipple and hadn't needed to ask. He grabbed a chair from another table and sat down. 'Didn't the other girls want to come?'

'Nah.' Lucy gazed from one man to the other. 'I wanted to keep you three handsome men to myself.'

Simon had been drawn to Lucy from the moment he'd seen her and was happy to be spending an evening in her company. 'So, what do you think of the pub?'

She gurgled with amusement. 'I've never seen or heard anything like it. I think I'm going to like it here.'

I hope you do, Simon thought. He couldn't remember when he'd been so attracted to a girl. He wanted to ask her out, but he'd wait for a while until she'd found her feet in the ATA. As her instructor at the moment, he wanted her whole attention focussed on what she had to learn. There would be plenty of time to get to know her better.

Chapter Sixteen

There was a knot of excitement churning in Ruth's stomach as she walked towards the Blenheim bomber. This was the last step towards her new rating, and then she would be able to fly all the twins.

Once she had strapped herself in the nerves vanished. There was nothing to worry about. All she had to do was take off, do a circuit around the airfield, and land. She wouldn't think about all the eyes watching her.

A young RAF boy was standing with a group of others, his mouth open in disbelief. 'She ain't going to fly that, surely?'

'Why not?' Simon asked.

'Well, she's a blooming girl!' He watched as the engines roared in to life and Ruth taxied for take-off. 'My God, she is!'

Jack joined Simon as the Blenheim soared into the air.

'Go girl!' Jack murmured, never taking his eyes off the plane. 'Nice smooth turn . . . that's it . . . perfect . . .'

This was a tense time for any pilot, Simon knew only too

well, but he had complete confidence in Ruth's ability. He'd known from the start that she was going to be a competent pilot, and not only was that true, but she had surpassed all his expectations.

'Now, start your approach.' Jack was still murmuring instructions under his breath. 'Wheels down . . . right . . .'

Simon watched with everyone else as the Blenheim touched down in a faultless landing, and taxied over to the parking bay. Captain Anders gave Simon a thumbs-up sign as he waited for Ruth to join him.

'You can breathe now, Jack,' Simon joked.

The tall man beside him gave a grunt of satisfaction. 'Even I would have been proud of that landing. Our Ruth certainly has steady nerves. She did well.'

'I never had the slightest doubt.'

'Yeah.' Jack watched Ruth jump down, walk beside the examiner and disappear into the building. 'She'll have passed. Do you know how Gussie's getting on?'

'She went up two hours ago and has her new rating.'

'Great.' Jack glanced at his watch and pulled a face. 'I should have been at Cowley ten minutes ago.'

'Had engine trouble, did you?' Simon asked dryly.

'Hmm, strange noise coming from the engine, so I thought I'd better land here and get it checked before continuing.'

'Very wise.'

They gave each other knowing looks, and then Jack thumped Simon on the back. 'We'd better get going then. Looks like we've got two more pilots for the twin-engine bombers.'

He started to walk away when Simon called him. 'The American girls are about to be sent to their pool at Ratcliffe.

They've all been passed as Class 2 single-engine pilots, and are ready to start work.'

'Lucy told me. They're raring to go.' Jack was about to continue walking when an Airacobra swept low over the airfield.

'What the hell?' Simon shaded his eyes, watching the plane bank, turn, and fly over again at treetop level.

'Trouble.' Jack tipped his head to one side, listening. 'Sounds OK. I'll bet the instruments are saying that the nose wheel isn't down. It happened to me in one of those. I took a chance and was lucky, but it's a tough decision.'

'Well, it's down, but is it locked?'

'That's something the pilot will have to decide. It's a choice between setting it down without any wheels, or risking a somersault if the nose wheel collapses.'

An RAF flight sergeant joined them. 'What do you think's wrong?'

'Nose wheel,' Jack stated. 'Next time round we'll have to signal somehow that it's down.'

The plane came over again very low and the sergeant gave the signal. 'Hope he understood that.'

'Looks like it. He's coming in this time.' Simon noted that the fire trucks and rescue teams were already in place.

The Airacobra touched down and they held their breath, eyes fixed on the nose wheel.

'It's OK,' Jack said in relief as the plane slowed to a stop.

'I heard that we're sending these to Russia.' The sergeant glanced at Jack. 'Sorry, mate, but the RAF boys don't like this American plane.'

'Not many do,' Jack agreed. 'It looks good in the air, but it's got a few unpleasant habits.'

They all walked over to the plane and waited for the pilot to get out.

'Hello, Sally.' Jack helped her down. 'Were you worried about the nose wheel?'

'Yes, there was a chance that it wasn't down.' She patted the wing. 'Temperamental beast, isn't it? I just prayed that the signal I'd received meant all was well and I could come in.' She smiled at the sergeant. 'Thanks.'

'You're welcome.' He was eyeing her with some respect. 'I'll get it checked.'

'Glad it turned out all right.' Simon looked at his watch. 'We must get going, Jack. Oh, and Sally, you'll find Ruth and Gussie here. They've taken the final test for their new rating.'

'Wonderful! I'll find them at once – and I could do with a strong cup of tea after that flight!'

As they walked towards their waiting aircraft, Jack nudged Simon. 'That young boy must be a new recruit. He's staring at Sally as if he can't believe his eyes. Girls flying combat aircraft is not something he expected to see.'

Simon's mouth twitched in amusement. 'Someone should have told him, but he'll soon get used to it.'

Now there was a Hurricane making its approach and Jack couldn't resist calling the boy. 'Hey, buddy, here comes another woman. Better make a fresh pot of tea.'

The boy giggled. 'Why don't we scramble a squadron of women pilots? Jerry would run for his life.'

'Cheeky sod,' Simon snorted.

As soon as the Hurricane landed, Sylvia jumped down, spotted Jack immediately, and began waving frantically.

Simon gave Jack an amused glance. 'I hear she's been chasing you.'

'She does have a habit of turning up quite often, but I'm not interested. Can't you get her sent up north somewhere out of the way?'

'Coward!'

'You bet.' Jack paused in the act of climbing into the Spitfire. 'You interested in my little sister?'

'Might be. Do you mind?'

'Nope, she makes her own decisions. Good luck, though.' With a wave of his hand he got in the plane and wasted no time taking off.

Simon followed in the Anson. He had pilots to pick up.

It was two hours later when Simon arrived back at White Waltham and found Lucy waiting for him.

'Hi, teacher. We're off to Ratcliffe in the morning and I wanted to thank you. You're a great instructor.'

Simon nodded in acknowledgement of the compliment. 'Where are the others?'

'Off celebrating, but I wanted to see my brother and Ruth before I leave.' She gave him a teasing smile. 'And you, of course.'

'Jack was here a while back, but you were all out on training flights. He should be back any minute now. He's bringing pilots in the Fairchild.' Simon glanced up. 'Sounds like him now.'

Lucy watched the plane land and disgorge its pilots. There was a wistful smile on her face as her brother walked towards them, his parachute over his shoulder. 'You know, Simon, he's a different man now. I believe he's truly happy for the first time ever. He loves this country, and feels he's making a worthwhile contribution to the war effort by using his talent for flying.'

Simon said nothing as Jack reached them. He had the feeling that Lucy was right, and from what he'd seen today, it was more than the love of this country keeping him here. Ruth was another reason.

Before even greeting them, Jack turned straight to Simon. 'Have you had confirmation yet about Ruth?'

'Yes, Captain Anders phoned me. She passed with flying colours.'

'Great.' Jack smiled and said, 'Hi, Lucy.'

She gave him a hug, and then stepped back, almost dancing with excitement. 'Are you saying Ruth has her new rating?'

'Sure she has. We both watched her fly the Blenheim, didn't we, Simon?'

'She did well, and Gussie passed as well.'

'Wow! We must all celebrate. Can we go over to Hamble now? It's the only chance I'll get because I'm leaving early in the morning.'

'I was about to nip over there now the day's flying is over. There's a Lysander sitting there doing nothing.'

'Let me check in and I'll be right with you.' Jack strode towards the ops room.

They were in high spirits when they took off, looking forward to seeing Ruth and Gussie.

The smoke was visible as they approached Hamble. Simon circled over the airfield to get a good look at the burning plane.

'Get down!' Jack ordered Simon between clenched teeth.

'Not possible.' The airfield was littered with wreckage,

people were running around and fire trucks were on the scene. 'It's only just happened by the look of it.'

'There's a field over there. Use that.'

'Jack—' Simon protested, but got no further.

'I don't bloody care where we land. Just get down!'

Lucy gripped hold of her brother's arm when it looked as if he might try and take over the controls. 'Easy, big brother. Simon's right. We can't land there.'

Jack closed his eyes for a moment to steady himself. 'Dear God, it's damned stupid to get fond of people in this war. Sorry, pal.'

'It's all right, Jack, I know how you feel.' Simon circled again, noting two other planes doing the same thing. 'We'll hang on. They'll clear the field as quickly as possible.'

Jack nodded, not taking his eyes off the frantic scenes below. 'Whoever was in that didn't stand a chance by the look of it.'

'It's a risk we all take.' Simon spoke calmly as he banked to go round again, not voicing the fear they all held, knowing it was going to be someone they knew. A picture of Ruth's parents flashed before Simon's eyes. They would be inconsolable if they lost their daughter as well – and it would be his difficult job to tell them . . . He blanked out the thought and focussed his whole attention on flying.

'Can you make out what plane it was?' Lucy asked in hushed tones.

'A twin.' Jack wiped a hand over his eyes to clear his vision. 'Could have been a Hudson.'

Two more circuits and enough room had been made to allow the waiting aircraft to touch down. Simon allowed the others to go in first in case they were low on fuel, and then he followed them in.

As soon as Simon cut the engine, they all jumped out and stood silently as a stretcher was loaded into an ambulance – a stretcher completely covered.

Lucy held on to her brother and Simon as they made their way to the operations building. Like the two men, she was silent.

There were a group of people standing around and Simon scanned the faces anxiously for someone who was missing.

'Over there,' Lucy pointed, a quiet sob in her voice. 'By the doorway.'

Without a word, they all walked towards the two women. They were wearing the one broad and one narrow stripe of a second officer – a recent promotion. Their heads were bowed and they didn't look up.

'Who was it, honey?' Jack asked, reaching out to grasp Ruth's hand.

She shook her head, unable to speak.

Gussie spoke. 'It was Rob.'

'Oh, dear God, no!' Jack gasped.

Ruth seemed to recover enough to say, 'Tricia's parents are going to be devastated. They were fond of him. We all were.'

'I'll go and break the news to them.' Simon didn't relish the task, but it had to be done.

'I'll come with you.' Jack ushered them all inside, away from the scene of the accident.

All thoughts of celebration were forgotten. This was the time to grieve for the loss of a fine man.

Chapter Seventeen

It was nearly midnight when Simon and Jack arrived back at White Waltham. Tricia's parents had been so upset by the news of Rob's death they hadn't wanted to leave them alone. They still hadn't recovered from the loss of their only child, and now the man who had comforted and supported them through that dreadful time was also dead. They were distraught.

Neither Jack nor Simon had wanted to go back to their lodgings – sleep would be impossible – so they'd headed for the Mess. There were still a few people on duty in the ops room preparing the list for tomorrow's deliveries, but apart from that the place was quiet.

'I don't know about you, Simon, but I could do with a stiff drink.'

'I've got a bottle of whisky in my locker. I'll get it while you scrounge a couple of glasses.'

Jack soon found them and sat down, staring into space,

still not able to believe that Rob was gone. He closed his eyes, hurting so much it was like a physical pain. Rob had been liked and respected by everyone. What a waste.

'Jack?'

The sound of his sister's voice made his eyes snap open. 'What are you doing here? You should be asleep.'

She sat opposite him and rested her arms on the table. 'I guessed you'd come back here. I stayed with Ruth and Gussie for a while.'

'How are they?'

Lucy shrugged, giving her brother a puzzled look. 'I don't understand. They clearly thought a lot of Rob, and were shocked by his death, but there were no tears, no sobbing, no anger at a life cut short.' A large tear trickled down her face. 'I didn't know him very well, but I cried. They didn't.'

'Lucy,' Jack reached over and took hold of her hand, 'you must remember what the British people have to cope with. Their young men are dying on land, at sea and in the air. Young and old are being killed in air raids. This is the reality of their lives, and they are dealing with it in their own way. They grieve quietly, and I'm positive that many tears are shed in private. They keep their feelings to themselves, but they hurt just like everyone else.'

She drew in a deep breath. 'You have to be here before you can grasp the enormity of the struggle against the Nazis, don't you?'

'And until now it's been a struggle they've had to face on their own.' Jack released his sister's hand and sat back. 'Get some sleep, Lucy.'

'You do the same.' She stood up and wrapped her arms

176

around him, giving him a fierce hug. 'You're a different man now, do you know that?'

'Am I?'

'Yeah, you're quite something, big brother. No wonder Ruth's crazy about you.'

When he just raised his eyebrows, she lifted her hands in surrender. 'I'm not prying into your love life, but the pair of you are no good at hiding how you feel about each other.'

Jack sat back and folded his arms. 'You're imagining things. We're friends, that's all.'

'That's a shame.' Sadness flashed across Lucy's face. 'Gussie told me that Rob had been in love with the girl who got killed. Perhaps they're together now.'

'Who knows.'

'It's a nice thought though, isn't it?'

'Yeah, now get some rest. You've a busy day ahead of you tomorrow.'

'OK.' She gave her brother an affectionate tap on the shoulder. 'I'm glad I came over here. I missed you.'

Lucy had just left when Simon appeared with a bottle of whisky. 'Sorry I took a while. I was talking to Jane. Was that your sister I caught a glimpse of?'

Jack nodded, took the bottle from Simon, poured two generous measures, then screwed the top back on. 'One will do. We're both flying in the morning.'

'I'm going to ask you to take on some of Rob's pupils, Jack.'

'Sure. God, but we're going to miss him.'

'We certainly are.' Simon emptied his glass in one go. 'It's a bloody tragedy. But he isn't the first ATA pilot we've lost, and he won't be the last.'

'True, and something we have to face.' Jack took a mouthful of whisky and grimaced. 'Lucy was puzzled because the girls didn't wail and cry over the loss of Rob.'

'If we did that every time someone was killed in this country, we'd be forever weeping into our beer.' Simon's mouth was set in a determined line. 'But it hurts, Jack. Believe me, it hurts.'

'That's what I told Lucy.'

Early next morning, Lucy and the other American girls were ready and waiting to be taken to the No. 6 ferry pool at Ratcliffe, near Leicester. They were now all eager to get on with the job.

'Do you know who's taking us?' Pat asked Lucy.

'No, it would probably have been Rob . . .' Her words tailed off.

'He seemed like a great guy.' Pat glanced around. The airfield was buzzing with activity. Pilots were leaving to pick up their first ferry of the day, and various planes were taking off and landing. 'But everyone's just getting on with the job. I sure admire that. It's something we've all got to learn to do if we're going to win this war.'

'We'll win.' Lucy was adamant. 'It's going to be a long, hard struggle, but at least we'll be doing something to help. Who would have thought women would get the chance to fly operational aircraft during a war!'

'Yeah, this organisation is quite something.' Pat nodded with satisfaction. 'I think I'm going to like it here.'

'Me too.' Lucy watched Simon walk towards them and felt a warm glow of pleasure. He was one lovely man.

She just adored his quiet sense of humour and air of calm efficiency. He was someone she felt you could lean on in difficult times.

'Ready, ladies? Number 6 ferry pool is awaiting your arrival with anticipation.'

That caused a laugh as they followed him out to the Anson.

On arrival they were taken to a large house and allotted rooms. This was to be their home while they were at Ratcliffe.

Once they'd stowed their luggage, they made their way back to the airfield to meet some of the other pilots. They were a mixed bunch of different nationalities, but there were still a few Americans, and they were the first to welcome the girls.

There was a Spitfire on the airfield, and Lucy couldn't resist having a look at it. She'd seen quite a few of them, of course, while they had been taking the tests, but it was a fascinating plane. She ran her hands over it, loving its feel and smell.

'Go and sit in the cockpit.'

Lucy spun around, startled. There was an RAF officer watching her. A group captain, she noted. 'Can I?'

He inclined his head. 'That's what you want to do, isn't it?'

'Very much.' She held out her hand. 'I'm Lucy Nelson.'

'Dave Sullivan.'

When he held out his hand and grasped hers, she saw him flinch. She looked down and noticed angry scars on his hand. She released her grip quickly. 'What happened?' she asked, always open and direct.

'I got shot up, and the hand is still sore.'

'I'm sorry. Has that put a stop to your flying?'

'I was grounded for a while, but I'm operational again.' He tipped his head to one side, looking thoughtful. 'Nelson, and by your accent I'd say you're American. Are you any relation to Jack?'

'He's my brother.' There was pride in her voice.

'Ah, then you are more than welcome.' He indicated towards the plane. 'Go on, sit in her.'

'Thanks.' Lucy didn't need a second invitation and clambered up, then eased herself into the cockpit. With her *Handling Notes* open at the Spitfire, she began to check the controls, running through the procedure for take-off in her head.

Dave jumped up and began to explain the flying capabilities of the Spitfire to her, and she couldn't help picking up his enthusiasm.

'Are you cleared for flying the fighters?'

She nodded, not taking her eyes off the instruments. 'All single engines. We start work tomorrow, but it might be a while before they let us loose on one of these.' She looked up, excitement in her eyes. 'Are they as good as I've heard?'

'Probably better.' Dave patted the plane affectionately. 'One of these babies saved my life. I was injured and unable to bail out and, although riddled with bullets, she still got me down.'

Lucy gazed into the grey eyes of the young man who had seen and done incredible things – and she fell in love. It was as quick as that.

He held out his uninjured hand. 'Come on, I'll buy

you a cup of tea, and you can tell me all about yourself.'

When they walked into the Mess, Lucy didn't miss the knowing smiles from the other American girls, but she didn't take any notice. All she wanted to do was spend some time with Dave. They sat at an empty table.

'I want your whole life story,' he told her, when they were settled with tea in front of her. Like her brother, Lucy had taken to this national drink, really enjoying it.

'How long have you got?' she laughed.

He glanced at his watch. 'Half an hour.'

'I'd better start when I was about sixteen, then.' She told him briefly about their home, her love of flying and the barnstorming she did with her brother, making him smile at some of the crazy antics of the flying circus.

The time whizzed by, and Dave was checking his watch again. 'I've got to go, but you can tell me the rest next time we meet.'

They walked out together, Lucy reluctant to let him go so soon.

Outside, Dave studied her face intently. 'I'm very pleased I landed here today to refuel. It's been a pleasure meeting you, Lucy.'

'Yeah, same here.' She watched him stride towards the Spitfire she had been sitting in a short time ago. In no time at all he was airborne and had disappeared from sight. She hoped she would see him again, but she hadn't even asked him where he was stationed. Stupid idiot!

The rest of the day was taken up with learning all about the day-to-day working of the ferry pool. They were told to be there by eight the next morning ready for their first deliveries. Even though she was keyed up, Lucy slept soundly.

Lucy's first ferry was a Harvard from Cosford to Ternhill. She had been meticulous in planning the route and was bubbling with a sense of achievement when she landed safely without getting lost. From Ternhill she picked up another trainer – and that was how her day went.

She was delighted to see Jack at Ratcliffe when she arrived back in the taxi Anson. 'Hi, Jack!' She slipped her hand through his arm and gazed up at him.

'Hmm, I don't have to ask how you got on today. From the expression on your face, I'd say you've thoroughly enjoyed yourself.'

She gave a little hop as they walked along. 'I never got lost once. Can you stay?'

He shook his head. 'Sorry, this is only a brief visit.'

The Mess was noisy with chatter as everyone talked about the day's flying. Jack and Lucy sat outside where it was quieter.

'Tell me what you've been up to since you arrived here.'

Lucy launched into vivid descriptions of the house they were staying in, and how unappetising the food was. 'What we used to eat at home in one day would last someone here a week.'

'That's an exaggeration, Lucy,' he told her wryly. 'Rationing is strict, but you'll soon get used to it.'

'Sure we will.' She examined the minuscule amount of cheese in her sandwich. 'If we don't we'll starve, and I've got no intention of doing that. What an organisation the ATA is, Jack.'

'It's quite something, isn't it. So, what did you fly today?'

'Two Harvards and a Magister. They're easing us in gently, but we can't wait to fly the fighters.' She then went on to tell him about Dave Sullivan and how he'd let her sit in his Spitfire. When she'd finished her brother was studying her intently, a deep frown creasing his brow.

'What's that look for?'

'You sound as if you liked him.'

'I did. Anything wrong with that?'

'Not if that's all it is. I've met Dave and he's a nice guy, but he's from No. 11 group at Biggin Hill.'

'So?' Lucy swallowed the last of her sandwich.

'They're always in the thick of things and lose pilots quite often.' Jack didn't know how to put it, but he baulked at saying that their pilots' life expectancy was not good. He only wanted to warn his sister. He caught Lucy's hand in his and turned her to face him. 'Don't get too fond of him.'

She'd always thought she knew her brother's every mood, but as she looked at his serious expression, she knew this wasn't the man she had grown up with. 'Jack, we can't hide from our feelings, even if there is a war on. Shouldn't we make the most of every moment?'

He looked into space for a moment, and then began to talk softly. 'I've known ATA pilots who've been killed. Tricia and Rob the most recent. I've delivered priority Lancasters and seen why they were needed so urgently. Early one morning I stood on an airfield and watched the bombers returning from a raid over Germany. The ground crew were anxiously counting them in as they landed, and scanning the sky for the next one. Then there was nothing.

The sky was empty and silent. I didn't ask how many hadn't returned, but it was the most heartrending thing I have ever experienced.'

'And is this why you keep your distance from Ruth? You're afraid that one of you might not make it through the war?'

'It's a possibility we have to face. I wouldn't want to cause Ruth such pain. I think it's best to wait until this mess is all over before making a firm commitment.'

'You're wrong, big brother.' Lucy shook her brother's arm. 'So very wrong. We can't put our lives on hold for the duration of the war. This is a time to savour the good moments, and deal with the bad.'

He shrugged. 'You're probably right, but that's how I feel at the moment.'

'Have you told Ruth any of this?'

'She knows how I feel about her, but I've said we must wait.'

'This war could go on for years. What makes you think Ruth won't find someone else?'

'It's a chance I'll have to take.' He stood up. 'I must get back now.'

Lucy also stood up and gave her brother a fierce hug. 'I can't be like you. I'll take my happiness where and when I find it, and so should you. You've got this whole thing wrong, and you're probably hurting Ruth more by your attitude than you realise. You mustn't let fear of the future stop you from loving.'

'I'm not afraid,' he protested firmly. 'I'm just trying to be kind to Ruth.'

Lucy gazed up at him in astonishment. 'Gee, have you got this all muddled up! Let the future take care of itself. If there's pain in it, then we'll have to deal with that when it comes. That's what I'm going to do. It's the only way to get through this war, Jack,' she admonished gently.

'You always were the sensible one out of the two of us, weren't you?'

'You only just realised that?' she teased.

He kissed her cheek. 'No, I've known it from the time you were a toddler, but I've never told you. Thanks for the lecture.'

She watched him get in the plane and take off. He'd obviously been shaken by the deaths of Tricia and Rob, and other things he'd witnessed since coming to this country. But boy, was he wrong! Her mouth set in a determined line. She'd have to see if she could change his mind.

Chapter Eighteen

It was three days later when Ruth had her first Blenheim to deliver to Hawarden, near Chester. From there she was to collect a Wellington for Brize Norton. It was a glorious day, without a cloud in the sky, but her mood didn't match the brightness. They had all been at Rob's funeral the day before, and she had been overwhelmed with sadness that his family from America couldn't be there. But the friends he had made in this country had all been present, including Tricia's parents. He had been a greatly loved man, and everyone felt his passing dreadfully.

There didn't seem a lot to smile about at the moment. The news from the desert war in North Africa was not encouraging. There was a long way to go before this war was won. And it had to be won – there was no other alternative. And another irritation was that she needed a new pair of shoes and didn't have enough clothing coupons for them.

She laughed out loud, her gloom lifting. What a daft

thing to think about! Her head came up – that was enough of gloomy thoughts – and she marched out to the waiting Blenheim. This was no time to fret about the state of things at home or abroad. She had planes to fly.

The flight to Hawarden was uneventful and Ruth thoroughly enjoyed the challenge of handling the larger planes. After checking in she was told that the Wellington wouldn't be ready for another hour, so she went to the Mess. There were several newspapers around and she picked one up to read while she had a cup of tea and a bun. There was no telling when she would have time to eat again. With good flying weather they delivered as many planes as possible during the day. There were only four men around taking a break, and they were playing cards.

The hour soon passed and Ruth was about to see if the plane was ready, when two RAF pilots walked in.

They glanced around the room. 'We've been told there's a Wellington going to Brize Norton. Is the pilot here? We'd like to cadge a lift.'

Ruth folded the paper carefully, holding it so it covered her wings, then walked towards the men. 'That will be all right. I'll just check that it's ready.'

'Thanks, we'll wait outside.'

Everything was now in order and Ruth collected the delivery chit. The men were waiting by the plane. 'Hop in, we can leave at once.'

They were now staring at the wings on her jacket, looking apprehensive.

The tallest one said, 'Er . . . where's the pilot?'

'You're talking to her.'

The other pilot swore quietly under his breath. 'Since when have women been flying bombers? How many of these have you flown?'

'This is my first Wellington.' She smiled brightly, thoroughly enjoying herself. Some men were still finding it hard to believe that women were doing this kind of work. She took the *Handling Notes* out of her pocket, flicked it open at the appropriate page. 'I've got all the instructions here.'

When they still didn't move, she said, 'Frightened to fly with a woman?'

That shook them up and they gave each other sheepish glances.

Ruth made a point of checking her watch. 'If you're coming then get on board, please. I've got another one to collect for Cowley.'

Giving a slight shrug they got into the plane.

From then on Ruth ignored them as she went through the pre-flight checks, and when satisfied that everything was all right, she took off. The men were silent, but she knew they were watching her every move with apprehension.

The weather was perfect and they had a smooth flight. She set the plane down, and when she climbed out the men were waiting for her.

'Sorry we doubted you,' the tallest one said, 'but we didn't know the women of the ATA were flying planes of this size.'

'Nice going,' the other one said. 'What's your name?'

'Ruth.' She headed for the check-in, and they fell into step beside her, all smiles now they were down safely.

'Can we buy you lunch?'

'Thanks all the same, but I've got another delivery to make.' After giving them a brief smile, she headed for the ops room.

Jack was there looking highly amused. 'Hi, Ruth. Picked up a couple of passengers, did you?'

She grinned. 'I thought they were going to change their minds when they realised who was flying the plane.'

'Scared, were they?'

'White as sheets.'

Jack gave a deep, amused chuckle, and then raised his hand. 'See you.'

'Damn it, Jack! Will you stop walking away from me?'

He paused and turned his head. 'I've got pilots to collect, honey.'

'I know, but you can spare me a few minutes, surely?'

He nodded.

'Have you seen Lucy? Is she getting on all right?'

'Sure, she's having the time of her life, and fallen for an RAF pilot, Dave Sullivan. I've warned her off.'

'That was quick. She's only been here five minutes, so to speak.' Ruth hesitated, frowning. 'What do you mean, you've warned her off?'

'He's from Biggin Hill and always in the thick of the fighting. She shouldn't get too fond of him. I don't want to see her get hurt if anything happens to him.'

Ruth stared at him in astonishment. 'Does she always do as you say?'

'Nope, never. She told me she's going to live her life to the full and let the future take care of itself.'

'Good for her!' Ruth moved forward until she was almost

toe to toe with him, then said firmly, 'Don't you think you ought to take a leaf out of your sister's book?'

'Meaning?' His gaze narrowed.

'We're not just friends, Jack. We're attracted to each other physically as well. It would be nice to find out how deep that attraction goes. I'd like to know how it feels to be held in your arms; to be kissed *properly*.' She emphasised the word properly, because the only time he'd kissed her had been more in anger than like a man in love. Then she stepped back. 'And that, Jack Nelson, is all the running I'm doing. I swear that you're a difficult man to pin down, but I'm not waiting around for years while you get over this daft notion of yours. I love you, and I'm hoping you feel the same about me. I'm embarrassing myself here, Jack, but I'm not prepared to go on like this. If you feel no great affection for me, then say so, and I'll never mention it again. But say something or our friendship ends here.'

When he just stared at her, taken aback by her outburst, she gave an exasperated sigh. 'I'm not asking for a lifelong commitment. When this blasted war is over you can go back home and never look back, if that's what you want.'

'You think I'd take advantage of you and then leave?' The words came out in a growl of disbelief.

Making him angry seemed to be the only way of getting through his defences. 'Oh, I'm not offering to let you take advantage of me.'

A glint of amusement replaced the anger in his eyes. 'That's a shame, honey. I'd sure like to take advantage of you . . . But, as that isn't on offer, would you like to come to the cinema with me this evening?'

'Only if we can sit in the back row.'

His mouth twitched at the corners. 'I'm sure that can be arranged. I'll pick you up at seven.' Before walking away, he said, 'Remember, honey, whatever happens between us, you started it.'

'I know what I'm doing, Jack.' As she watched him walk away, she wondered if she really did know what she had just done. She could get more than she'd bargained for. Although her life had been one of parties and functions, she had never taken the step of sleeping with anyone she'd met, preferring to wait for the right man. Was that right man Jack? Only time would tell, but she certainly wasn't going to jump into bed with him until she was sure how they both felt. She placed her hand over her heart, feeling it thud in her breast. She had just taken a chance. Jack could have shrugged at her ultimatum and walked out of her life. But he hadn't. Something Lucy had said must have made him think again. She'd thank her next time she saw her.

Gussie came into the kitchen. 'You sound happy this morning. What picture did you see?'

Ruth gazed into space, then back at her friend. 'I haven't the faintest idea.'

There was a smell of burning and Gussie lunged for the grill to save their toast. 'Ah, I take it that Jack's making up for lost time.'

'Hmm.' Ruth picked up a slice of scorched bread and began scraping off the blackened part, then handed it to Gussie, changing the subject quickly. 'You've never said, but have you ever heard from Don?'

'No, and I didn't expect to. He didn't belong here, Ruthie. He wasn't like Jack and Rob.'

Ruth chewed thoughtfully on a piece of toast. 'You're right. Rob had made this his home, but Jack will return to his family when this is all over. He thinks the world of his mother. He told me she brought them up on her own, and he loves and respects her for that.'

'I expect you're right.' Gussie poured them another cup of tea. 'How will you feel about that?'

'Lucy told Jack that she's going to live for the now and let the future take care of itself. That's what I'm going to do. I love Jack and need to be with him while it's possible. If he walks away at the end it will hurt like crazy, but at least I'll have had him for a while.' She gave a shrug of resignation. 'Does that sound selfish of me?'

'No, those are my sentiments exactly. We can't put our feelings on hold. We've got to make the most of what we have now.'

Ruth sighed. 'Jack's trying to put his feelings on hold. I've broken through his defences a little, but I don't believe he's truly convinced that we should have a serious relationship at this time. Perhaps he never will, but that's something I'll find out some time in the future.'

'And you'll handle it in your usual sensible way. I was upset when Don left without a backward glance, but I think he was just having fun with me. We liked each other, but our feelings never went any deeper than that.' Gussie's eyes gleamed. 'I've found someone else now, and this is the real thing!'

Ruth stopped with her cup halfway to her mouth, and

then put it down hastily. 'That's terrific! Who is he? Where did you meet him? What's he like?'

'Whoa!' Gussie laughed. 'Save your questions, you'll get to meet him tonight. Now, come on, move, Ruthie, or we'll be late. Looks like decent flying weather today.'

That evening, Ruth, Jack and Simon met in the local pub to wait for Gussie and her new boyfriend. Sally and Jane joined them and they began to speculate who Gussie's friend might be.

'Have you any idea?' Sally asked Ruth. 'She's kept this romance very quiet.'

'She certainly has. I didn't even know she was seeing anyone.'

'I hope it isn't another American.' Jane pulled a face. 'Sorry, Jack, I keep forgetting you're American. I don't mean to offend you, but Gussie was more upset than she let on when Don left.'

'No offence taken. I also hope she's found someone who won't up and leave her. Gussie's a lovely girl and no one wants to see her hurt.'

'He's bound to be someone lively like herself.' Ruth chuckled as she thought of her extrovert friend. 'She'll soon get tired of him if he isn't.'

The door opened and a group of RAF airmen came in. They were all sporting wings on their jackets, and Gussie was in the middle of them. One of the men was Dave Sullivan.

'Oh, hell!' Jack cursed quietly under his breath when he saw Dave.

Gussie waved and towed her entourage to their table. She introduced each one in turn – Paul, Dave, Stan and Harry. Then it was bedlam as more chairs were commandeered and pints ordered.

Ruth managed to grab Gussie's arm. 'Which one is yours?'

'Harry.' She sighed blissfully. 'Isn't he the most gorgeous man you've ever seen?'

'Absolutely.' Ruth studied Harry as he stood at the bar with Jack and Simon waiting for the beer to be served. There was nothing spectacular about him; in fact he was quite an ordinary looking man with brown hair and dark eyes. But when he came back to the table she could see that there was a glint of devilment in his eyes. Oh, yes, she could see what had attracted Gussie to him. He was well over six feet, and Ruth couldn't help wondering how he squeezed himself into a fighter. Then she felt a cold chill creep through her when Gussie announced that Harry was a bomber pilot. She silently uttered Jack's curse – Oh, hell! Being part of a bomber crew was a precarious occupation.

'Hello, Jack.' Dave put a pint in front of Jack. 'I met your sister at Ratcliffe.'

'So she told me.' He picked up the beer. 'Thanks. You with Gussie?'

'No, Harry's her fellow. We met outside the door and she insisted we join her party.'

'Ah, she would. Are you going to see Lucy again?'

'I've got a couple of days' leave and I thought I would.' Dave sat back. 'Do you mind?'

'Would it make any difference if I said I did?'

'None at all.'

'I thought not.' Jack nodded and took a mouthful of beer. 'My sister's her own person and will do as she pleases. I think she'd like to see you again.'

'Good, I'll go tomorrow.'

Ruth had listened to the exchange, and knew she couldn't love Jack more than she did at that moment. Even though he was protective of his sister, he had just told Dave that the way was clear for him if he wanted to see Lucy. It looked as if he had taken Lucy's words to heart and was now prepared to let the future unfold as it would. They were living in dangerous times and, in her opinion, the only thing they could do was take each day as it came. If they worried about what tomorrow would bring, they would never leave the house.

It had turned out to be a lively evening, Simon thought wryly, his head thumping slightly, but the couple of Aspirin he'd taken would soon clear that – in fact it was already fading. He climbed into the Anson. Those RAF boys really knew how to enjoy themselves, but no one could blame them. They were risking their lives every time they took off. And Gussie's boyfriend, in bombers, never knew if he was coming back after every raid. No, he wouldn't deny them any happiness they could snatch.

He took off, pleased the weather was clear today. One of the Ansons was out of service and he'd been asked to cover a lot of the country today. Pilots everywhere needed to be picked up and dropped at their next destination. His first call was Shawbury, then Litchfield and on to Ratcliffe. He was pleased about that as he might have a chance to see Lucy. He couldn't get Jack's sister off his mind, and with some leave coming up, he was hoping to take her out. It would give him a chance to get to know her.

He was, therefore, pleased when he saw her waiting for the taxi at Lichfield.

'Hi, Simon.' Lucy laughingly started to thumb a lift. 'You going to Ratcliffe?'

'My next stop.' He turned to the group of pilots – men and women. 'Little Rissington after that, and all stops on the way to White Waltham.'

Four, including Lucy, hoisted up their parachutes and followed Simon to the plane.

At Ratcliffe, Simon decided to take a break and see if he could persuade Lucy to come out with him. Perhaps he'd take her dancing.

They'd just got out of the plane when he heard Lucy give a squeal of delight. Simon recognised the man she was waving frantically to – Dave Sullivan.

'Do you know him?' he asked.

'Sure do. Thanks for the lift, Simon.' Then she was rushing towards Dave.

The disappointment Simon felt was more than he would have expected. He'd seen Dave talking to Jack last night, but he'd never guessed that Lucy knew him as well.

That served him right. While he'd been hesitating, someone else had stepped in.

Chapter Nineteen

The summer months had flown by, and it was now the end of September. As Ruth looked back, she realised that on a personal level it had been a good few months. She now knew for certain that her love for Jack was strong and lasting, and Lucy had become a good friend. Because of the volume of work they had only been able to meet now and again, but both Lucy and Jack would be spending Christmas at her home. Her parents had met Lucy and were looking forward to it enormously. Things were going well for Gussie and Harry as he continued to return from his bombing raids. But as far as the war was concerned things were not encouraging.

In June Tobruk had fallen to Rommel's Afrika Korps, with thousands of allied troops being taken prisoner. American troops were engaged in fierce fighting in the Pacific, and in August there had been an attempt to raid Dieppe, with disastrous results.

'Ruth!' The sound of Sally's voice broke through her reverie. 'Jane wants to see you.'

'Right.' She noticed that Sally was looking very pleased about something. 'What's going on?'

'You won't find out if you stand there.'

That was enough for Ruth and she hurried to Jane's office. Sally was very steady and usually calm. It took something really special to stir her up like that. Ruth knocked on the open door.

'Come in, Ruth, and sit down. Has Sally told you?'

'No, she just said I should get in here quickly.'

'Well, I've got good news. You and Sally have been recommended to go on a course for the four-engines.'

Ruth gasped in surprise. 'You mean try for our Class 5 rating?'

'You're going to do more than try. You are going to succeed.' Jane leant forward. 'The choice of the first pilots to convert to four-engines has been given careful consideration, and we are sure that you and Sally are the most suitable candidates. Some men still believe that women can't handle the big planes. We're going to prove them wrong!'

'We certainly are!' Ruth couldn't stay in her seat. 'When do we start?'

'The day after tomorrow. You will go to Leavesden. Captain Anders will be your instructor, and he's on your side. He believes that women *can* fly the large bombers.'

Ruth nodded. 'I like him, and he's one of the best instructors in the ATA.'

'I agree, and we're also going to train some flight engineers.' Jane gave a satisfied nod. 'Now, back to today's business. I'd like you to take the Anson, pick up pilots from Lyneham and return them to White Waltham.'

After thanking Jane, Ruth couldn't get out of the office quickly enough. She had been chosen! It was hard to believe.

Sally was waiting and they grinned at each other, then the full import of what they were about to do hit Ruth. 'Wow!' was all she could say.

'Wow, indeed!' Then Sally sounded a note of caution. 'This isn't going to be easy, Ruth. If we don't make it on the four-engines then that will be the end, and the doubters will say, "I told you women weren't strong enough."'

'We'll prove them wrong,' Ruth declared with complete confidence. She picked up her parachute. 'But first, I've got some pilots to collect.'

One of the pilots waiting for the taxi was Gussie. Ruth was bursting to tell her, but decided to wait until later when there weren't so many people around. She wasn't sure if anyone else knew about this yet, but Jane hadn't told them to keep it a secret. She hoped Simon and Jack were around when she landed at White Waltham.

She was in luck. They were both there checking in when she went to do the same. She pulled them out into the corridor to give them a bit of privacy. 'I've been chosen to go on a conversion course for the four-engines.'

The two men looked at each other, then back to her, but said nothing.

'Class 5!' She spread her arms out as wide as they would go. They didn't seem to be getting the message. 'Big bombers!'

Suddenly she was lifted off the ground by Jack and spun

round. 'We know, honey, and that's great. Don't take any notice of us, we're just teasing.' He put her down again.

Simon kissed her cheek. 'Congratulations, Ruth, you'll do just fine.'

'What am I missing?' Gussie rushed up to them. Ruth told her, and her friend erupted with pleasure. 'Wonderful! Do well and that will give the rest of us a chance later on.'

Ruth grimaced. 'There's no pressure then.'

But during the winter as one delay after another held up the training, the pressure built. Ruth had only completed six of the required solo landings when the Halifax had problems and the course was stopped. She worried about the time it was taking, and doubts crept in as to whether the idea of women flying the large bombers had been abandoned. Sally was confident that it hadn't.

Ruth tried to relax over Christmas, and having Jack and Lucy with them helped. Her parents were in their element making a fuss of their guests.

Sally proved to be correct, and in February 1943 the course resumed, and Ruth finally completed the required solo landings. Handling large planes did not prove to be too difficult. With a flight engineer on board, all they had to do was concentrate on the flying. They had proved that women were capable of doing this, and the way was now open for more women to progress to the large aircraft. It had been a long haul due to the many delays, and now it was over, Ruth felt quite drained.

Jack was in Perth on a priority delivery, and Ruth longed for him to be with her. She wanted him to hold her in his arms and just talk in his deep, soothing American voice.

Sally wandered into the Mess and sat beside Ruth. 'We've just heard from Gussie and she won't be back tonight. She's grounded by bad weather and she'll try to complete the delivery tomorrow. It's a priority again.'

'Jack's on one of those as well. Blast!'

'We ought to celebrate our new rating.' Sally spoke gently. 'Tricia and Rob would have expected it. Let's you and I do something crazy.'

Sally was quite right, Ruth realised. Neither of those lovely friends would have expected them to be gloomy after their achievement. She sat up straight. And it was an achievement to be proud of. 'I agree. What shall we do?'

'We've got tomorrow off so why don't we go to London and dance until we drop? We could spend the night at the Savoy and have breakfast in bed before coming back.'

'That's a wonderful idea,' Ruth laughed, 'but hardly crazy.'

'Ah, but who knows what we'll get up to while out on the town!'

'True,' Ruth agreed. 'We'll have to go by train because I haven't got enough petrol for the car.'

'As it happens, there's an RAF truck going to London. I've already cadged a lift.' Sally winked at Ruth. 'We're not the only ones looking for a night out.'

'That's terrific.' She stood up. 'When is it leaving?'

Sally consulted her watch. 'In about fifteen minutes.'

'What? We can't be ready by then!'

'Of course we can. You keep an overnight bag in your locker, don't you?'

'Yes . . . but I haven't got a dress in it.'

'Neither have I, and it doesn't matter, everyone will be in uniform, Ruth.'

'So they will.' Ruth pulled a face. 'I've almost forgotten what it's like to go out all dressed up and looking feminine. Do you think anyone will ask us to dance when they see the stripes and wings?'

'Let's find out, shall we?'

They both made a dash for the lockers and had just collected their bags when a voice shouted that the truck was leaving.

'I'll just leave a note for Gussie in case she gets back and wants to join us in London.' This was hastily written and left with ops.

When they climbed into the back of the truck, it was crowded with a mixture of ATA pilots and servicemen. They were the only women and Sally was already joking with the men. Ruth had never seen her in such a relaxed mood, but she obviously felt she had earned a bit of fun. And she was right. Ruth squeezed in between two men and smiled, now ready for a good night out and a little flirting. This was another thing she had almost forgotten how to do, but would soon get the hang of again. And she'd forget Jack for a while. Since his sister had talked to him, he'd become more affectionate and relaxed with her. When they were alone together – which wasn't nearly often enough – he held and kissed her, but as soon as their passion mounted, he stepped back. It was damned frustrating. Sometimes she wished she didn't love him quite so much. Still, she couldn't change her feelings for him, and didn't want to. He was everything she wanted in a man, and if he drove her mad at times, then that was just the way he was. Whatever he did was because he felt it was the right thing to do, and she couldn't argue with his motives.

When they arrived in London, the first thing they did was book into the Savoy Hotel. They were busy and only had a twin room free, so they took that.

After dumping their bags and freshening up, they had a meal in the restaurant and then went to the American Bar for a drink.

'Do you know where we can go dancing?' Sally asked the barman.

'Try Covent Garden. They hold dances in the Opera House sometimes.'

'Really?' Ruth was surprised and turned to Sally. 'Let's try that. We can walk from here.'

They quickly finished their drinks and were on their way.

There was indeed a dance being held there and, when they stepped inside, the place was packed. They'd hardly set foot in the door when two army officers moved in on them. One was Major Alan Brewster and the other Captain Pete Hammond, both in the parachute regiment.

'Told you it wouldn't matter if we were in uniform, didn't I?' Sally managed to whisper before they were swept on to the dance floor by the men.

Pete was Ruth's partner. He was tall with polished manners, but he was clearly a strong man. No doubt they had to be ultra-fit to jump out of planes and be ready to fight. Ruth glanced around at the sea of uniforms and studied some of the faces, everyone intent on having a good time. She couldn't help wondering what many of them had seen and done. They were ordinary people being called upon to do extraordinary things.

'You don't talk much, do you?' Pete remarked dryly.

'Oh, I'm sorry.' She smiled up at him. 'I didn't mean to be rude, but I couldn't help looking at the crowd. There must be servicemen of many nations here tonight.'

'Including the Yanks. That's why we moved in as soon as we saw you. Our American friends have a way with the ladies.'

Ruth bit back a smile. 'So I believe.'

He held her away from him so he could examine the gold wings on her jacket. 'Air Transport Auxiliary. I've heard about the women pilots, but you are the first one I've met. What do you fly?'

'Anything that needs delivering.'

'You mean trainers?'

She shook her head, but didn't have a chance to answer as Sally and Alan danced up to them.

'Would you believe it, Pete, these little girls fly fighters and bombers! Isn't that something?' Then they danced away again.

'Four-engines?' When she nodded he was clearly impressed. 'But aren't they heavy to handle?'

'Women are quite capable of flying them, and we do have a flight engineer on board to help us with the undercarriage and any controls that are out of the pilot's reach.'

Amusement flickered across his face as he asked, 'Ever jumped?'

'Not yet, but I wouldn't hesitate if I had to.' She looked

up at his face. He had nice grey eyes and was handsome in a tough way. 'How many times have you jumped?'

'Too many.'

The dance ended and they went to find Sally and Alan. They caught up with them at the bar. They spent the entire evening together and had a thoroughly good time. The officers were excellent dancers and had a wicked sense of humour. Ruth and Sally hadn't laughed so much for ages, and it did them both the world of good.

'Where are you staying?' Alan asked when it was time to leave.

'The Savoy.'

'Right, we'll walk you back.' When he saw they were about to say it wasn't necessary, he said, 'And it's no good you protesting.'

Ruth and Sally thought the least they could do was buy them a drink at the hotel. The soldiers wanted more, but on receiving a firm refusal, they took it like gentlemen.

They walked into the bar laughing, not at all eager for the evening to end.

Chapter Twenty

The sound of a familiar laugh made Jack glance towards the door. Seeing Ruth on the arm of an army officer shook him so badly that his first instinct was to leap out of his chair and tear her away from him. He took a deep breath. That wasn't the way to handle this. After all, he was the one who kept insisting that a firm commitment between them would be wrong at this time. She was free to do whatever she liked.

They were at the bar now and having too much of a good time to notice him. What a blasted fool he was. He'd been so sure she wouldn't look at anyone else. Arrogant sod! He could think of more colourful expressions to describe his stupidity, but that would achieve nothing. He closed his eyes briefly as he marshalled his thoughts. He was going to have to make sure she didn't want to turn to anyone else for her pleasure. And the best way to do that was to make her his – in every sense of the word. She was a well brought up girl who didn't sleep around, he knew that well enough – and he'd respected her for that.

But seeing her with someone else had shaken him, and called for drastic action on his part, or he was going to lose her.

His mouth twisted in a wry grimace as he thought, Ma, you tried to make a gentleman of me, but I'm about to throw all that teaching out of the window.

He stood up and walked towards the bar, and stopped right behind Ruth. 'Hiya, honey. Had a good time?'

She nearly fell off the stool she was sitting on, and he steadied her as she spun round.

'Jack, what are you doing here?'

Not the most encouraging greeting, but he let it go. 'I saw the note you left for Gussie, so I thought I'd come and join you.'

Ruth was still flustered. 'I thought you were stuck with a priority delivery. How did you get back?'

'The weather was rough, but I managed to complete the trip. I got a lift part of the way, and finished the journey to White Waltham by train.' He gave a forced smile. 'Aren't you going to introduce me to your friends?'

'Sorry.' Sally made the introductions.

Jack shook hands politely and bought them all another drink. He stood so close to Ruth that their bodies were touching, and he knew the soldiers had got the message. He was also aware that this irritated Ruth because she kept glaring at him, but he didn't move.

They talked for about an hour, and then Pete and Alan prepared to leave, thanking Ruth and Sally for making their evening so enjoyable.

Jack walked with them to the door where the captain faced him. 'Ruth is a lovely and talented girl. You've made it plain that she belongs to you, though I'm not so sure she feels the same about you. You'd better sort that out, mate, because if you don't, I'll be back. I know where to find her.'

'You won't need to do that. I'll get it "sorted", as you say. It's sure nice to have met you both.'

Alan and Pete grinned as they shook hands with Jack. 'You too. Take care of those girls. They're something special.'

'They sure are.' Jack watched them march away, then turned and went back to the bar.

Ruth was furious. 'What the blazes do you think you were doing?'

'Doing?' He shot Sally a glance of mock surprise. 'Do you know what she's talking about? I was perfectly polite. I bought them drinks and even saw them on their way.'

Sally smothered a laugh. 'Oh, Jack, you're incorrigible, do you know that? You smiled, but your attitude said, "Hands off, buddy, she's mine."'

Sally's American accent was so bad that Ruth saw the funny side of Jack's actions. In a way it showed he cared about her, although he never put it into words. She yawned. 'Where are you staying, Jack?'

'Here.'

'I thought they didn't have any vacancies? We could only get a twin room.'

'They found me one. Sally can have the room to herself. You'll be sharing mine.'

'*I beg your pardon?*' Ruth lowered her voice, not wanting anyone else to hear, relieved that Sally was occupied ordering a newspaper for the morning. 'You dare come here radiating disapproval because I've been dancing with a charming man – and that's all I've been doing – then you have the nerve to *tell* me I'm sharing your bed! Well, you've had a wasted journey!' She took a deep breath to steady herself. 'You are a complete mystery to me, Jack.'

He watched her storm away, collecting Sally on the way, and leave the bar. He gave a snort of disbelief at his crass conduct. He'd really loused that up! She was furious with him, but not as angry as he was with himself. If he didn't do something to redeem himself in her eyes, he was going to lose her. He had come to this country to fly planes, not fall in love. But that's what he'd done, and there was no point trying to run from that fact. Goodness knows he'd tried hard enough to do just that. And as for her not understanding him – join the queue, he thought. His family had never understood his restlessness, and the way he shied away from making a commitment. He had a dislike of being tied down in any way. That's why the freedom he felt in the air was right for him.

This self-analysis was all very well, but it wasn't solving his immediate problem. Wandering over to the bar he sat on a stool and beckoned the barman. 'Would it be possible to get some flowers – preferably roses – in the next ten minutes?'

The barman was having difficulty keeping a straight face, having witnessed the exchange. He poured Jack a whisky from a bottle he kept under the counter. 'Put your foot in it, have you?'

Jack tossed back the fiery liquid and grimaced. 'Yeah, big time.'

'I'll have a word with reception and see what we can do.'

'Thanks.' Jack stayed where he was as the barman disappeared. It was late now – or rather, early morning – and the bar was nearly empty. He ordered another drink and stared at it gloomily.

The barman was gone for some time, but when he returned he was carrying an enormous bouquet of mixed flowers tied with a golden bow.

'My God!' Jack gasped. 'Where did you get those at this time of night?'

The man smirked. 'There're ways. We couldn't get all roses, but there are a couple of red ones in the bunch. Would you like to attach a note, and then the bellboy will take them up to the young lady's room.'

Jack wrote five words – I'm sorry, please forgive me – then tucked it in the flowers.

The bellboy was hovering, ready to carry out his errand. Jack tipped them both generously, and then made his way up to his room. That was all he could do tonight. He might as well try to get some sleep.

He was sprawled on the large double bed trying to read a newspaper when there was a knock on the door. With a sigh, he got up. That was probably the boy to tell him Ruth had refused the flowers. If he was in her shoes, he'd throw them right back as well.

When he opened the door Ruth was standing there, a rose in one hand and her toilet bag in the other. He was too stunned to move or speak.

She nudged him aside and walked in. Turning to face him she said, 'You are a difficult man to stay mad at, Jack Nelson.'

Relief flooded through him. For once in his life he'd done the right thing. He moved towards her but didn't dare take her in his arms, for he doubted he would be able to stop if he did. He carefully reached out and ran his fingers down her cheek, caressing gently. 'Thanks for coming to tell me, honey. I'm real sorry, but I was so damned jealous when I saw you with another man.'

'Were you?' She leant her cheek against his hand, and held up the flower. 'I like a man who isn't afraid to say he's sorry.'

His hand moved down to caress her shoulder. He wanted her so much, and that realisation scared him half to death. He was in territory he'd never been in before. His girlfriends had come and gone without a pang of regret. Her hesitant demeanour told him that it had taken a great deal of courage on her part to come to his room like this. Her inexperience was showing.

Lowering his head he brushed his lips over hers. 'Stay with me tonight, honey. You can trust me. I won't get you into trouble.'

Ruth studied his face for a moment, then put the toilet bag on a chair next to her, and tossed the rose on to the bed, her decision made. She wrapped her arms around him and held on tightly.

Unable to hold himself in check any longer, Jack kissed her until they were both lost in passion.

Breaking the embrace he undid the top button of her blouse and murmured, 'Let's get rid of these clothes, shall we?'

* * *

When Ruth opened her eyes she found Jack leaning on his elbow and looking down at her. He kissed her gently. 'Morning, honey.'

'Is it morning already?' She stretched and smiled at him before realising that he was dressed. She couldn't hide her disappointment. After the night they had just shared it would have been lovely to wake in his arms and savour the closeness. 'You're up early.'

'Yeah, sorry, but I've got to leave now. I've ordered breakfast for you, and I've taken care of the check – *bill*,' he corrected. After kissing her again he swung himself off the bed and stood up, looking anxiously at his watch.

'You'd better not be late.' She didn't know how she managed to keep her voice so normal. There wasn't a hint of the passion of last night. He just wanted to be on his way. He was going to leave without a word of love. But then, he had never said he loved her. She knew it was something she was going to have to accept. This was how Jack Nelson was. It was either take it or leave it. She would take it.

He picked up his bag. 'I'll see you when you get back, then.'

She nodded.

With his hand on the door, he turned. 'Thanks for last night.' Then he was gone.

As soon as the door closed behind him she burst into tears. It wasn't supposed to be like this, was it? For her it had been a glorious experience, but Jack clearly didn't feel the same. Calling herself all manner of names, she dried her eyes and blew her nose. She had come to him willingly, without any pressure from him, knowing what he was like. He obviously wasn't a novice at making love, and she couldn't help wondering how many women had fallen for his charm. Quite a few, she imagined.

Ruth got up, washed and dressed. There was no way she was having breakfast here by herself. And she had to stop feeling sorry for herself. It was selfish. Since Rob had been killed, Jack had taken on more and more work as an instructor and, no doubt, had lessons lined up for today. When she'd made the decision to sleep with him, she had been fully aware of the step she was taking. And she couldn't regret it. Whatever happened in the future, she would always have wonderful memories of their night together. And, to be honest, she hoped there would be many more.

There was a tap on the door and she opened it to find the waiter there with her tray. She gave him Sally's room number, asking him to take it there, and walked along the corridor with him.

She opened the door and peered in. 'You up, Sally? I've brought my breakfast with me.'

Sally was sitting up in bed with a tray on her knees and beckoned Ruth to join her.

When the waiter had left, Sally studied Ruth's face. 'Where's Jack?'

'He had to leave early.'

'Hmm, are you all right?'

Ruth nodded. 'Yes, I am. I don't regret my decision. I love that difficult man so much.'

'Good.' Sally managed to squeeze another half a cup of tea out of her pot. 'My boyfriend's in the navy, and we make the most of every moment we get together.'

'I didn't know you had a steady boyfriend.' Ruth was surprised, for Sally never said much about her private life.

'We met about two years ago, and will probably marry if we both survive this war.'

'Not before?'

'No. Too many people are jumping into hasty marriages. We feel it's best to wait until things quieten down before taking that step. We all react differently to the danger of this war. Some forge ahead without thinking about the future, and others are more cautious.' Sally gave Ruth an understanding smile. 'I suspect Jack is the cautious type, like me. Any decision taken in the heat of battle, so to speak, could turn out to be a dreadful mistake. Don't be upset by Jack's refusal to make a firm commitment. From what I've seen of him, he's a man with a strong sense of honour, and won't want to cause you more heartache than is absolutely necessary. Who knows how we'll all feel after this conflict is over, when the danger and tension has gone. Just enjoy being with him.'

Ruth thought about Sally's words and smiled wryly. 'You're quite right. I'm usually quite sensible, but Jack seems to scramble my thoughts.'

Sally laughed out loud. 'I know exactly what you mean. Now, what are we going to do for the rest of the day?'

'I don't know. Have you any ideas?'

'Let's go out and take the day as it comes, shall we?'

Ruth nodded in agreement. 'That sounds like a recipe for every day, doesn't it?'

'It helps.'

* * *

He was running behind time. Jack put his foot down hard on the accelerator. He'd managed to borrow a car for this trip to London or he would never have been able to stay overnight. He should have been on his way an hour ago, but hadn't wanted to leave before Ruth woke up. She had looked so lovely, and it had taken all his self-control not to make love to her again, but he doubted if he'd have made it back before afternoon if he had. She had been disappointed when he'd left so early, but once she got over that she would see that he'd had no choice.

Once he was out of London, he drove like a bat out of hell. If he didn't come across any delays on the way he might just about make his first appointment.

As the car hummed along his thoughts went back to last night. Ruth must love him or she would never have come to him like that. He was pretty damned sure it had been her first time – and he had never experienced anything like it before. Oh, he'd had one or two women in the past, but making love to them had been quite different from Ruth. Dear God, but she was wonderful! He hoped he'd been able to show her how much she meant to him. He didn't know why it was so hard to say those simple little words – I love you – but they seemed to stick in his throat. He'd just have to show her by his actions.

Chapter Twenty-One

It was a beautiful spring day, but Lucy was oblivious to this. She was in trouble. The Hurricane she was flying sounded terrible, and the instruments had gone haywire, showing she was almost out of fuel, which she couldn't be. She had been in the air less than half an hour. She had collected the plane from Rochester for delivery to the repair unit at Henlow.

A nasty crunch came from the engine, making it shudder. Lucy didn't know how much longer she could keep this plane in the air. As far as she could see, she had two alternatives: find somewhere to land, or jump. She was reluctant to do the latter because there was no telling where the plane would come down. There was always the danger of hurting someone on the ground, and no ATA pilot liked to lose a plane.

The Hurricane was becoming hard to control. The noise from the engine didn't seem to be getting any worse though, so she'd see if she could get the plane down. But where? It had to be quick or she was going to have to jump before she lost too much height. That thought didn't thrill her one bit!

Suddenly, a Spitfire appeared on her wing, and then another. They circled the Hurricane, obviously inspecting it, and then one flew in front of her and wiggled its wings. The other plane stayed on her wing, the pilot looking across at her. She was concentrating too much on holding the plane level to be able to see who it was, but she did wonder if it might be Dave. When she glanced across quickly, he pointed straight ahead, indicating that she should follow the plane in front. With a ragged sigh of relief she let them escort her to an airfield.

But her troubles weren't by any means over. As she approached the airfield the undercarriage wouldn't come down. Try as she might, it wouldn't budge. Lucy had never been one to panic, and she didn't now. You could lose your life like that. She'd never landed a plane without an undercarriage before, but her brother had taught her the procedure and she was sure she could do it. Anyway, there wasn't any alternative; she was now too low to do anything else. She was committed to this landing.

The Spitfires stayed with her until she was almost down, and then shot up and away. Her whole concentration was on getting down without somersaulting the plane, but she knew they were up there watching. They couldn't do any more to help; this was entirely up to her, but it was strangely comforting to know they were willing her on.

The plane touched down, tore along for what seemed like an age, then spun sideways before coming to a halt. But she was still the right way up. She was very aware of the danger of fire and pushed back the hood immediately. Hands reached in, released her harness and pulled her out.

'Bloody hell!' she heard a man exclaim. 'It's a woman!'

Now she had firm ground under her feet, she braced herself, standing straight, refusing to let her legs shake. Pushing a strand of hair away from her eyes, she managed a smile. 'Thanks, guys. Where have I landed?'

'Biggin Hill, miss.' The man who had pulled her out was studying her with interest. 'You ain't English.'

The Spitfires had landed and the two pilots were walking towards her. One of them was Dave. 'No, she's American,' Dave told him. 'Nice flying, Lucy. This is Greg.'

'Hi.' Lucy shook hands. 'Thanks for your help.'

'You managed that landing well.'

She looked at the badly damaged Hurricane and grimaced. 'Oh gosh, I've made a mess of that. There will be an inquiry over this.'

'Nothing for you to worry about.' Dave spoke confidently. 'Now, I expect you could do with a strong cup of tea?'

'Please, but first I must phone my ferry pool and report this.'

'I'll show you where the phone is and, while you're doing that, Dave can get the teas.'

'You've got that round the wrong way, old pal. I'll show Lucy where the phone is, and *you* can get the teas.'

Greg shrugged and winked at Lucy. 'Oh well, it was worth a try.'

Lucy got through and explained the situation. 'I'm OK, but I've broken the Hurricane. What do you want me to do now?'

She listened to the instructions. As she was at Biggin Hill she had been hoping to be able to spend some time with Dave, but that wasn't possible. It was a shame because it would have given her a chance to unwind. Nothing ever seemed to ruffle his composure and she found that soothing. After putting down the phone she found Dave in the corridor waiting for her.

'Can you stay tonight?' he asked.

'They want me back at Ratcliffe and are sending a taxi for me. They're going to start the investigation at once.' She chewed her lips anxiously.

Dave placed an arm around her shoulders. 'It wasn't your fault, Lucy. We could see fuel streaming out. You did well to even get that plane on the ground. You send them to me and I'll tell them.'

'Thanks.' Her worry lifted slightly. This was the first plane she had damaged, and she didn't want to have a black mark against her record.

'Let's get that—Oh, damn!'

There was a bell ringing and the sound of running feet. Dave disappeared without another word. Lucy rushed over to the window and saw fighters already taking off and pilots clambering into others.

There was nothing Lucy could do now but to wait for the taxi aircraft to arrive.

Simon was about to enjoy a sandwich and a cup of tea when the operations officer found him.

'Ah, good, I'm glad someone's around. We've just received a request from Ratcliffe to pick up one of their pilots from Biggin Hill. She crash-landed there and they haven't got a taxi available at the moment.'

Simon took a quick gulp of tea. 'Do you know who it is?'

'Lucy Nelson,' they said. 'She's one of their Americans.'

'I know her. I'll go straight away. The Anson is fuelled and ready to go.' Simon wasted no time in getting airborne. Lucy must be all right or they would be calling for an ambulance, not a taxi. Nevertheless, he was anxious to see her.

She was standing on the airfield waiting for him as he landed, and walked straight up to the plane as soon as it came to a stop. He was relieved to see her looking calm after her experience. But she was a good pilot and, in his opinion, one of the best of the American women. She had a lively, outgoing nature, but once in the air she was unflappable and focussed.

'Simon.' She smiled when he jumped out. 'Have you come to take me back?'

He nodded. 'But first I want to have a look at the plane you were flying.'

'They've dragged it over to the hangar.' Her expressive face clouded with worry. 'It's a mess, Simon, but I didn't have any choice.'

'I'm sure you didn't.' He spoke reassuringly. No pilot liked to damage a plane, and Lucy was no exception. The first one was always the most worrying.

When Simon saw the plane his heart jumped uncomfortably. Lucy could have been badly injured or killed. The fact that she was unscathed was testament to her skill as a pilot.

'I've never asked you before, but who taught you to fly?'

'Jack.'

Simon nodded, satisfied. 'You had a good instructor. Jack's one of the most natural pilots I've come across. He's almost as good as Ruth.'

'Don't ever tell Jack that,' Lucy laughed. 'It might dent his ego.'

'I don't believe he has one.'

Lucy was still grinning as they joked. 'Do you know, I don't think he has. He's always seemed to be unaware of how good he is, and has never hesitated to praise someone else for their skill.'

Seeing that Lucy was now more relaxed, Simon began to examine the plane. He checked the cockpit and climbed over every inch he could reach. He couldn't get underneath, but the crash investigators would do that.

'Dave and his friend said they could see fluid coming out.' Lucy was following Simon round, looking at everything as well.

He straightened up. 'Dave? Did he see you?'

'Yeah, I was in real trouble. They flew beside me and guided me to this airfield. I was too busy trying to control the plane to take note of where I was exactly.'

'Well, I'm pretty sure you had a fuel leak.' Simon wiped his hands on a handkerchief. 'And a lot more if you couldn't lower the undercarriage. You won't have any trouble over this, Lucy. In fact, you'll probably be commended for getting down safely. The one thing the ATA hates more than wrecking a plane is losing a pilot.'

She blew out a pent-up breath of relief. 'Gee, Simon, you don't know how glad I am to hear you say that! This is the first accident I've had, and I don't know how severe the investigations are. It would break my heart if they sacked me.'

'There isn't the slightest danger of that.' Simon took her arm. 'You're too good a pilot.'

She gave him a grateful look and squeezed his arm. 'Do you know, you're the nicest man I've ever met?'

He laughed. 'I'm sure that isn't true, but thanks anyway. Let's get you back to the ferry pool.'

They were no sooner airborne than a Spitfire zoomed past, did a victory roll and then came up beside them.

Lucy began to wave frantically. 'That's Dave. I know his number now.'

'Crazy bugger!' Simon muttered under his breath, as the plane rolled away and out of sight. It was probably because of Dave Sullivan that Lucy was so anxious to stay in this country. He found that fact unpalatable.

When they landed at Ratcliffe, Lucy leant across and kissed Simon's cheek. 'You're a pal. Thanks for the reassurance.' Then she jumped out and headed for the ops to report in.

He sat there for a moment. Oh, well, a friendly peck on the cheek was better than nothing, he supposed. But he wanted to be more than a pal to her. But that was out of the question with the charismatic Dave in the picture. Feeling thoroughly disgruntled, Simon got out of the Anson. Every time he'd tried to eat today, an emergency of one kind or another had stopped him. He wasn't going anywhere until he'd had something to eat and drink. He was blasted well starving!

There were two ATA pilots in the Mess. 'You're a welcome sight, Simon. Can you take us to Little Rissington?'

He nodded. 'Give me fifteen minutes.'

It was late afternoon before he arrived back at White Waltham, and the first person he saw was Jack. He'd climbed into the plane, not giving Simon a chance to put his feet on the ground.

'I've just heard about Lucy. Is she OK?'

'She's fine, and completely unruffled by the experience. The only thing worrying her is the investigation, but I saw the plane, and any lesser pilot would have had to bail out. You taught her well, Jack.'

Jack visibly relaxed, nodding in satisfaction. 'She's one

hell of a pilot, isn't she? When she was a kid she used to beg and beg me to take her up. I'd only just earned my pilot's licence then, and Ma refused to let me take her until I was more experienced. When I finally did fly with her, she went crazy, loving every minute. From then on she just had to become a pilot, and there was no way anyone could have stopped her. She was a big draw at the air shows.'

'Not only is she a good pilot, but she's also a very nice girl.'

Jack cast him a thoughtful look. 'Dave Sullivan's a fine young man, but somehow he doesn't seem right for my sister. I'm sorry she ever met him.'

'Me too, but she has, and is very fond of him. I just hope it works out for them.'

'You English are far too polite. Most Americans would wade in and try to take her away from him.'

That made Simon laugh. 'How do you compete with one of "the few", as Winston Churchill has named them?'

'Yeah, how indeed.' Jack slapped Simon on the back. 'Come on, chum, I'll buy you a drink.'

A week later, Lucy was completely cleared of any responsibility for the crash. She was also highly praised for her handling of the stricken plane, just as Simon had predicted. She was ecstatic and Dave took her out dancing until the early hours. It was a lovely way to celebrate, and she couldn't have been happier than she was at that moment. What more could she ask for than to have the crash worry lifted from her, and to spend the night in the arms of the man she loved?

Chapter Twenty-Two

'Ah, good, you've made a pot of tea. I'm gasping.' Ruth sat down at the kitchen table and closed her eyes for a moment, then opened them again. 'I haven't stopped all day.'

'Nor me.' Gussie poured the tea and sat opposite Ruth. 'Hope the weather's as nice as this in two weeks' time.'

'What's so special then?'

'I'm getting married.'

Ruth coughed on a mouthful of scalding tea. 'Say that again, Gussie. I don't think I heard you properly.'

'I'm marrying Harry in two weeks.'

'Gussie!' Ruth was on her feet hugging her friend. 'That's wonderful! When did he ask you?'

'Yesterday. He's finished his tour of ops and won't be flying for a while. We decided to grab the chance and get married.'

'I'm so pleased for you. Harry's a lovely man, and you suit each other.'

'Yes, we do. I'm very lucky, Ruthie.' She gave her friend an understanding look. 'There's no sign of Jack popping the question?'

Ruth shook her head. 'I doubt if he ever will. I've come to know him well now and there's a part of him that is a free spirit. I don't know if he could make such a binding commitment at this time. I know he loves me in his own way, but he won't say the words – not even in the heat of passion. And he is a very passionate man. But Jack is Jack. This is how he is and I've accepted that now. I don't know what will become of our relationship when the war is over. Only time will tell.'

'You'll be left with a broken heart, won't you?'

'Bruised, Gussie, not broken. I love that difficult man, and I'm making the most of the time we have together, just as you and Harry are. Nothing is certain in this war, but for the moment, I'm happy.'

'Jack doesn't deserve you, Ruthie. Not many women would be so understanding.'

'Perhaps not, but he's got me for the duration. Now, tell me about your wedding plans.'

'I haven't had time to make any.' Gussie tapped Ruth's arm. 'You're a good organiser, so I thought I'd enlist your help.'

'Right.' Ruth took a pen and paper out of the drawer. 'Let's get down to it. We haven't got much time.'

The wedding was the first Saturday in June and the weather was glorious. They would all be in uniform, but Ruth had insisted that her friend walk down the aisle in a white gown.

She had managed to get hold of a damaged parachute and, with her mother's help, had made Gussie a beautiful wedding dress. Ruth's mother was expert with a needle and had embroidered golden wings over the bodice. Gussie, who had no close family to help her, had wept in gratitude when she'd seen it.

Ruth watched her friend walk up the aisle on the arm of her new husband, and she sent up a silent prayer that Harry wouldn't have to go on any more bombing raids. Gussie had lost her parents when she'd been about fifteen, and this was a chance to have a family of her own. *Please let them have a long and happy life together,* she pleaded silently, and hoped someone up there was listening. There had been some girls who had married and found themselves widows in a matter of weeks.

One of the ushers was Jack and he was busy urging the guests outside so the photos could be taken. She wondered if he was right about not making a commitment while the war was still on. Would it be harder to lose a husband or a lover? That was difficult to answer, but she felt she was beginning to understand Jack a little better. She might not agree with him, but she could see his concerns.

Someone laughed and shook her out of her gloomy musing. This was a day to forget the war and be happy. She walked outside and joined everyone else. While the bride and groom were being photographed, Ruth pulled Jack and Lucy to one side. 'I've got one precious film in my camera and I want photos of you together so I can send them to your mother.'

They couldn't be serious, but she managed to take a couple of shots. Film was hard to come by and she didn't want to waste any of it. Once Lucy had arrived in this country, Ruth had begun writing to their mother, Bet, knowing how difficult it must be for her to have both of her children so far from home.

'That's enough of us.' Lucy darted off, telling them to wait there. She returned with Dave and Simon. 'Come on, I want a picture of my favourite men together.'

Ruth did this for her and then asked Dave to take one of all of them with her parents.

'Mom will be so pleased with those. I hope they come out.'

The reception was being held in the church hall. It hadn't been easy gathering enough food together, but there was a modest spread, and no one expected a sumptuous banquet. The cake was a simple sponge, but they'd put a frill around it and even found a bride and groom to place on the top.

Harry's parents were there, pleased to see their son so happy. It was obvious that they approved of his choice of wife. And no doubt they were relieved that he was grounded for the time being. Listening to the bombers droning overhead night after night, wondering if your son was up there and if he would be coming back, must be a kind of purgatory.

The wedding had been a time of rejoicing. They all waved as Gussie and Harry left for a quiet honeymoon, refusing to tell anyone where they were going. They all had smiles on their faces. It had been a lovely day.

Over the next week Ruth was very busy. She was getting a few four-engine bombers now, and some men still shook their heads in disbelief when she climbed out, but mostly they were glad to get the replacements and didn't care who was flying them. Unfortunately they were going to be short of a few pilots now as in America there was a new organisation called the Women's Air Force Service Pilots (WASPS). A few of the women were preparing to return home and join them. Lucy was staying though. Another milestone for the ATA women had been reached. They were now receiving the same pay as the men. But in Ruth's present mood, even that couldn't bring a smile to her face.

She hated coming back to an empty cottage at night. It seemed strange not having anyone to talk over the day's work or have a laugh with. In the beginning this place had always been full of girls, now she was the only one living here, and she missed the company.

She wandered out to the kitchen and put the kettle on to boil. She ought to ask if any of the other girls would like to share, but it would never be the same.

She had just made tea when there was a knock on the door, and she was delighted to see Jack standing there. She hadn't seen him since the wedding.

'Hiya, can you spare a thirsty traveller a drink?'

'I'm sure I can manage that.' She stood on tiptoe to kiss him, loving the feel of his arms around her, then she stepped aside to let him in. When she saw the strange car outside she couldn't help grinning. 'Where did you borrow that from?'

'It's mine. I bought it yesterday. Not bad, huh?'

After studying the small Austin for a moment, she pursed her lips. 'Can you actually get in it?'

'Sure, and it's easy on the gas. I'll get something bigger soon, but it'll do for now.'

He followed her into the kitchen. 'Did you get the photos printed?'

'Yes, Dad took the camera home with him.' She handed him an envelope. 'These are for you and Lucy, and I've sent a set to your mother.'

He shuffled through them, smiling. 'They're great. Mom will just love these. Thanks, honey.' He drew her close again and studied her face. 'You look glum. Had a tough day?'

'Before you arrived I had been feeling lonely here on my own, and I was wondering if any of the other girls would like to share with me.' Her eyes gleamed with mischief. 'I would have asked Sylvia, but she's been moved to Cosford. I wonder how that happened . . . ?'

'Nothing to do with me.' He kept a perfectly straight face. 'Someone in charge must have thought she'd be useful there.'

'Hmm,' was Ruth's only comment. Sylvia was a nice enough girl, and a good pilot, but she did love the men. Many didn't mind, of course, but others, like Jack, found it tiresome. She was rather persistent when she set her eyes on someone.

'Why don't you wait a while before asking someone else to share with you?' He gave her an enquiring glance. 'You could let me stay.'

'You can't move in here with me, Jack. My God, think of the talk that would cause! And—'

He held up his hand to stop her. 'That's not what I'm suggesting. I was hoping that you'd let me stay overnight now and again. We haven't had much time together since we were in London, and I'd sure like to make love to you again.'

The very thought made her heart leap. He was right. This was a good opportunity to be alone, something not easily achieved with the kind of life they led. 'I'd like that too. Can you stay tonight?'

He reached across for her hand and squeezed it. 'I was hoping you'd say that.' Standing up, he pulled her into his arms and kissed her lingeringly. 'Let's go out and eat first, shall we?'

'Good idea. I'm starving.'

'Me too!'

When the photographs fell out of the envelope, Bet gave a cry of delight. Ruth had written names on the back to show who they all were. She had even included one of the bride and groom. As Bet studied the smiling faces, especially those of her children, her vision blurred and tears trickled down her cheeks. She had been so worried when they had gone to a country fighting a desperate war, but Jack and Lucy looked happy. She missed them so much. They had been her whole life for many years, but she would never have tried to stop them from doing anything they thought was right for them. Ruth was such a thoughtful girl sending her regular letters to give assurance that her children were OK. There had never been the slightest hint of a romance between her and Jack, but Bet couldn't help hoping that there was. She was just the kind of girl Jack needed.

The picture of Lucy smiling up at the RAF pilot, Dave, made Bet sigh. He looked such a lovely boy. She picked up another picture. Ah, and here was Simon. He was constantly mentioned in letters from all of them, but this was the first time she had seen what he looked like. Bet wished the pictures were in colour, but saw he was quite good-looking and more mature than Dave. She liked him. Her children had obviously made some fine friends, and she was very happy about that. She was also delighted to have a picture of Ruth's folks. It was lovely to see the couple who were being so kind to Jack and Lucy.

Her neighbour, Kathy, would love to see these. Her son was in the army and somewhere in England. Scooping up the photos, Bet hurried across the yard and into Kathy's kitchen.

Bet sniffed appreciatively. 'I'm just in time. You're making pancakes and I haven't had breakfast yet.'

Kathy rolled her eyes. 'I don't know how you do it, Bet. I've only got to start mixing, and there you are.'

'No one makes pancakes like you.' Bet sat at the table and waited. They had fallen into the habit of doing this on a Saturday morning. They made a joke about it, but the truth was, they were both a little lonely and enjoyed talking about their children over pancakes and maple syrup. Kathy was a widow like Bet, and only had one son, Al. He wasn't much of a letter writer, so Bet shared any news she had.

'Ruth sent me some photos and I thought you'd like to see them.'

'Oh, yes please! But let's eat these before they get cold.' Kathy put a plate of hot pancakes on the table and they started on them straight away.

When the plate was empty, Bet sat back and sighed with pleasure. 'Mine never taste as good as that.'

Kathy began clearing the table. 'Al always liked them.

Do you think they're getting enough to eat over there?'

'Of course they are. Lucy says the food isn't anything like ours, but they aren't starving.' Bet spread out the pictures for Kathy to see, pointing to each one in turn and giving their names.

'They're great, Bet. And they look as if they're having fun.'

'My two have only ever wanted to fly, and the ATA is giving them the chance to do that with lots of different planes. Lucy flies Spitfires,' Bet said proudly. 'Jack is working as an instructor, and Ruth flies bombers as well. Jack says she's very good.'

'Nice-looking girl.' Kathy studied the picture carefully. 'Do you think Jack's in love with her?'

'I'd be really happy if he was, but as far as I can tell, they're just friends. You know my Jack, he wouldn't say anything even if there was a romance between them.'

Kathy nodded understandingly. 'Your Jack's always been too difficult to pin down, though one or two girls have tried.'

'Yeah, that's true enough. Lucy says he's changed, but I doubt he's changed *that* much. It's a shame, though. Ruth seems a real nice girl, and her family have been good to my two.'

'Your Lucy looks taken with that RAF pilot, doesn't she?'

'That's Dave Sullivan, and from the way she goes on about him, I'd say she's in love.'

'I had a letter from Al yesterday.' Kathy beamed with pleasure. 'He said the local people are very friendly and often invite them into their homes. Though they're careful not to eat too much, because of the food rationing. It's hard to imagine what it's like not being able to go out and buy what you want, isn't it?'

Bet nodded, and let Kathy continue.

'And they throw a party for the children sometimes, and invite all the young girls to their dances. They're doing all right, aren't they?'

'Sure they are.' Bet squeezed her hand. 'They say the war will be over by the end of next year, and then they'll all be coming home.'

'Won't that be great? It's tough having them so far away, but we're not the only ones, are we? Families are separated all over the world.'

Bet gazed at the photos, a wistful expression on her face. 'Yeah, it's hard, but we'll get through it. We've got to.'

Kathy nodded glumly. 'We don't have much choice.'

'Isn't that the truth!'

Chapter Twenty-Three

The evenings were getting cold now November had arrived. Where had the summer gone? Ruth put a match to the fire and sat back on her heels to watch the flames take hold. It was such a comforting sight. She was going to spoil herself this evening and curl up on the settee to read a book. She still didn't like being here on her own, and Jack's suggestion that he would stay overnight quite often had not worked out. He was so busy – they all were. It had been recorded that in two days at the beginning of November the ATA had ferried over 800 aircraft. The delivery of heavy bombers had also increased, and a few more women were now cleared to fly them in an effort to meet the demand for qualified pilots. Gussie was one of them. There was no denying that Ruth missed her lively friend, but they met up occasionally at some airfield. Gussie was obviously blissfully happy, and that was all that mattered.

There was a knock on the door, making Ruth jump to her feet. That couldn't be Jack because he had his own key.

She smiled with pleasure when she opened the door. 'Lucy! What a lovely surprise. Come in. What are you doing down here?'

'I've got two days off, so I thought I'd come and see you. I hope you don't mind.'

'Of course I don't.' Ruth took Lucy's bag from her and placed it on a chair. 'Are you able to stay the night?'

'I'd like to, if that's OK?'

'That would be lovely.' It was then Ruth noticed that Lucy looked rather unhappy, which was more than unusual, for she had such a sunny disposition. 'Sit down and tell me what's the matter.'

'Dave's asked me to marry him.'

'And what did you say?' Ruth spoke gently as Lucy didn't seem overjoyed by the proposal.

'Well, I was pleased, of course, but I told him there was a lot to consider, like where would we live when the war's over – England or America. He waved that aside and said we could sort it out when the time came.' Lucy clasped her hands together tightly. 'I didn't like that, Ruth. I told him that when I married it would be for life, and it was sensible to get everything straight first.'

Ah, there was a touch of her brother's caution in her after all. Ruth hadn't noticed it before. Bet had obviously brought up her children to think before they took action.

Lucy stood up with her back to the fire. 'He just laughed and told me I worry too much. He took me to meet his family last Sunday.'

When she lapsed into silence, Ruth waited, then asked, 'How did you get on with them?'

'They didn't like me. They were very posh. I didn't think anything about it at first.' Lucy gave Ruth an affectionate smile. 'After all, you and your family are posh, so is Simon, and you treat us real good. Your mom and pop are the nicest folks we've ever met. Not once have you ever made us feel out of place.'

Ruth was surprised to hear that. Her father was a successful barrister and they were quite wealthy, but she'd never considered that they were 'posh', as Lucy put it. Her family had worked hard for what they had. Dave's parents must have hurt Lucy very much for her to be so upset. 'And they did make you feel out of place?'

'They made it clear that I wasn't good enough for their son. Boy, did they know how to snub without being too obvious. All it took was a sly remark here and there. They had belittling someone down to a fine art. And they kept shoving some other girl down my throat all the time, saying how wonderful she was.' Lucy's mouth thinned into an angry line. 'I told Dave I wasn't going to be treated like a piece of dirt. I've had a fine education and I'm as good as they are. Better, in fact!'

'Of course you are. By the sound of it they're the ones who need a lesson in good manners. Don't let them upset you.' Ruth put an arm around the unhappy girl, angry at the way her friend had been treated. 'Want a cup of tea and something to eat?'

'Please.' Lucy opened her bag and took out a box. 'I brought you some eggs.'

'Gosh, thanks! Fancy scrambled eggs on toast?'

'That would be great.' Lucy was smiling now. 'I feel better for telling you.'

'Lucy, you mustn't let people like that upset you. It sounds as if they've lined up a suitable wife for their son, and you've thrown a spanner into their plans. I'm sure it wasn't anything personal. They would dislike any girl but the one they had chosen to be their daughter-in-law.'

'I expect you're right, and Dave just looked bored when they went on about this other girl. He didn't seem at all like his parents – stuffy, you know?'

'No, he isn't *stuffy*.' Ruth broke the eggs in a pan, her annoyance disappearing when she heard Lucy use that word. 'And don't forget that he is facing danger each time he takes off. He must have a very different outlook on life. What did he say about his parents' rudeness?'

'He just shrugged and told me to ignore them. They were always like that, he said. But I was hurt and suggested it would be better if we didn't see each other again. He exploded. It was his life, he told me, and he'd go out with any girl he wanted to. He begged me not to leave him because he loved me, and we could still get married without telling his family – it was none of their business anyway.'

Ruth stared at her in alarm. This was a recipe for disaster.

'It's all right, Ruth. I told him that was out of the question, but we would still go out together. Once the war is over his family might feel differently, so we'd discuss it then.'

'Did he accept that?'

'Yeah, he seemed happy with that. He said he'd try to be patient and wait for the right time. I love him, Ruth, and don't want to hurt him. His folks ought to realise that he's facing danger each time he takes to the air, and they shouldn't begrudge him any happiness. And he's happy with me.'

'We know he is, Lucy, but you've done the right thing by saying you should wait before taking such an important step.' Ruth dished up the eggs, relief surging through her as they sat at the table. Thank heavens she was a sensible girl – many weren't, and had got themselves into great trouble by making a hasty decision. That was the nature of war. The uncertainty of wondering if you were going to live through the next day made some people reckless, allowing themselves to be swept away on the moment. It was a happiness that could turn sour in a short space of time, and she didn't want that for Lucy. 'Dave isn't a fool, and I expect that deep down he agrees with you.'

'He does.' Lucy took a mouthful of egg. 'Gee, this is great. Nearly as good as Mom's.'

'A compliment indeed.' Ruth was relieved to see Lucy more cheerful again.

'Don't tell my big brother about this, will you? If he found out I'd been treated bad, he'd be round there telling them what he thought of them.'

Ruth couldn't agree more; he would be furious if he thought his little sister was being treated with disrespect. 'I'll bet he would, but I promise not to say a word to him. I'll leave that for you to do in your own time.'

'Thanks, you're a real pal.' Lucy cleared her plate and stood up. 'I'll make the tea.'

'That's all right, I'll do it.'

Lucy gave her a hurt look. 'I do know how to make proper English tea. Jack taught me.'

Ruth was immediately on her feet. Jack's tea was atrocious, and she wouldn't let him near a teapot.

'I'm only kidding,' Lucy joked. 'Simon showed me how it's made.'

'That's a relief!' She watched carefully though, but Lucy even warmed the pot first.

'Anyway, I thought to hell with his folks.' Lucy returned to the subject troubling her. 'It was Dave I loved and I'd stay with him, even if they did disapprove.'

'Good for you! And really, it's their problem, not yours.'

'I never thought of it that way, but you're right. It was silly to let them upset me.' Lucy poured the tea and handed a cup to Ruth, smirking with pride. 'Try that.'

Ruth made a show of savouring the brew. 'That's excellent.'

'Told you.' She put her arms around Ruth and hugged. 'Thanks for letting me talk. It was what I needed to do, and I knew you'd be the one to come to. You're so sensible.'

Ruth pulled a face. 'I'm not so sure about that, but thanks for the compliment.'

'But you are. Jack always says you've got your head screwed on right.'

'Jack!' Ruth just had to laugh at that. 'He's very expert at *unscrewing* it.'

'Don't I know it! He's so damned persuasive. If he ever starts a sentence with the words "Will you—?" it's time to run for your life. When I was in the air strapped to the wing at the show, all I could think of was how did I ever agree to this? Come to think about it, I'm not sure I ever did.'

They were both laughing when there was a knock on the door, and Ruth opened it to find Simon standing there.

'How lovely, two visitors in one evening. Come in, Simon.'

Lucy beamed when she saw him. 'Great to see you, Teach.'

'Am I interrupting anything? I could hear you laughing from outside.'

'We were talking about my big brother, and I was giving Ruth some sisterly advice on how to handle him.'

'Ah,' was all he said.

'Sit down.' Ruth took another cup off the dresser. 'The tea's fresh and if you're hungry I could do you scrambled eggs on toast. Lucy brought some eggs and there's two left.'

'I wouldn't say no to that.' Simon sat at the table while Ruth busied herself at the stove.

'What brings you here?' she asked.

'There's a bit of reorganising going on, and I said I'd come and let you know. In fact, it's good you're both here, because it concerns you as well, Lucy.'

Ruth put the plate in front of him and sat down, expectantly. 'Sounds intriguing.'

'You're needed at White Waltham, Ruth. We're getting an increasing amount of Halifaxs and Stirlings to ferry and need all the four-engine pilots we can find at the moment. And things could get even busier next year as the build-up to the invasion begins.'

'What about me?' Lucy's eyes were wide with excitement. 'Can I come to White Waltham as well?'

'That has already been agreed.' Simon didn't get any further as Lucy erupted.

'What do you want me to fly?'

He gave Ruth an amused smile, and then looked back at Lucy. 'Well, there's the Typhoon and the new Tempest coming on to our books. Also the Mosquito . . .'

Lucy stilled, a question in her eyes. 'But that's a twin . . .'

'How about doing a conversion course for twins?'

'Wow! Can I, Simon?'

'I'll teach you myself.'

That was too much for Lucy. She was on her feet dancing around and hugging Simon and Ruth in turn.

'These Americans are so emotional,' Simon remarked dryly.

'Aren't they? But it's really quite refreshing.'

Lucy sat down, her smile as wide as it could get. 'You English,' she chided, 'you ought to let your emotions out. It's good for you. Isn't it wonderful, we'll be at the same ferry pool, Ruth! Won't that be great?'

'It certainly will.' Ruth couldn't be more pleased, and she was delighted to see Lucy so happy again. Dave's parents had upset her, but she doubted if anything could keep Lucy down for long. All she had needed was a chance to talk over the situation and get it clear in her mind. Once she'd done that she had been able to see how unimportant it was at this point. She had a zest for life that really *was* refreshing.

'Could we rent a little place like this and share it?' Lucy gazed hopefully at Ruth.

'We'll see what we can find.' She couldn't help wondering what Jack was going to say about that arrangement.

Their secret nights together would end. That would be a disappointment for both of them, but she wouldn't be sorry to leave this cottage. Since Gussie had moved out, Jack had only been able to come a few times, and she didn't enjoy coming back to an empty place each night. She had never lived on her own before, and she didn't care for it much.

'That's great! Wait till I tell Jack!'

Ruth fought to hide a wry smile. Lucy evidently didn't have any idea that her relationship with Jack was so intimate. Still, the move to White Waltham was an exciting prospect, and they would be able to see more of each other when they were working at the same ferry pool.

Lucy had become serious. 'Simon, do you really think there will be an invasion next year?'

'It's a strong possibility. The raids on Germany have intensified, and the build-up of troops and equipment here is already under way.'

'We're going to be busy, aren't we?' Ruth could just picture the amount of aircraft they would have to shift. 'When do we come to White Waltham?'

'You are both to report there the day after tomorrow.'

'Oh, this is so exciting! I can't wait to tell my brother I'll be working with him.'

Ruth tipped her head to one side at the sound of a key in the door. 'You'll be able to tell him now.'

'Jack!' Lucy, as excitable as ever, was on her feet talking to her brother, hardly stopping to take a breath as she told him everything in the shortest possible time. It didn't seem to have occurred to her that her brother had let himself in with his own key.

Simon and Ruth smiled at each other, knowing they both loved these two engaging Americans.

Jack ruffled his sister's hair, indulgent amusement shining in his dark blue eyes. 'I guess you're pleased?'

'You bet ya! Simon's going to be my instructor for the twins, and me and Ruth are going to find a house to share.' She flung her arms out wide, her earlier distress completely forgotten in the joy of the moment. 'What more could I ask for?'

'That about covers it,' Jack said dryly. 'Now, can I say hello to Ruth and Simon?'

'Oops, sorry.'

They spent the evening talking about their hopes for an invasion next year, and the extra work that would mean for the ATA. It was eleven o'clock before Jack and Simon made a move to leave.

Lucy was outside talking to Simon and Jack kissed Ruth longingly. 'I'm sorry about tonight,' she told him, 'but Lucy wants to stay.'

'No problem, honey. I'll find us a little hotel somewhere so we can have time alone together.'

Ruth waved the two men off. Things were changing, and she couldn't help wondering what 1944 would bring. Perhaps the end of the war?

Chapter Twenty-Four

By the end of May 1944 it was obvious that plans for the invasion were going ahead at a pace, and there was much speculation about the date. The weather was unusually hot for the time of year when Ruth took off in a priority Stirling for a new airfield in Wiltshire. Her flight engineer was Joyce Hammond, newly qualified and good at her job. Ruth was happy with her calm demeanour and businesslike way of carrying out her duties.

When they landed and climbed out of the aircraft, they gazed around in amazement at the huge gliders assembled there.

'What do you think these are for, Ruth?'

'I really don't know, but they'd carry an awful lot of troops and equipment. They must be planning to use them for the invasion. We'd better go and check in.'

They'd no sooner done this than a taxi Anson landed, ready to take them back to White Waltham. There was an air of expectancy everywhere, with an increased workload for all of them. Days off were forgotten, but no one minded.

Joyce's stomach gave an audible rumble and she pulled a face. 'We're not even being given time to eat.'

'That isn't unusual. We'll make sure we get something when we get back. Now you mention it, I'm hungry as well.' Ruth smiled when she recognised the tall man waiting beside the aircraft. 'They've put you on taxi duty, then.'

'Hiya.' Jack gave his usual lazy smile. 'I'm only doing this one trip. There's another Stirling waiting for you.'

'My goodness, I am being spoilt. Two four-engines in one day.' Ruth touched his arm and pointed across the field at the gliders. 'Looks like the invasion's on, doesn't it?'

'No doubt about it. This country is bursting at the seams with troops and equipment. Let's hope the Luftwaffe keep away, because they wouldn't be short of targets. I can't understand why they aren't coming across in waves to put a stop to this.'

'When do you think it will be?' Ruth knew this was the question on everyone's lips, but she still asked.

'Soon, it must be soon.' He opened the door for them. 'In you get. The aircraft are stacked up, waiting to be moved.'

As soon as they arrived back, Jack was off in a Lancaster. Ruth wished she'd been given that. They all agreed that it was a lovely plane to fly.

'Good, you're back.' The head of ops handed Ruth a ferry chitty for the next delivery. 'It's all ready for you.'

Joyce cast Ruth a pleading look, and she knew what her flight engineer was asking. 'We need to grab a sandwich first. Breakfast was our last meal, and that was six hours ago.'

'All right, but make it quick. Your delivery is a priority again.'

The girls headed for the food at top speed. They were just finishing their hasty snack when Lucy bounced in and sat with them.

'Food!' Lucy pinched the last sandwich. 'I'm starving. No one seems to realise that *we* need refuelling as well.'

She shot off and quickly returned with three mugs of tea and more sandwiches, which she shared out.

'Thanks.' Ruth watched as Lucy demolished the food. 'Where have you been today?'

'All over the place, but I've just delivered a Mosquito to the maintenance unit at Hullavington, and do you know what they were doing?'

Ruth and Joyce shook their heads.

'They were painting black and white stripes on the wings of gliders and fighters.'

'Did you find out why?'

'No, but I'll ask Dave when I see him. He'll know.'

Ops came into the room. 'I'm sorry to rush you, girls, but there's a Stirling and Spitfire we want to get out of the way.'

'Whoops.' Lucy carried on eating as she stood up. 'The Spit's mine.'

'Be careful when you land at Brize Norton, Lucy,' ops warned. 'You might find gliders parked near the runway.

'I'll watch it.'

'More gliders,' Joyce said, as they hurried out to the Stirling.

During the rest of May they worked hard, ferrying as many planes as they could during daylight hours. The weather was good, and all the time it held, they flew.

But with the arrival of June, the weather broke.

They were in the Mess waiting for the weather to clear so they could fly, when the door opened and a bedraggled pilot walked in. Ruth was immediately on her feet, ushering her into a chair. 'Gussie, you haven't been flying in this weather, surely?'

She waved at everyone in her usual boisterous way. Marriage hadn't changed her and, although soaking wet, she still smiled happily. 'I only had a short flight so I thought I'd give it a go.' She shook the water out of her hair and then fingered it back into place. 'Visibility was worse than I'd thought, so I decided to land here and come and see you.'

'Wonderful. I'm so pleased you did. How's married life treating you?' Ruth settled down for a good gossip with her friend.

'Just fine, Ruthie. I've got myself a good man in Harry.' She glanced around. 'Any chance of a cuppa? I'm gasping.'

'Coming right up.' Ruth got her a mug of tea, delighted with this unexpected chance to see her friend. They had seen very little of each other since the wedding. They had kept in touch by letter, but Gussie wasn't much of a letter writer, and they'd all been so busy.

The rain was lashing down, making Gussie sigh as she looked at the streaming windows. 'I'm not going anywhere tonight.'

'Stay with us, we've got a spare bed.' Ruth studied her friend's wet clothes. 'Have you got your overnight bag with you?'

'Never go anywhere without it, and thanks for the offer of a bed, it will be like old times. I'll just let my pool know where I am. Is Lucy around?'

'Gone to find Simon. She believes he knows everything

and is keeping the date of the invasion to himself.'

Gussie's face lit up with interest. 'Is there something between them?'

'No, I wish there was. She's still crazy about Dave, even though his parents don't seem to approve of her. They appear to have picked out a suitable wife for their son, and his involvement with Lucy has upset their plans.'

'Oh, Lord, that poor girl could be in for a rough flight.'

Ruth nodded. 'She finally told Jack about the meeting with Dave's family. He wasn't pleased, as you can imagine, but he says she's got to make her own decisions. As much as he would like to interfere, he won't do it.'

'Wise man. And talking about the big man, where is he?'

'No idea, but like everyone else, he's pacing around like a caged lion.'

'I expect they're thinking they might be able to go home soon.' Gussie saw Ruth's expression and reached out to touch her hand. 'I'm sorry, Ruthie, that was clumsy of me.'

'Don't apologise. You've only put into words what is constantly on my mind. Everyone's thinking about the future. Simon's going to start his flying school again and has asked me to join him. I'll get my instructor's rating as soon as I can.'

'That won't be any problem. You're a damned good pilot.'

'Thanks.' Ruth smiled at her friend. 'And what are your plans?'

'Lots of children. We both want a large family. As soon as the war's over we're going to find a large house somewhere quiet, and create our own noise by filling it with kids.'

'Sounds idyllic, and you'll make a terrific mother.'

'I think so too.'

They were both laughing when Lucy came in with Jack and Simon. They were all delighted to see Gussie. 'How's Harry?' Simon asked.

'Wonderful, and he's grounded after completing another tour of ops. Which is a relief, I can tell you. So many of those bomber crews don't come back. It's heartbreaking.'

Simon nodded, and then lit a cigarette. 'Germany's taking a terrible pasting.'

'So did London and other British cities,' Jack pointed out.

'I know, but you can't help feeling sorry for the ordinary people who are suffering in this madness. Let's hope the invasion starts soon.'

Jack grimaced as he glanced at the rain on the windows. 'Everything must be in place now. Troops and equipment have been moving towards the coast for days, but they can't go in this weather.'

'And neither can we go anywhere.' Gussie stood up. 'So put away your gloomy faces and let's find a pub with food and drink.'

'You're not going anywhere until you get out of those wet clothes,' Ruth scolded.

'They're only damp.' Gussie ran a hand over her sleeve. 'I ran as fast as I could from the plane to here.'

'Change!' Ruth glared sternly.

'All right, Mum.' She grinned and held up her bag. 'I'll change in the ladies', and then the food is on me.'

'Now there's an offer we can't refuse.' Simon stubbed out his cigarette. 'I'll go and get my car.'

* * *

Later that night the three girls sat around the kitchen table enjoying a cup of cocoa, talking about their hopes for the future, and catching up on all the news.

'Have you and Dave made any plans?' Gussie asked.

'Not really. Dave did say he'd come to America with me. I know his folks don't like me much, but they adore him, and it would be hard on them if he did live so far away. I'm not sure I would be happy about that.' Lucy sipped her drink. 'Or I could stay here, but I'd miss Mom so much, and I'd hate being parted from Jack. We've always been together, and we're more than brother and sister. We're real good friends.'

Gussie studied Lucy carefully. 'Want a bit of advice?'

'Oh, please! I keep going over and over everything in my mind, but there doesn't seem to be a happy solution.'

'Don't make any definite decisions yet. Even if the invasion begins soon, there will still be a long fight ahead. It could be another year before it's all over, so you've got plenty of time to work out the best thing to do. Don't try to cross your bridges before you get to them.'

'Yeah, you're right, Gussie. And what a great saying. I must tell that to my mom.'

Ruth had listened to all this and said nothing. Jack hadn't mentioned what he intended doing after the war, but Lucy seemed sure he would go back home. She'd always known this, of course; after all, he'd been away for a long time now.

If she were in his position she'd be longing to return to her family. She couldn't blame him for that, but when the time came it was going to be so damned painful. But she would also take Gussie's advice and try not to cross that particular bridge until she came to it. A lot could, and probably would, change before this war was over.

Gussie yawned. 'Let's get some sleep. Hopefully the weather will be better in the morning and we can get back to work.'

By morning the cloud had lifted enough for Gussie to complete her delivery. It had been lovely to be together again, and had given Ruth the lift she needed. Speculation was rife about an imminent invasion, making everyone on edge.

'She's happy.' Simon stood beside Ruth as they waved to the departing plane.

'Yes, I'm so pleased for her and Harry.' Ruth gave Simon a wistful smile. 'After all the loss and separation people have suffered it's comforting to see that it's worked out for some.'

There was amusement in Simon's voice when he spoke. 'Tell you what, Ruth, when our American friends have left us, we could get married. We'd make a good team.'

'Now that's a sensible idea.' She laughed, knowing he was joking. They were good friends, but that was all they would ever be. The physical love she felt for Jack, and she was sure Simon felt for Lucy, didn't exist between them. While marriages had been successfully based on friendship alone before, that wouldn't work for them, and they both knew it.

'I'm full of sensible ideas.' He placed an arm around her shoulders as they walked back to the Mess. 'We must see about getting you that instructor's rating.'

Chapter Twenty-Five

'Switch on the wireless!' Simon hurtled into the Mess where they were all waiting for the clouds to lift so they could fly.

Ruth was startled, she'd never seen Simon so animated. 'What's going on?'

'Shush!' Sally motioned to Ruth to be quiet.

The tension in the room was palpable as they listened to the announcement. The invasion was under way and troops were already moving into France. There was much rejoicing as the wireless was switched off, and then silence as they all digested the news.

Jane broke the quiet. 'I never expected them to go in this weather.'

'Neither did the Germans,' Jack said, nodding approval. 'That was a smart move. They're going to need planes in France, Simon, let's go and see what we can find out.'

As the men left, Sally turned to Jane. 'Do you think there's any chance of them allowing women to ferry planes to France?'

'Not at the moment. The RAF will probably handle that at first, but we might be needed later. We'll have to see how things work out, but it will be the men who get the first flights.'

'Now there's a surprise,' Sally said dryly, making them all laugh.

'I wonder where Dave is.' Lucy gazed out of the window. 'We were supposed to meet two days ago, but he sent a message to say he couldn't make it. Now I know why.'

'The invasion fleet would have been given a fighter escort.' Ruth joined Lucy at the window. 'I expect he's nipping back and forth across the Channel.'

'Yeah, I expect he's going to be busy for a while.'

'And so are we, as soon as this blasted weather clears.'

'Look!' Sally pointed. 'There's a break in the clouds. I'll go and see what the Met has to say. We might be able to get one delivery in today.'

Everyone got to their feet, eager to be doing something. They all knew the next few weeks would be crucial to the outcome of the war, and none of them wanted to be standing around wasting time.

One week after the start of the invasion, London was once again under attack from V1 flying bombs. These unmanned aircraft were coming over at any time, night or day. Every effort was being made to shoot them down before they reached their targets. The fighters were chasing them and trying to bring them down over the sea, and this was dangerous. Any that got through then came under fire from the ground guns, but many were still making it to London.

Ruth and the other pilots were ready to start deliveries for the day, but first they had an update on the situation.

'Plan your routes carefully,' Jane advised. 'Stay away from the gun emplacements or you might come under fire if there is a flying bomb around. Be careful if your flight takes you anywhere near what is being called "Bomb Alley".'

With their maps meticulously checked they set off for the day's work. The invasion had been under way for nearly three weeks now, and although the news was encouraging, it was clear that there was not going to be a speedy end to the war. Ruth's destination was Redhill, the group support unit, which had been set up to keep the Air Force supplied with aircraft. She had hardly brought the fighter to a halt when a man climbed on to the wing.

'We're right in line with Bomb Alley,' he shouted above the roar of the engine. 'You've got to take this to Bognor right away.'

She nodded, waited for him to jump down, and then turned immediately to take off again. When she arrived back at White Waltham and reported in, they were already aware of the situation.

The next morning all available pilots of No. 1 ferry pool at White Waltham were called together.

'We've got a big job on our hands today,' Captain Anders told them. 'The GSU at Redhill has got to be moved to Bognor. The flying bombs are too close for comfort. If one lands there it would cause havoc.'

'What, *everything*?' Lucy gasped. 'That place is packed with planes. How long have we got?'

'One day.' Andy looked around at the stunned

expressions. 'Simon and Jack will be needed for the ferrying, so I'll fly the taxi. And Jane will help with the ferrying. We're going to need every pilot we can muster.'

Ruth smiled at Captain Anders, or Andy, as his friends called him. He was going grey at the temples now, but he was a very impressive man. She had been lucky enough to have him as her instructor for the four-engines, and she admired him enormously.

'Right.' Jane, who was standing next to Andy, glanced at the clock. 'Let's get this show on the road by nine o'clock. It's going to be one hell of a day.'

Never a truer word had been spoken. It was ten that night before they stopped. The day had become a blur of trips to Bognor, then in the taxi back to Redhill, then to Bognor again.

When Ruth and Lucy finally arrived home, they were too exhausted to speak. They just flopped in chairs with a groan of relief.

After some minutes, Lucy muttered, 'I don't think I had any lunch.'

Ruth gave an inelegant snort. 'I'm *sure* I didn't.' She tried to stir herself but couldn't seem to make herself move. 'We ought to get something to eat, my stomach's complaining.'

'Yeah, so's mine.'

Neither of them moved until there was a knock on the door.

'I'll go.' Lucy dragged herself up, staggered slightly, and then lurched for the door.

Ruth opened one eye as Simon and Jack walked in. Then her nose twitched. 'Food?'

'Hi.' Jack leant over and kissed her, then whispered the magic words – fish and chips.

She was suddenly awake. 'Where did you get those at this time of night?'

'We have friends who took pity on a group of exhausted pilots.' Jack pulled Ruth to her feet. 'Come on, let's eat before they get cold.'

They didn't bother with plates or knives and forks. They just unwrapped the paper and dived in after sprinkling salt and vinegar over the feast. The pieces of battered fish were small, but there were plenty of chips. Not a word was spoken, and when Jack pinched a few of Ruth's chips, she was in too mellow a mood to object. She just grinned happily at him. 'Come on, where did you get this?'

'We pleaded with one of the RAF cooks.'

'Well, thank him next time you see him, and tell him he's a wonderful cook.'

'Sure will.'

Soon there wasn't a scrap left, and Simon groaned in satisfaction. 'That was the best fish and chips I've ever tasted.'

Not one of them could disagree with that. They just hadn't had time to stop for food.

Ruth then made a large pot of tea, and they sat around the table, talking about the day. 'I didn't believe we could shift that amount of aircraft in one day, but we managed it.'

'Yes, it was a good team effort.' Simon drained his cup and held it out for a refill. 'Does anyone know exactly how many planes we moved today?'

'No idea, I haven't bothered to check yet.' Jack sat back.

'I felt sorry for Andy in the taxi. How many landings and take-offs did he do today?'

'I dread to think.' Ruth made some more tea. 'But we had the right man for the job.'

Their meal finished, they retired to the other room and more comfortable chairs. There they talked and laughed about the day, and one thing was clear: it had been the most frantic day of ferrying, but a satisfying one.

The news was worrying. England was being attacked again by unmanned flying bombs, and Bet's children were right in the thick of the danger. Her insides fluttered uncomfortably. When the Blitz had stopped she had been relieved, but now it had all started again. Just when she had begun to think that Jack and Lucy were safe, they had a new danger to face.

'Bet?' Kathy was looking in the back door and waving a letter, a huge smile on her face. 'I've heard from Al.'

'That's great.' Bet pushed away her own worries. Ever since the invasion had begun, Kathy had been worried out of her mind, knowing that her son would be part of the action. 'Come in and tell me what he says.'

'He's in France, but he can't tell me where, of course. He says they're moving forward, and the French people are really happy to see them. I was scared to death that he wouldn't survive the landings, but he's OK.'

'That's wonderful news, Kathy.'

'Yeah, but that bloody man Hitler won't give up, will he? He's bombing London again. Poor devils. Have you heard from your two?'

'Not for a couple of weeks. Even Ruth hasn't written, but I expect they're all being kept busy.'

Kathy sighed. 'They must be. I won't be able to rest until the fighting's over and our children come home for good. I don't suppose Al can wait to get back to his horses. They're keeping his job open at the stud for him, which will give him something to look forward to. What do you think Jack and Lucy will do when they come home? They'll probably have had enough of flying by then.'

'I doubt that. My two will always fly. It's like lifeblood to them. Lucy might get married and settle down, but I think Jack will always be involved with planes. You know how I worried about him when he was growing up. His teachers said he had a fine mind, but all he cared about were engines.'

Kathy nodded in agreement. 'He was only twelve when he took our car engine to pieces because Chas was having troubles starting it. "I'll fix it," he told us with such confidence. Chas couldn't bear to watch as he spread the parts out in the yard. He was sure Jack wouldn't get it back together again, but he did, and it worked like a dream.'

Bet chuckled as she remembered the incident. Chas had been sure he would have to buy a new car. 'I had to watch him like a hawk. If he could get his hands on anything mechanical it ended up in pieces, always needing to find out how it worked. And he was so damned restless. I was sure I'd lose him to a big city somewhere when he was old enough, but flying gave him something he craved. And Lucy wanted to do everything her brother did. There's four years between them, but they're more like twins. I wasn't surprised when Lucy wanted to follow Jack to England. It near broke my heart to see them both leave.' Bet gave a helpless shrug. 'But what can you do? They've got to follow their own paths in life, haven't they?'

'They sure have. Chas wanted Al to become a doctor or something, but he only ever wanted to be around horses. He could ride almost before he could walk.'

They fell silent for a moment as they remembered the happy times when their children were young. Now this terrible war had taken them away, but with the invasion under way, there was hope that things would soon return to normal.

Bet broke the silence. 'I think we ought to go somewhere for the weekend. Find a lovely spot, relax and spoil ourselves.'

'Great idea!' Kathy was on her feet. 'It'll only take me ten minutes to throw some things in a bag.'

Within half an hour they were driving along the highway, smiling like a couple of kids sneaking off for a forbidden treat.

Chapter Twenty-Six

Simon was dealing with some paperwork when Lucy walked in. As soon as he saw her strained expression he was instantly on his feet. 'What's the matter?'

'I can't find Dave.' Her lips trembled.

'Sit down, Lucy.' Simon urged her into a chair and crouched in front of her. 'Tell me about it.'

She gripped his hands tightly. 'I was supposed to meet him last night at a pub in Maidenhead. It's where we always go when he can get away for a few hours. I waited all evening and he didn't come. Jane let me phone Biggin Hill today, but they were very cagey and wouldn't tell me anything.'

'You know they won't give out details about personnel over the phone,' Simon pointed out gently. He was sure she had got herself worked up for nothing. These pilots could be called upon at a moment's notice, not giving them a chance to contact anyone.

She looked at him in anguish. 'Then why did they tell me to contact his parents?'

That shook Simon. 'Are you sure they didn't mean he was on leave?'

'He'd have told me if he was going home.' She became agitated. 'Something's wrong. Can you find out for me? Please, Simon!'

'I know the station commander at Biggin Hill. I'll see if I can reach him, but I'm sure you're worrying unnecessarily.'

'I hope so,' she whispered. 'I'll wait here.'

He stood up. 'I expect Dave got caught for an unexpected trip across the Channel and wasn't able to let you know.'

'That's what I thought at first, but it doesn't feel right. When I asked about Dave there was a moment of silence on the other end of the phone before the man spoke again. He was very evasive. Something's happened and I don't think his folks would be too pleased if I contacted them. I wouldn't want to upset them if I'm imagining this.' Lucy took a deep breath. 'But I don't think I am. I'm worried and need to know if he's all right.'

The stricken look in her eyes tore Simon apart, and he hurried to the ops room for the telephone. The invasion had been under way for a few weeks now and the troops were making their way into France. There was an air of hope around that it would all be over by the end of the year. Lucy had been so buoyant and happy just lately, but if anything had happened to Dave, she was going to be devastated.

Simon had met the station commander on several occasions and hoped he would talk to him. When the phone was answered he asked for Commander Young, gave his own name, and waited.

'Hello, Simon. What can I do for you?'

'I've got a favour to ask, Ian.'

'Fire away.'

'Can you tell me if Dave Sullivan is all right?'

Ian hesitated. 'What's your interest?'

'I'm a friend of Lucy Nelson. She's his girlfriend, and is worried.' When he was greeted with silence, Simon continued, 'They've been dating for some time, Ian, and are serious about each other. If something has happened she ought to be told.' He now had a very nasty feeling about this. Lucy was right: they were being evasive.

'She phoned earlier, but we couldn't tell her anything until the next of kin had been informed.'

A cold chill crept through Simon. 'He's dead?'

'Yes, he was killed yesterday when his plane crashed in France. I'm sorry, Simon, I thought his parents would have contacted her.'

'They haven't, but I'll break the news to her.' He'd had to face many distressing times in this war, but this was going to be one of the hardest.

When he returned to where he'd left her, Lucy searched his face, pleading with her eyes for good news. But she knew at once that there wasn't going to be any.

Simon sat beside her and placed an arm around her shoulders. 'Dave's plane crashed yesterday in France. I'm so sorry, Lucy, he was killed.'

She let out a stifled moan and began to shake. Simon

drew her into his arms, not knowing how to comfort her as she sobbed in grief.

They had been like that for some minutes when Ruth walked in. 'Oh, God, what's happened?' she asked, rushing over to them.

'Dave's been killed.' Simon spoke softly.

'Hell!' Ruth swore with feeling. 'I'm so sorry. Lucy, let me take you home.'

Still holding tightly on to Simon, she nodded. 'Simon comes too.'

'If that's what you want.' He helped her to her feet. Her expression was grim, but he was relieved to see that she was more in control. And he was also grateful to have Ruth take over.

Ruth supported her on the other side and they walked with her to Simon's car. 'Do you know where Jack is?' she asked him.

'He's taken a Spit over to France. I'm not sure if he'll be back tonight.'

Once at the house, Ruth made Lucy eat a piece of toast and drink two cups of tea, then, seeing how exhausted she was, helped her to bed.

'How is she?' Simon wanted to know when Ruth came downstairs again.

'Asleep already.' She sat down opposite him. 'Tell me what happened.'

He then told her the little he knew, not being able to hide his annoyance. 'Dave's family should have sent her a message. They know she's in the ATA, and a call to any ferry pool would have been forwarded to her. But perhaps they're too distraught to have given his girlfriend a thought. I'll give them the benefit of the doubt.'

'I expect that's it.' Ruth gave Simon a sympathetic look. 'So the unpleasant task was left to you.'

He grimaced. 'God, Ruth, I hated doing that. It hurts to see her so upset.'

'She'll be all right when she gets over the initial shock,' she assured him. 'She's resilient and, like her brother, made of strong stuff.'

He stood up, feeling drained. 'Take care of her, Ruth. I must get some sleep if I'm going to function properly tomorrow.'

'I will, and don't you worry.' She watched him leave, then went back indoors. It was doubtful if she was going to get much rest tonight, but she had to try because she was flying again in the morning.

Ruth was surprised to find Lucy in the kitchen the next morning, and in uniform. 'No one will mind if you don't come in today, Lucy.'

'No, but I would mind.' She spoke firmly. 'We have a job to do, Ruth, and I've seen you all carry on when tragedy strikes. Not one of you has ever let your personal feelings get in the way of what has to be done, and I'm not going to either.' She gave a sad smile. 'It hurts like mad, but he's gone, and no amount of wishing is going to change that. I'll come to terms with the loss in time, just like everyone else has to. In the meantime, I want to fly and be with my friends. When I'm in the air all I have on my mind is flying. It will help me through this.'

Ruth didn't try to persuade her otherwise because that was exactly how she would feel and act. 'I learnt to fly after my brother was killed in a racing car accident. Being in the air was like balm to my soul.'

'Exactly.' Lucy spread margarine on the toast. 'We're very lucky to be able to fly, aren't we?'

'Very.'

'I've written a letter to Dave's folks. It was the least I could do.'

'That's thoughtful of you, and I'm sure they'll appreciate it.'

'I hope so, because I want to go to the funeral and say my goodbyes properly.'

After finishing their breakfast they made their way to the airfield, ready for another day. The only thing allowed to interrupt their routine was the weather.

Jack returned that evening to the sad news, and although Lucy cried on his shoulder as she told him, it was Simon she turned to continually for support and encouragement.

Two days later, Lucy received a note from Dave's father, thanking her for her letter and giving details of the funeral to be held in ten days' time. It was to be a military funeral in his hometown of Windsor.

Jack, Simon and Ruth had all known Dave, so they went with Lucy, not wanting her to face this ordeal alone. They made sure they were all smartly dressed in their ATA uniforms. Lucy stayed close to Jack and Simon during the service, and Ruth watched her anxiously, but she stood with her head up, straight and controlled. When the coffin was lowered into the ground, silent tears ran down her cheeks.

Dave's mother was so distraught she couldn't stand on her own and had to be helped to the car.

When Lucy made a move to go and speak to her, Jack shook his head. 'I wouldn't, Lucy. The poor woman isn't in any state to meet people. I'd say she's been sedated and probably wouldn't recognise anyone at the moment.'

His sister nodded, and the four of them stayed where they were as the mourners drifted away.

A man walked towards them as if every step was an effort. 'Thank you all for coming. Your letter was much appreciated, Lucy. My wife would have thanked you herself but, as you can see, she's too grief stricken to do anything at the moment.'

'I understand, Mr Sullivan. Dave was a lovely man and a brave one. His loss is a terrible tragedy.' Lucy's voice was husky with distress as she introduced Dave's father.

He shook hands with each of them, thanking them for coming, and inviting them back to the house.

'That's kind of you, sir,' Jack spoke first, 'but I'm afraid we have to get back.'

'Yes, of course. Dave was always singing the praises of the ATA. He said that without you the RAF would have had a job to keep flying. We never wanted him to fly, you know, but it was what he wanted to do.' He gave a strained smile. 'I suspect that you are all like that as well.'

'Yes, sir, our mom didn't want us to fly either, but no one could have stopped us.'

Mr Sullivan nodded, and then studied Lucy sadly. 'You made our son very happy, and I'm sorry we didn't welcome you as we should have done.'

Without saying a word, Lucy gripped one of his hands in both of hers, and then stepped back. It was an action of silent forgiveness, and understood as such by Dave's father.

They watched while he walked back to the waiting car and drove away.

Jack placed an arm round his sister's shoulder and gave her a squeeze. 'Let's get back. We've got planes to fly.'

Later that day, as Jack made pickups in the taxi, his thoughts went back to the funeral. He had been proud of Lucy. She had acted with dignity, and he was glad Mr Sullivan had come over to talk with them. It had given his sister a chance to put her first unfortunate meeting with Dave's folks behind her. Lucy had a generous nature and forgave easily. He'd felt so sorry for the Sullivans. It must be unbelievably hard to lose a child, as he had noticed with Ruth's folks. He doubted that they would ever fully get over the loss of their son. It could be a cruel world at times.

Lucy now had her own battle to deal with in trying to come to terms with Dave's death. He knew it wasn't going to be easy for her, but they were all here for her. She wouldn't lack love and support.

Chapter Twenty-Seven

Lucy threw herself into her work as she tried to deal with the loss of Dave. Ruth's admiration grew for the lovely American girl who had become a treasured friend. Jack and Simon were also there to support when needed. It was only five weeks since the tragedy and it was clear that Lucy was making a huge effort to move on with her life, and Ruth knew just how difficult that was. It had taken her a long time after her brother's death. Flying had been her way to healing, and Lucy was finding it the same. She flew constantly, only taking a day off when she was ordered to do so. But no one worried about her flying, for she was far too good a pilot to take unnecessary chances. Like all of them, if the conditions were bad she wouldn't take off.

Making her approach to Little Rissington, Ruth set the plane down and taxied to the parking area. As she jumped out it was obvious that the men were all talking animatedly. Wondering what was going on, she went straight to check in. There was an air of excitement around the place.

'What's happened?' she asked, as she handed over the delivery chit.

'Haven't you heard? Paris has been liberated!'

'That's wonderful!' She glanced at the date of the ferry chit – 25th August. This was a day that would go down in history. It was a milestone in the war.

'Berlin next,' the officer said.

Ruth couldn't wait to get back to White Waltham. They'd all go out and celebrate tonight. 'Have you got something else for me?'

'There's a Dakota for Luton. Can you take that? We've got a flight engineer who needs to get to Luton, and he can come with you.'

She nodded. It always amused her that the plane was named after the state Lucy and Jack came from. 'I need to phone my ferry pool and let them know where I'm going and see if a taxi can pick me up from Luton.'

Arrangements were soon made and Ruth was once again in the air, singing quietly to herself. Things were going well, and she hoped Jack was back from his jaunt across the Channel. He'd been there overnight and was expected back sometime today.

As it happened, she was able to pick up an Oxford from Luton and didn't need the taxi. It was late in the afternoon before she arrived back at her ferry pool.

When she walked into the Mess it was as if a dark cloud was filling the place. The atmosphere was completely different. No one was celebrating the liberation of Paris. Lucy was as white as a sheet and everyone else seemed stunned.

'What's happened?' Ruth asked, the words barely audible.

Simon left Lucy's side and came to her. He didn't mess about, but told her the news straight away. 'Jack's missing, Ruth. The Spitfire he was delivering never arrived. The weather turned nasty evidently and he might have landed at another field. We're waiting to hear.'

She felt as if someone had hit her very hard and rocked her back on her heels. She gathered her senses together as best she could. 'But you'd have heard from him if he had.'

'Yes.' Simon's expression was grim. 'Let's hope he didn't come down in the sea.'

'Oh, God!' The room began to sway.

Simon stood in front of her, shielding her from the rest of the room. 'Breathe deeply,' he murmured.

As she did this she steadied again. Touching his arm to indicate her thanks for his understanding, she straightened up and walked towards Lucy. There was no need to give up hope so soon, and this double blow was going to tear Lucy apart. Ruth sat beside her, taking hold of her hand. She was shaking badly from the shock. 'They'll find him,' was all she could think of to say.

When Lucy looked up she was dry-eyed with terror. 'Not Jack as well,' she moaned. 'That's too much, Ruth. Too much. How am I going to tell Mom?'

'I wouldn't say anything just yet. Wait until we have some definite news.' Ruth steeled herself to offer comfort, but all she wanted to do was find a place on her own and curl into a tight ball until the pain disappeared. The man she adored might never come back. All she'd have left were blissful memories of his lazy smile and spending nights in his arms. She had always known that after the war he would return to America, but she didn't want to lose him like this. *Please God*, she pleaded silently, *not like this*.

Her whole being rebelled at the direction her thoughts were taking. He wasn't dead! She wouldn't accept that. Many things could have happened, and he would probably turn up tomorrow, quite unaware of the distress he had caused. She clenched her teeth together in an effort to gain control. The last thing she must do is fall apart. Lucy needed her to be strong and positive.

'My car's outside.' Simon was bending down in front of them. 'I'll take you home.'

The next day Ruth and Lucy were back at work, needing to be kept busy. They were anxious for news, but at the same time afraid that when it came it would be what they didn't want to hear.

Lucy had said very little, but Ruth knew neither of them had slept. She had listened to the muffled crying from the other bedroom and hadn't been able to stop her own silent tears from soaking the pillow. When dawn had finally arrived, Ruth had wanted nothing more than to stay where she was. Fear swamped her, but she could hear Jack saying, 'Come on, honey, there are planes to fly.'

Simon was already at the airfield when they arrived. Without them saying a word, he just shook his head to let them know that there wasn't any news yet.

One day stretched into another, and the longer they went without news, the more chance there was that Jack was lost to them for ever.

'Four days,' Lucy said, when they returned home after another long day. 'I haven't told Mom yet, but I can't leave it much longer, Ruth. I asked the ATA to let me tell her. I can't bear the thought of her just receiving an official letter saying he's missing. They have given me the letter, but I haven't had the courage to send it. The news should come from me.' The tears began to trickle down her cheeks. 'This is going to break her heart.'

'Would you like me to write to her as well?' Lucy was right; they had delayed too long. Jack's mother had a right to know.

'He's dead, isn't he, Ruth?' The words came out in a sob.

'We don't know that.'

Lucy lifted her tear-stained face, her mouth set in a straight line. 'Yes, we do. I'll try and write that letter to Mom, and I'm sure it would be a comfort to hear from you as well.'

'All right, but we might receive news soon. He can't have disappeared. Someone must know something. Give it one more day, Lucy.' Ruth knew that sounded silly. Many people had just disappeared in this war, but she was clutching at any thin sliver of hope.

The next morning, they were collecting their ferry chits when Simon caught them. 'Lucy, there are a couple of American pilots who have ferried bombers across. They're going back today and have said they'll take you.' He tipped his head to one side enquiringly. 'Would you like to see your mother? They'll bring you back in two days' time.'

'Oh, that would be a blessing. I've tried many times to

272

write to Mom, but I just haven't been able to put it into words. It seems so impersonal.'

'It'll be better if you can see her, won't it?'

She nodded, her bottom lip trembling as she hugged him. 'Thank you, Simon. I don't know what I'd do without you.'

'You'd manage,' he said as he removed the ferry chit from her hands. 'I've fixed it for you to have some time off and I'll do your deliveries today. Now, you'd better hurry. They're leaving in fifteen minutes.'

Lucy turned to Ruth and clasped her hands. 'I'll be back.'

'Give your mother my love, won't you, and tell her I'll be writing soon.'

'Sure will.'

Simon and Ruth watched her run out to the waiting plane, climb in, and it immediately taxied for take-off. Lucy was on her way home to America.

'Hi, Mom.'

Bet spun around at the sound of her daughter's voice. She had the wireless playing Glenn Miller and hadn't heard her arrive. She stared for a moment, too stunned to move or speak as she took in the sight of Lucy standing in the kitchen. She was wearing her ATA uniform, and Bet felt as if her heart would burst with pride. She'd raised a couple of fine children.

'Lucy!' she squealed and threw herself at her daughter, hugging with all her might. The questions poured out. 'Where did you come from? Where's Jack, is he with you? Are you home for good?'

'I'm only here for two days . . . and Jack isn't with me.'

It was only then Bet realised that something was terribly wrong and her joy turned to sickening dread. She gripped Lucy's arms fiercely. 'Tell me.'

'He was delivering a plane to France, but he never arrived. They haven't found him, Mom. He's officially listed as missing.' Lucy's eyes misted with tears.

'Missing?' Bet had been steeling herself to hear that her darling son was dead, but the word missing ignited a spark of hope. 'Then he could still be alive.'

Lucy shook her head miserably. 'It's been five days, Mom. If he'd been alive they would have found him by now.'

'No! I can't accept that. If my boy had died I would have known.' She wanted to yell and know why the hell she hadn't been told about this at once, but when she saw the tears rolling down Lucy's face, she hugged her again, her own tears mingling with those of her daughter. 'Ah, sweetie, you've had a terrible time, haven't you, what with losing Dave, and now this. But don't give up hope. Jack will turn up alive and well, you'll see. You're tired out. Stay home and have a nice rest.'

'I have to go back the day after tomorrow. Simon's managed to get me a lift in a bomber being ferried to England.'

Bet nodded, desperately needing Lucy to stay, but she understood her need to get back. For that is where Jack would go. 'I wish I could come with you.'

'Once this war's over you must come and meet everyone, Mom. Ruth's folks have been so kind to us.' Lucy wiped a hand over her eyes, tired beyond belief. 'They lost their son in an accident just before the war, and they loved Jack as their own.'

'Don't talk in the past tense!' Bet spoke sharply, and immediately regretted it. This dear child of hers had been through so much, and it showed. There were dark circles under her eyes, showing both grief and weariness.

'I'm sorry.' Lucy bowed her head.

'You're worn out. Why don't you try and get some sleep? Your room is just as you left it.'

Lucy stood up and began to walk towards the stairs.

'Lucy, I won't believe that Jack is dead unless I see a body. And neither should you. I gave birth to the two of you –' Bet placed a hand over her heart '– and if anything happened to either of you, I'd know it. I don't know what has happened over there in France, or wherever Jack might be, but he'll be coming back alive.'

'I hope you're right, Mom. I must sleep. I might be able to see things clearer then.'

Bet watched her daughter climb the stairs as if every step was an effort, then she picked up the framed photo of her son. 'Be safe somewhere,' she whispered.

Ruth leant on the table, relieved that the bar was quiet this early in the evening. 'That was kind of you to get Lucy a lift home, Simon. But do you think she'll come back?'

'I'm sure she will. This is where Jack belongs, and she knows it. If he's out there somewhere then he'll make his way back to White Waltham, even if he has to crawl the whole way.'

'What do you think the chances are that he's survived?' Simon sounded as if he believed Jack was still alive, and Ruth prayed that he was right.

'Very slim, but as long as he didn't come down in the Channel there's always a chance.'

She nodded. But if he came down on land then he might be out there injured and in need of help. The thought that he might be somewhere alone and in pain frightened Ruth. Then something Simon had said penetrated her weary mind. 'What do you mean, this is where Jack belongs?'

'Just that, Ruth. Jack loves this country and I believe he now considers England as his home. If he survives this then he will probably go back to America for a while when the war's over, but he'll be back because this is where he wants to be.'

'He's never said that to me.'

'He hasn't said anything to me either, but I'm sure that's how he feels.' He gave Ruth a tired smile. 'You know Jack never talks about his inner feelings, but he thinks things through very carefully before talking about or acting on any decision. But you already know that, don't you?'

'It's really hard to know what's going on inside his head.' Ruth fought back the tears, determined not to let them spill over again. 'He's got to come back, Simon. There's going to be a great hole in many lives if he doesn't.'

'I know. He arrived in this country at the beginning of the war, and over the years he has gained respect from all the people he's dealt with.'

'And love,' Ruth added.

Simon covered her hand with his. 'Respect and love,' he repeated. 'Have you told your parents yet?'

'Yes, I nipped home last night. They're both dreadfully upset and are praying for his safe return.'

'It's obvious that he ran into trouble and has come down somewhere. He's a strong man, Ruth, and if he survived the crash then he'll get back somehow.' Simon picked up their empty glasses. 'I'll get us another drink.'

While he was away, Ruth thought over what Simon had said about Jack. They had become firm friends, and Jack may well have talked more freely to Simon than he had to her. But was Simon right when he said that Jack would want to stay in England when the war was over? She knew he loved it here, but did he love it enough to settle here permanently? Could he leave his own home, leave his mother and sister, for Lucy was sure to return home as soon as she could now? Brother and sister had always been close and, in her view, it was unlikely they would live so far apart now. She clenched her hands into tight fists. If he didn't come back then these were questions she would never have answered.

Chapter Twenty-Eight

The sound of the front door opening had Ruth surging to her feet and rushing into the hall. 'Lucy! I'm so glad to see you. I was afraid you might not come back.'

'Not a chance. Is there any news?'

Ruth shook her head, her expression grim. 'They're still looking for him. If only we knew where he came down. But worrying and letting our imaginations run riot is getting us nowhere, except adding to our fear. Come on, you look tired, I'll get you something to eat.' If only she could take her own advice, Ruth thought wryly.

'Tea and toast will do. Mom's been feeding me up, and she sends her love to you.' Lucy sat at the kitchen table. 'She wanted to come back with me.'

'I expect she did. How is she?'

'Devastated, but she's adamant that Jack is still alive.' Lucy sipped the tea Ruth had just placed in front of her. 'She insists that she would know if he'd been killed.'

'I don't want to believe it either, but after seven days it's hard to remain hopeful.' Ruth's hand trembled as she spread margarine on the toast. 'Where the hell is he, Lucy? Why haven't they found any trace of a crashed plane? Simon's made two trips to France while you've been away. He won't let it rest until he finds out what happened.'

'Bless Simon, he's such a wonderful man to have on your side in times of trouble, isn't he?'

Ruth nodded. 'He's a very kind man.'

They talked until midnight as Lucy told Ruth about her trip back to America, and how brave her mother was being. Then they went to bed, hoping to get some sleep.

The next morning Lucy insisted that she was going to work. 'I need to keep busy, Ruth.'

'Of course, and so do I.' She dragged up a smile. 'Come on then, we've got planes to fly, and the weather looks good.'

When they arrived at the airfield, Simon was preparing to take off for France, and didn't try to hide his delight at seeing Lucy back from America.

They waved him off, but there was little hope in their eyes. It had been too long now and they feared the worst. Nevertheless, painful as it would be, they had to know what had happened to Jack.

The weather held good and for the next three days they ferried plane after plane. Only when Ruth was in the air did she have a respite from the gnawing worry and grief. She knew Lucy felt the same. Flying needed total concentration and they spent as much time in the air as possible. Only when the light faded did they pack up for the day. But they made sure that they both got back to base each evening as they waited for news of the man they loved.

They were both in the taxi on their way back to White Waltham when Lucy shook Ruth's arm, drawing her attention to another Anson following them. 'Who's in that?'

'Jane,' Ruth called to the pilot, 'there's another Anson following us in. Do you know anything about it?'

'As far as I know we're the only one in this area, but they're using some Ansons as cargo planes at the moment, ferrying equipment over to France. It might be one of those.'

'It might be Simon,' Lucy said hopefully.

As soon as they were on the ground they waited for the other plane to land. If it was Simon and there was no news after ten days, they would have to give up the tiny glimmer of hope they'd tried to keep burning. Lucy's mouth was set in a straight line as she grasped Ruth's hand in a crushing grip. It was Simon. His familiar figure was immediately recognisable as he reached up to help another man out of the plane.

Ruth blinked rapidly, sure her eyes were deceiving her. Suddenly the grip on her hand was released as Lucy began to run, her squeal of joy startling. 'Oh, dear God!' Ruth ran as well. Her eyes hadn't been mistaken. It was Jack.

He saw them coming and held out his arms as they hurtled towards him, nearly knocking him off his feet. 'Whoa there, steady on, I'm a bit shaky.'

After checking that her brother really was all right, Lucy launched herself at Simon. 'Thank you, thank you for finding him!'

Jack was leaning against the plane for support and ran

his fingers gently down Ruth's cheek. 'Hiya, honey.'

She didn't bother to hide her relief as tears brimmed over and clouded her vision. 'Where have you been, Jack? We've been out of our minds with worry.'

'I'll tell you later.'

Quite a crowd had gathered now to welcome him back. Everyone was overjoyed to see he was safe.

Simon stepped in. 'All right, everyone, you'll hear all about Jack's adventures in time, but now he's exhausted and needs to rest.'

'Come home with us.' Lucy placed a hand through her brother's arm. 'We'll look after you. Ruth, take his other arm.'

'Gee, a beauty on each arm. How lucky can a man get?' he joked.

Ruth was very aware of the strain in his voice. He was thinner and looked several years older. Whatever he'd been doing over the last ten days, it had clearly been an ordeal.

'I've got to report in,' he said as they reached the Mess.

Jane greeted him with a hint of moisture in her eyes. 'We're relieved to have you back in one piece, Jack. The place hasn't been the same without you. I want you to go to hospital for rest and a thorough check-up.'

'There's no need for that.' The lazy smile was still there. 'I'm fine; all I need is rest and food. Lucy and Ruth have offered to take good care of me.'

Jane looked reluctant, but knowing Jack, she relented. 'All right, but you're to find a doctor at once if you feel bad at any time.'

'We will, Jane,' Lucy assured her.

'Very well. When you feel up to it, Jack, we'd like a full report of what happened.'

'Will do.'

'Take your brother home with you, Lucy, and I don't want to see him climbing in a plane for at least a week.'

When he was about to protest, Captain Anders, who had just arrived, said, 'It's no use you arguing, Jack, that's an order. We're damned glad to see you, but you're done in. Rest, and when you're feeling stronger, come and see me.'

'On your feet,' Simon urged. 'You've caused the girls a lot of worry, now it's time to let them make a fuss of you.'

Back at the house, Ruth went straight up to the bathroom, hoping the temperamental water heater was going to behave itself. Ignoring the regulation of five inches of water for a bath, she filled it halfway, and then went back downstairs. 'There's a hot bath ready for you, Jack. Have a nice soak in that while we get you something to eat. Then you're going straight to bed.'

'I don't want anything to eat at the moment. I was practically starving and the American troops gave me far too much food.' He dragged himself to his feet and slapped Simon on the back. 'Thanks, pal.'

'I was damned relieved to see you get out of that American Jeep. Now, don't let your bath get cold. I'll bring your other uniform and clothes here in the morning. Sleep well.'

'I will.' He started for the stairs, and then stopped, looking slightly puzzled. 'What am I doing here instead of my own digs?'

This alarmed Ruth. Jack was obviously suffering more than he was letting on. Perhaps he should have gone to the hospital after all.

Simon urged him towards the stairs. 'Because this was nearer, and you refused to go to the hospital. Lucy and Ruth are going to see that you eat and rest.'

'My God,' he muttered, 'I spent my time dodging Germans and shells, and now I'm being treated like a kid.'

'Stop being so ungrateful,' Lucy said, a smile of amusement on her face. 'Your bath's getting cold.'

When he'd disappeared up the stairs, Ruth frowned at Simon. 'What did he mean by dodging Germans?'

'He came down behind enemy lines. That's all he would tell me, but by the look of him, he's had a rough time getting through to the allies.'

'That's for sure,' Lucy agreed. 'Simon, I've got to let Mom know he's safe. There's a small store near our house and they've got a telephone. Is there any chance we could phone from ops? The storekeeper, Bud, would go and get Mom. He often let us use it when we had shows to arrange. I've got the number.'

'I'm sure it will be all right. Why don't we go there now? We could ask the storekeeper to bring your mother to the phone at a certain time so Jack can speak to her himself.'

'That's a great idea.' Lucy's eyes filled with gratitude as she looked at Simon. 'You're really something, do you know that?'

'I'm not going to ask what you mean by that,' he laughed.

When Simon stood up, Ruth caught his arm. 'Would you just check on Jack to see he hasn't fallen asleep in the bath?'

He ran up the stairs, coming back almost at once. 'He's in bed and fast asleep. I doubt he will move until morning.' He held his hand out to Lucy. 'We won't be long, Ruth.'

The house was very quiet after they left, and Ruth made her way upstairs. She'd just check on Jack again and then go to bed herself; she was exhausted. He was in her bedroom, but she didn't mind; she could easily sleep in the spare room. He was sprawled out with only a sheet covering him. She crept forward and began to carefully cover him with a blanket as well. A hand reached out and pulled her down beside him, wrapping his arms around her and making it impossible to move.

'Stay,' he murmured.

She was exactly where she wanted to be, so she laid her head on his chest and listened to his steady breathing. Relaxed at last after days of worrying, she was instantly asleep.

'Hello, Bud, can you hear me? This is Lucy Nelson and I'm calling from England.' She paused. 'Oh, good, I'm coming through OK. Could you ask Mom to come to the phone at nine o'clock tomorrow morning? Ask her to wait for my call. It might take us a while to make the connection, but keep her there. It's very important.'

Lucy nodded as she listened to Bud on the other end. 'Thanks a lot.'

She replaced the receiver and turned to Simon. 'There was a lot of noise on the line, but he heard me. All we've got to do now is get Jack to the phone early tomorrow afternoon.'

'He'll be awake by then. I'll take you back home now.' He studied her tired face. 'You need sleep as well.'

When they arrived back there was no sign of Ruth

downstairs. 'She's probably gone to bed,' Lucy said. 'I'll just creep up and see if Jack's OK.'

Simon went with her. He was still concerned for Jack, and thought he should have gone for a check-up as soon as they arrived back. When the American Jeep had arrived at Le Bourget airfield, Simon had hardly recognised his friend. He had been dressed in US Army combat gear, had lost weight and looked years older. The sergeant with him had explained to Simon that Jack had walked up to their tanks, his hands in the air, and shouted in an American accent that he was a downed pilot. After eating and changing out of his tattered uniform, he had asked to be taken to an airfield.

All Jack had wanted to do then was get back to England, and no amount of prompting had made him talk about his experiences. Hopefully, they would learn more when he submitted his official report.

Lucy stopped in the doorway of one of the bedrooms. 'Look at that,' she whispered, a huge smile on her face.

Simon's reaction was the same. Jack and Ruth were locked in each other's arms and sound asleep.

They tiptoed downstairs again, and Lucy giggled. 'Ruth's going to be sorry she slept in her clothes all night. I'd better get her other uniform ready for the morning. Want some cocoa, Simon?'

'No thanks. I'll be back tomorrow with Jack's clothes.' The corners of his mouth twitched when he thought about the scene upstairs. 'Your tough guy of a brother might not say much, but he obviously needs the comfort of having Ruth close after his ordeal.'

'And it has been an ordeal. That's clear for anyone to

see, but if I know Jack, he'll soon recover.' Lucy yawned and handed him a spare key. 'You'll need this if we aren't here. I don't think sleeping will be any problem for me either tonight. Thanks for everything you've done for us, Simon.'

'My pleasure.' He kissed her cheek gently. 'See you in the morning.'

The sun was streaming through the window and resting on his face. Jack stretched, revelling in the comfort of a proper bed. Then his eyes shot open and he sat upright, groaning at the pain caused by the sudden movement. Every muscle in his body was aching, but that was hardly surprising. He'd spent days hiding in ditches, barns or anywhere there was cover. It had been his bad fortune to come down behind the German lines and, as he'd only been able to move at night, the journey to the allies had been long and dangerous.

He rested back against the pillows. He remembered pulling Ruth down beside him before sinking into oblivion. How long had she stayed with him? He tipped his head to one side and listened to footsteps on the stairs.

'Ah, good, you're awake at last.' Simon came in with an armful of clothes.

'Hi, Simon, where are the girls?'

'Halfway through their working day.'

Jack frowned. 'What time is it?'

'Midday, and I need you to get up. We've made arrangements for you to speak to your mother. Your storekeeper friend is going to make sure she's by the phone when we call.'

'That's great.' Jack was already out of bed. 'Thanks a lot, Simon, she must be worried sick.'

'Worried?' Simon shook his head. 'Jack, everyone's been frantic about you, not only in America, but here as well. You've made a lot of friends since you came here, and you'd have left a large hole in many lives if you'd died in France.'

Jack was touched by Simon's words. Joining the ATA was the best thing he'd ever done. Being here had helped him sort out what was important in life, and what wasn't worth bothering about. He'd also learnt the value of each life, and had been damned determined not to lose his. He was no longer gazing over the next hill, wondering if it was better on the other side. He'd found all he wanted here.

'What are you going to do when the war's over?' Jack asked Simon as he shaved.

'Start my flying school again. There will be a big demand for pilots, especially with the airlines making plans for the future of air travel. My planes are still in Cornwall where someone's been looking after them for me.'

'They'll need a good overhaul before they're fit to fly again.'

Simon gave Jack a studied look. 'I know. Want a job?'

Razor poised in the air, Jack turned to look at him. 'You serious?'

'Completely. Think about it, Jack, we could go into partnership. We'd make a good team.'

'I sure will give it serious thought.' And he would. That was something he would really like to do, but he had a lot to sort out before he could make a decision. This wasn't just about him; there were other people to consider.

'Good, now, do you want something to eat before we go to the airfield?'

'Not just at the moment, but how about a meal after I've spoken to Ma?'

'We'll see what we can get.'

It took some time to make the connection and Jack had begun to worry they wouldn't be able to get through. He knew his ma would be worrying, and he wanted to let her know he was safe. A phone call would be the quickest way. Finally, Simon gave him a thumbs-up sign. 'Hello, Mrs Nelson, this is Simon from England. I've got someone here who wants to talk to you.'

Jack took the phone. 'Hi, Ma.' He listened for a few seconds. 'Yes, it's me and I'm fine. Now don't take on so, Ma. I haven't got a scratch on me. I'll tell you all about it in a letter . . . you still there, Ma?'

He handed the phone back to Simon. 'We got cut off, but she knows I'm OK. Thanks a lot. Now I'm hungry.'

Chapter Twenty-Nine

It was eight o'clock before Ruth arrived home, and the first thing she saw was Jack's little car outside the house. She found him in the kitchen writing industriously.

He looked up and smiled. 'Hi, honey, I'm just doing a letter to Ma. Is Lucy with you?'

'She'll be about another hour, we think.'

'Ah, in that case . . .' He stood up and wrapped her in his arms, kissing her like a hungry man. Breaking off the embrace, he sighed. 'Hell, but it's great to be home.'

A warm glow ran through Ruth. That was the first time she had ever heard him refer to England as home. 'It's wonderful to have you back. You scared us, Jack.'

He gave a dry laugh. 'I scared myself, but I couldn't get back any sooner. If I'd been caught I could have ended up as a prisoner or dead, and I didn't fancy either. I doubted if a retreating army would bother with prisoners. I was surrounded by them and it was damned difficult to move without being seen.'

Just then the front door burst open and Lucy erupted into the room with Simon right behind her. 'Jack, you spoke to Mom. What did she say?'

'Not much, we got cut off, but there was just enough time to let her know I was all in one piece and back here safely.'

'I bet she cried.'

He chuckled. 'Not enough to stop her asking what the hell I thought I was doing, frightening everyone like this.'

Brother and sister grinned at each other. 'That's Mom,' Lucy said, 'but I bet she had a good cry when she got back home.'

It was interesting to see the rapport between them, and Ruth gave Simon an amused glance. 'Want a cup of cocoa?' she asked him.

'No, thanks, I've come to remind Jack about the report, and to take you all out for a drink. That's if Jack feels up to it?'

'Sure, I'm great now.' He shuffled through the papers on the table and handed Simon a single sheet. 'I've done the report.'

Simon read it and then shook his head in disbelief. 'This is it?'

'Yep.'

'Jack, you were missing for ten days, and all you've said is that you got caught in a sudden storm, ran out of fuel and had to bail out. You were behind enemy lines and had to find the allies.'

'Well?'

'Couldn't you give a few more details?'

'Why?'

By now Ruth and Lucy were almost bursting with suppressed laughter at the puzzled expression on Jack's face. He obviously considered that his report was adequate.

'Simon,' Lucy took the paper from out of his hands, folded it neatly and tucked it in his top pocket, 'you're wasting your breath. I know my brother and that's all you're going to get. Once his sentences get down to one word you can forget it. He isn't going to budge.'

'All right, but do you think that if we get him drunk he'll tell us what really happened in France?'

'Not a chance.' She slipped her hand through Simon's arm. 'You said something about a drink?'

'Do you think we can get something to eat, as well?' Jack closed the front door behind them. 'I'm ravenous.'

'We'll get the girls to smile nicely at the landlord.'

'Great idea, Simon. Who can resist a woman in uniform? Especially when they're wearing golden wings.'

'Oh, this brother of yours is smooth, isn't he?' Ruth said, giving Jack a teasing glance. There had been a chance that she would never see him again, but here he was, walking beside her, and still the same man she loved. She couldn't stop smiling with happiness.

'Yep, back home he had the girls dropping at his feet in an effort to gain his attention.'

Jack looked up at the sky in mock despair. 'Let's get that drink before my reputation's in shreds. There's something you don't know about my sister, Simon: she exaggerates like hell.'

They were in luck at the pub. The landlord's wife had just finished baking a batch of vegetable pies for the next day, and quite happily agreed to give them a meal. They were regulars at the pub and always received the best service. There was huge admiration throughout the country for what the pilots had done, and were still doing. And although the ATA weren't

RAF, they still flew planes and kept the RAF supplied with aircraft, and that counted for a lot with many people.

'Gosh, this is great,' Jack said as he demolished the pie, mashed potatoes and carrots. 'I've got a few missed meals to make up for.'

It was noticeable that he was thinner so Ruth slipped half of her pie on to his plate, which quickly disappeared. He hadn't been very hungry when he'd first arrived back, but now he had rested he seemed to need the food.

The landlady bustled over to their table. 'Come back hungry, has he?' she asked Ruth, well aware that Jack had been reported missing for some days.

'I'm afraid so.'

'You look half starved. What have you been up to, young man?'

Jack gave her one of his engaging smiles. 'Got lost in France – without food,' he added, pointedly looking at his empty plate.

She picked up the plate, muttering about the young people doing dangerous things, and walked back to the kitchen. She soon returned with another portion of pie and mash. Placing it in front of him, she tapped his hand. 'You eat that now, there's a lot of you to fill up.'

'Why thank you, ma'am.'

The landlady chuckled. 'He's a right charmer, isn't he? Don't you go getting lost again.'

'I'll sure be careful not to.'

As she walked away, Lucy punched her brother on the arm. 'You're shameless, Jack Nelson. Fancy playing on her sympathy to get another meal!'

His only reply was a wide grin before making short work of his extra portion.

'I don't know how you can eat that much.' Simon handed Jack a cigarette when the second plate was empty. 'You had half of Ruth's as well.'

Drawing on the cigarette, Jack blew the smoke towards the ceiling, and then pulled Ruth close to him. 'She knows how to look after me.'

This outward show of affection came as a surprise to Ruth. He had always been careful to make it appear that their relationship was platonic, but it was as if he didn't care what people thought any more. This change made her think that he'd had a very bad time in France. Perhaps he had doubted that he would survive. Whatever his reasons, she was happy about it, and so was Lucy, by the look on her face.

They stayed until closing time and walked back to the house.

'Are you staying tonight?' Ruth asked, worried that he was doing too much too soon.

'Not tonight, honey.' He bent and brushed his lips over hers. 'I'd never be able to stay out of your bed, and with Lucy there it could be awkward.'

'You've got a few days' leave, so why don't you go and stay with my parents? They'd love to have you, and you'll be able to rest there. It might be better if you get away from planes for a few days. If you don't, I know you'll be back at work far too soon.' She looked up at him, not wanting to let him out of her sight, but she was just being silly: he was alive and back with them, and that was all that mattered.

'That would be great. If you're sure they wouldn't mind?'

'Positive. You're always welcome there, Jack, and you don't need an invitation.'

'I'll drive over and see them in the morning.'

Ruth's parents had always made Jack so welcome that he felt like part of the family. He'd readily accepted Ruth's suggestion. Not only did he need space to recover, but he also needed time to think. And this was just the place to do it.

'Jack!' Alice greeted him with obvious relief. 'Ruth told us you were safe, and we're so pleased to see you.'

George shook his hand. 'Welcome back, son.'

'Thank you, sir, it's good to be back. Would you mind if I stayed for a couple of days? Please say no if it's not convenient.'

'Of course you can stay.' Alice studied him carefully. 'My dear, you've lost weight. You can rest here for as long as you like.'

He kissed her cheek. 'I can see where Ruth gets her kindness from. They won't let me fly again until I've had a medical, and that's scheduled for the end of the week.'

'Have you brought a bag with you?'

'It's in my car. I'll go and fetch it.'

'No, you sit yourself down.' George urged him into a chair. 'I'll go and get it.'

'Take it straight up to Jack's usual room, George. I always keep it ready.'

George was soon back. 'What on earth have you got in here, Jack? It weighs a ton.'

'Something from Ma to help out with the food. She sends us regular parcels, though we don't always receive them. Some get lost on the way over.' Jack opened the bag and gave Alice several tins of various meats.

'Oh, that's very generous of her,' she said as she examined the tins. 'Anything we don't use you must take back with you.'

Jack shook his head. 'We don't need them. I'm sure you can make good use of them.'

Alice accepted with a smile. 'We know you need rest so we won't get in your way, but join us for meals.'

They were very perceptive. He needed some time to himself to relax. 'It's a nice day so I'll just go and enjoy the peace of your beautiful garden, if I may?'

'Of course, my boy,' George said. 'We'll call you when lunch is ready.'

Jack wandered down the garden to an old wooden seat he always used when he came here, sat down and gazed around him. The sun was pleasantly warm on his face. Alice really loved her flowers but, like everyone else, a section at the end had been dug over to grow vegetables. It seemed as if this whole country had been turned into a market garden in an effort to feed itself.

He closed his eyes, allowing his thoughts to drift back to his time in France. That storm had come out of nowhere. If he'd been in this country he would have turned back, but he didn't have enough fuel for a return trip to England, and coming down in the Channel was not an option. He'd tried everything to get out of it – up, down, sideways – but before he'd been able to find the edge of the storm he had run out of fuel. The Spit was being buffeted about and he'd had a hell of a job getting out of the cockpit, but somehow he'd managed it and tumbled down. He'd just missed some trees and landed in a field of cabbages. After rolling up his parachute and stowing it out of sight in some bushes, he'd started walking. The rain was still pouring down, and after about fifteen minutes, soaked to the skin, the sound of voices reached him. There were tanks ahead and he'd been about to call out when he realised they were Germans.

Diving for cover he'd waited for them to move off, which they hadn't done until morning. During the night the rain had stopped and his clothes dried on him. He'd been chilled to the bone and very hungry. He'd moved cautiously after that and it wasn't long before he came across more German troops. The rest of the day was spent in a ditch, giving him plenty of time to curse his bad luck for coming down in the middle of the enemy.

He'd soon discovered that the only time he could move with any safety was at night. The journey had been slow, but he'd been determined not to get caught. Neither had he been prepared to risk revealing himself to any civilians, so he'd lived on raw vegetables from the fields and water from any stream he could find. He'd known the allies were somewhere near Paris, so he'd headed in what he hoped was the right direction. He always carried a compass with him in his pocket, but it must have fallen out as he'd struggled to free himself from the cockpit, and he'd cursed the loss. Fortunately he still had the silk map and the lucky dollar he always carried with him. He wasn't normally a superstitious man, but this dollar had been given to him by a veteran of the First World War, and was a treasured possession. Day followed day, and he'd lost all sense of time, but he knew the allies must be close when the area was bombarded with shells . . .

Jack ran a hand over his eyes, opened them and gazed at the tranquil garden, absorbing the peace of this lovely spot.

As the shells had screamed around him, he'd begun to feel that his efforts to reach safety might have been in vain. He could still feel the great sadness that had engulfed him. Was he ever going to see Ma and Lucy again, or any of the friends he'd made in the ATA? And what about Ruth? The thought of leaving her caused him so much distress that he'd groaned out loud as he'd covered his head with his hands. The ground had rocked beneath him as one shell had fallen far too close.

Then, mercifully there had been silence, broken some minutes later by the sound of tanks and familiar American accents shouting orders. He'd crawled out of his hiding place – and the rest was a blur. He could remember asking them to take him to the nearest airfield. The next thing he knew Simon was there. He'd wept in relief and wasn't ashamed to admit it.

'Jack.' George came up to him. 'Lunch is ready. You can have it out here if you like.'

'Thanks, George, but I'll eat with you and Alice. I'm looking forward to hearing what you've been up to since I was last here.' He stood up, feeling refreshed already. He'd needed this time alone to clear his mind and think over what had happened to him. He could see now just how damned lucky he had been. He had survived and now he could put it behind him. And another thing he couldn't deny – life was now much sweeter for the experience.

Chapter Thirty

Ruth watched Jack strolling across the field carrying his parachute and couldn't help smiling. He had only taken three days off after his adventures in France and, within a week, was once again crossing the Channel. The only difference she had noticed in him over the last few days was that he was more relaxed, more openly affectionate, and seemed to enjoy everything he did. Their occasional nights together had taken on a new intensity. She was sure he loved her, but he'd still never uttered the words she longed to hear.

'Hi, honey.' He ruffled her hair as he walked past to report in. Then he stopped and turned. 'I saw Gussie today, and she said to tell you that number one is on the way.'

It took a moment for that to sink in, then she gasped. 'She's expecting?'

'Yep, and she said she's leaving the ATA at Christmas.'

'That's only a week away. I must ask Mum to make a christening gown for the baby.'

'What's this about babies?' Lucy asked as she came into the Mess.

'Gussie's pregnant.'

'Wow, that's terrific, Ruth! I'll write to her tonight and see what she needs.'

'Everything, I expect. She's leaving the ATA almost immediately, Lucy, so we must try and get over to see her soon.'

'First bit of free time we get.' Lucy followed her brother to report in then paused at the door. 'I thought they were going to wait until the war was over before starting a family?'

'So did I, but they must have decided not to wait any longer. This damned war can't go on for many more months.'

'That's what we all keep saying, but there's still a way to go yet,' Lucy said, and then disappeared.

Ruth knew Lucy was right. The faint hope they'd nurtured that the war would be over by Christmas had faded.

Not only had Hitler unleashed his V1 flying bombs on them, but the V2 rockets had followed. There was no warning with the rockets, and you didn't know they were coming until they exploded.

'Do you know where Simon is?' Lucy asked Jack as she came back to the Mess with him.

'Still in France. Why?'

She shrugged. 'I wanted to wish him a happy Christmas before we go to Ruth's folks for the holiday.'

'Well, if the weather doesn't improve he'll be spending it

in Paris.' His eyes glinted with amusement. 'I expect there'll be plenty of grateful girls to keep him company.'

'Yeah, I suppose.' She looked thoughtful. 'What are his folks like, Ruth? He never says much about them.'

'They're nice people, but Simon's relationship with his father has been rather strained in the past. He's a busy doctor and wanted his son to follow in his footsteps and join him in the practice, but Simon had other ideas. His family weren't at all happy when he said he was going to fly instead of going to medical school.'

'He ought to be proud of his son,' Lucy declared. 'He's a terrific pilot.'

'Yes, he is. From the age of seventeen Simon's made his own way in life, but he thinks the world of his parents and visits them regularly. He'll get home at Christmas if at all possible.'

'He's a strong character in a quiet way, isn't he?'

Ruth nodded. 'He knows what he wants, and sets about getting it with the minimum of fuss. In that way he's like his father.'

'Have his folks ever forgiven him?' Lucy seemed quite concerned about this.

'I'd say they've come to terms with it.'

'Hmm . . .' was Lucy's only comment.

Two days later, Ruth and Lucy managed to catch up with Gussie when she flew into Bognor with her last delivery for the ATA. The baby wasn't due until early May, but Harry wanted Gussie to stop flying until after the birth, and she had readily agreed. The most important thing in Gussie's life now was that she had a healthy baby. The first of many, she hoped.

'You keep in touch now,' Gussie told them. 'This baby is going to have heaps of godparents.'

'You bet.' Lucy couldn't stop smiling. 'We've got to look after a future pilot.'

Gussie ran her hand over her thickening middle. 'Let's hope the war is over before this little one puts in an appearance.'

'It looks as if it could be.' Ruth gazed into space. 'It's going to be strange, isn't it? This will be our fifth Christmas at war, and in all probability, the fighting will be over well before the next one.'

'Yes, and what an opportunity the war has given us, Ruthie. Who would have believed at the beginning that women would be given the chance to fly so many different planes?'

'We've done a good job.' Ruth smiled affectionately at Lucy. 'And so have the many nationalities who have flown for the ATA. And that includes the Americans who have become our friends. It's been a privilege, and we haven't finished yet.'

'No, but I have. Here comes my taxi.'

'You take care of our baby!' Lucy hugged Gussie. 'I can't wait to be a godmother.'

'Same here.' Ruth also hugged Gussie. 'Love to Harry and tell him we'll be around as often as we can to make sure you're not tossing a Spit around in the air.'

Gussie kept a perfectly straight face. 'You know that's against the rules, Ruthie.'

'Oh, come on, Gussie, are you trying to kid me you didn't? Pull the other one.'

Her friend tipped back her head and roared with laughter. 'And you didn't, I suppose?'

'You don't expect me to admit to a thing like that, do you? I'm still in the ATA. What about you, Lucy, have you ever been tempted?'

'Who, me?' Her mouth twitched at the corners, making them all chuckle.

They waved Gussie on her way, and then made for their next job.

Ruth's mother was in her element when they arrived late on Christmas Eve. She and George adored Jack and Lucy, treating them not like guests, but as part of the family.

'Come and look at this!' Alice towed them into the kitchen where the dresser was loaded with tins and boxes of delicious luxuries. 'All this arrived over the last few days. I thought the parcels were never going to stop coming!'

'Good old Mom,' Lucy nodded approval. 'She's been busy.'

'But my dears, this must have been very expensive.' A frown of worry creased Alice's brow. 'She really shouldn't have. It is so generous.'

Jack placed an arm around her shoulders. 'Don't worry, we've always seen that Ma isn't short of a dollar or two. You're feeding her children, and have made us welcome in your home ever since we arrived in England. We're grateful to you for that, and so is Ma. It's her way of thanking you.'

Ruth's father, who had just come downstairs after

insisting that he put their bags in their rooms, said, 'We don't need thanks; in fact, it should be the other way round. You've been the one bright spark in this terrible war. We were still hurting after losing our son, and then Ruth joined the ATA, leaving our house very empty. Then she brought you home, Jack. And when Lucy joined us as well we felt as if we had gained two more fine children.'

Lucy was quite overcome, and in her usual outgoing way, gave Ruth's parents a big hug. 'You're great folks.'

George was clearly pleased with the show of affection. He picked up one of the boxes. 'Let's have a nice pot of tea and some of these. Are they biscuits, Lucy?'

'Yeah, only we call them cookies.'

'Then it's tea and cookies,' he teased.

Ruth helped her mother while the others went into the sitting room.

'We're going to miss them when they go home.' Alice sighed. 'What about Jack? He's more than a little fond of you, and I know you're in love with him, Ruth. I see it in your eyes when you look at him.'

There was little point in denying it. 'I am, but I don't know what's going to happen when the war's finally over. Jack's been here since the beginning and must be longing to return home. He's not a man you could easily tie down and I wouldn't try. I'm not putting any pressure on him, and if he wants to take things further later, then that will have to be his decision. But it will be a tough one, Mum, with other people to consider. Jack and Lucy wouldn't want to leave their mother, and I wouldn't want to leave you and Dad.'

'Yes, I agree it isn't easy, and Lucy hasn't anything to stay here for after losing Dave.' Alice studied her daughter with respect. 'You've grown into a very wise young woman, darling. We'd let you go to America if that's what you really wanted to do, but I won't pretend it wouldn't break our hearts.'

'I couldn't leave you.' Ruth changed the subject. If her brother had still been alive then she might have considered going if Jack had asked her to, but he hadn't. It was a problem they were going to have to talk over soon, but they still had a little time yet. And the last thing you did to a man like Jack Nelson was try to tell him what to do.

'Everyone's looking to the future now. Simon's going to open his flying school again and has asked me to join him. I'm going to get my instructor's licence as soon as possible.'

'That will be lovely for you.' Alice arranged the cookies on a plate, clearly pleased her daughter was making arrangements to go into business with Simon. 'I met Simon's parents the other day and they were so proud of what he's been doing.'

Ruth filled the pot. 'He's one of the best pilots in the ATA, if not *the* best.'

'His father accepts that now. This war has changed a lot of our priorities, hasn't it? I've asked them over for tea on Boxing Day.'

'Oh, good. I haven't seen them for some time. And you're right, Mum, things we once considered important, no longer are.'

'And in many cases that's for the better.' Alice picked up the tray. 'We'd better take the tea through to the other room. I expect they're wondering what we're up to.'

* * *

Not only did Mr and Mrs Trent arrive on Boxing Day, but Simon was with them as well.

'Glad you made it back in time,' Jack said as soon as he saw his friend. 'How was Paris?'

'I wouldn't know; I never made it that far.' Simon introduced his parents to Jack and Lucy.

Ruth was amused to see that Lucy was regarding Mr Trent with unusual reserve. Simon took after his father in looks and manner, and there seemed to be very little of his mother in him. She was more talkative and dominated the conversation for some time.

During a short break when his wife went out to help Alice lay the table for tea, Mr Trent turned to Ruth. 'Simon tells me you fly anything from fighters to bombers, Ruth?'

'We fly anything that needs moving.'

Mr Trent shook his head. 'I don't know how you do it. And what about you, Lucy, what do you fly?'

'Fighters, trainers and twin-engines. Simon's been my teacher,' she said proudly. 'He's the best darned pilot in the whole world, along with my brother, of course.'

Simon's mouth twitched as he glanced at Jack, but they said nothing.

But they weren't the only ones amused by Lucy's declaration. Mr Trent had also discerned the way her mind was working. 'You don't have to defend my son to me, my dear. I am well aware of Simon's talents.'

'Oh.' Lucy hadn't been expecting that.

Simon's father winked at her, looking so like an older version of his son. 'I still think he would have made an excellent doctor, but I'm sure he's an even better pilot.'

'He is!'

Jack sighed pointedly, making Lucy turn to him with a frown on her face. 'What?'

'You don't need me to tell you.'

She thought for a moment and then looked slightly uncomfortable when she realised what she had been doing. 'I'm sorry, sir,' she said to Simon's father. 'I didn't mean to be rude. I have the habit of saying what's on my mind.'

'There's no need to apologise. I'm pleased my son stands so high in your estimation.'

Lucy glanced at her brother, puzzled, and then a sudden smile crossed her face. 'Oh, I get it; you mean you're pleased I think so much of him. Well, it isn't just me, we all do.'

'That is even more gratifying.'

'Jack, just listen to that accent.' Now Lucy was enjoying herself. 'You're posh, Simon, but you don't talk like that.'

'Neither does my father usually. He's teasing you, Lucy.'

'Are you?' She turned back to Mr Trent, now completely relaxed. 'Do you know, sir, I like you?'

Simon's father was having difficulty keeping a straight face. 'And I like you. You are a charming girl.'

'Gee, thanks.'

Ruth stood up. 'Come and help me get the tea ready, Lucy, and leave the men to have a chat.'

As they made their way to the kitchen, Ruth heard the amused chuckles coming from the other room.

'You know, Ruth, I thought I wouldn't like Simon's pa, but he's OK, and they're so alike. And what about his mother!' Lucy whispered. 'She's OK too, but she sure can talk!'

* * *

When the girls had left the room, Mr Trent turned his attention to Jack. 'Your sister is a remarkable young girl. She speaks her mind, and I like that. You have said very little, though, and I suspect that you are more reserved.'

Simon laughed. 'Jack's just the opposite to his sister. No one has been able to find out what really happened to him in France.'

Jack sat back, a slight smile on his face. 'You had it all in my report.'

'Which consisted of three lines. One day I want the whole story from you.'

'Perhaps I'll tell you when I'm sixty.'

Simon laughed out loud. 'I'll keep you to that, my friend.'

'Tea's ready.' Alice looked in to the room. 'You sound as if you're having a good time.'

'We are, my dear,' George said, as he stood up. 'But now we're ready for those luxuries Mrs Nelson has so generously sent us.'

Mr Trent walked beside his son into the dining room, and said quietly, 'I like your friends, Simon.'

'So do I, Father.'

Chapter Thirty-One

1945 heralded bitterly cold weather, but as the weeks passed it was obvious that the war in Europe was coming to an end. By the 19th of January the German army was in full retreat along the Eastern Front, and by the end of that month the Soviet troops were in Germany and only about a hundred miles from Berlin. All the time the British and Americans were carrying out raids on Germany.

Ruth, and all the other ATA pilots, continued with their work of delivering planes where they were needed.

It was late March when Captain Anders joined them in the Mess at the end of the day. 'I've just heard that the US forces have crossed the Rhine into Germany.'

A cheer went up and everyone began talking at once. Andy motioned to someone at the door and the room erupted into laughter as Jack rolled in a barrel of beer. He hoisted it on to a table and leant on it. 'The drinks are on the American contingent of the ATA.'

Ruth and Lucy were crying with laughter at the stampede to find glasses and get them filled.

'Where did he get that?' Ruth asked Simon, wiping her eyes.

'He sweet-talked the landlady at the pub. He can certainly turn on the charm when he needs to.'

Ruth rolled her eyes. 'Don't I know it!'

'This bloody war's nearly over, Ruth. But it's given us a flying opportunity we would never have had otherwise.'

'I agree. When I learnt to fly I never imagined that I would be flying fighters and bombers, but there's been so much death, destruction and suffering. It will be a relief to see the end of it.'

'Hey, you two!' Lucy was holding out glasses of beer to them. 'Stop looking so serious and have a drink with us.'

It turned into quite a party and Ruth and Lucy had to tear themselves away at eleven to get some sleep. They were flying in the morning, weather permitting. The war might be coming to an end, but there was still work to do, and they were just as devoted to the ferrying as they had been at the start. They wouldn't give up until they were told that the ATA was no longer needed.

A couple of weeks later the British and Canadian forces crossed the Rhine, and the excitement mounted. It wouldn't be long now.

Ruth had just delivered a Lancaster to one of the supply units and went to check in.

'Have you heard the news?' the ops officer asked her, as he stamped her chit dated 12th April. 'President Roosevelt has died. He was only sixty-three.'

'Oh, no!' Ruth was dismayed. 'We're so close to the end

of the war and he won't see it! What a dreadful thing to have happened.'

The officer nodded. 'It's a damned shame.'

'ATA taxi's here!' someone shouted.

Ruth hurried out to find Simon was the pilot. 'Have you heard the sad news?'

'Yes, at my last stop. Jack and Lucy are going to be upset. Harry Truman is being sworn in. The war in Europe is almost over, but it will be his task to bring the war with Japan to an end.'

Ruth climbed into the Anson and sat next to Simon. 'We're all excited about the war with Germany coming to an end, but we mustn't forget that there is still a fierce battle raging with Japan. And we have troops in Burma, and there are many who were taken prisoner by the Japanese.'

When they arrived back at White Waltham everyone was sorry about the death of the American President.

'He's worked so hard,' Lucy said, 'and he won't see the end. It's so sad.'

'He sure wouldn't like to see us sitting around here with long faces.' Jack stood up. 'He was the right man for the job, and we should celebrate his achievements.'

Every ATA pilot there agreed, whatever their nationality, and they all went to the pub to drink to his memory.

Jack was grabbing a quick snack at Luton as he waited for Sally to deal with her paperwork, when a young RAF recruit ran in.

'The bugger's topped himself!' he yelled, making sure everyone in the Mess could hear.

When no one responded he waved his arms around. 'Hitler's dead! He committed suicide!'

'You sure, son?' Jack asked.

'Course I am. Station officer's just told us.'

Jack closed his eyes for a moment. Just over two weeks since Roosevelt had died, Hitler had killed himself. Germany must surrender now.

'That's good news, Jack, isn't it?'

He opened his eyes and saw Sally smiling at him. 'Yeah, terrific. That leaves Japan to deal with, and that won't be easy.'

'I agree, but you and Lucy will be able to go home soon. What will you do, go back to barnstorming?'

'I don't think we could return to that kind of life after this. We'll stay with the ATA until it's disbanded.' He stood up. 'You ready to go now?'

On the way back to No. 1 ferry pool, Jack's mind mulled over Sally's words. He had been putting off making a decision about the future, but one thing was for sure: there was no way he wanted to go back to his old life. It would be wonderful to see Ma again, but he doubted if he could stay at home for very long. He gazed out at the countryside below him and felt the usual tug at his heart. He'd fallen in love with this country as soon as he'd arrived, and he still felt the same. And it wasn't only the country that would keep him here; there was also Simon's offer. He'd sure love to be a part of his flying school. They got on well together, and he'd really enjoy working with him. There was so much to keep him in this country, but could he leave Ma and Lucy? But just as importantly, could he leave Ruth? Simon had already told him that she was going for her instructor's rating as soon as possible so she could work with him. She had made her decision, and he couldn't blame her because he had never given any indication that he considered their relationship a permanent one. He was going to have to sort that out soon. He was being damned unfair to her, and she didn't deserve to be treated like this. He knew what he wanted to do with his life now, but how could he achieve that without hurting some of the people he loved?

White Waltham came into view and he put aside his dilemma to concentrate on landing.

He found Simon in the Mess and sat next to him. 'Where are the girls?'

'Lucy's back and has gone home. Ruth's making a final delivery to Bognor.' Simon checked the clock. 'I'm going to collect her in half an hour.'

'Right. Is that tea fresh?'

'Yes, help yourself.'

Jack poured the tea and drank it straight down. He loved it boiling hot. 'Is that offer of a partnership still open?'

Simon nodded, giving Jack his full attention. 'It will always be on the table. You can pick it up at any time.'

'I can't say yes or no at the moment. There are other people to consider. If I stay I'm going to upset Ma and Lucy. If I go back to America, I'm going to hurt Ruth, her folks and the friends I've made here.'

'You've got to think about yourself as well, Jack. What do you really want to do?'

He didn't get a chance to answer Simon's question because Jane hurried into the room. And the words he heard turned him cold with fear.

'Simon, get over to Bognor right away. Ruth's crashed. That's all I know at the moment.'

Both men were on their feet and rushing for the Anson.

'I'm coming with you, Simon.'

It was only a short hop and they were soon there.

'Oh, dear God!' Jack swore when he saw the fighter Ruth had been flying. 'She's flipped right over.'

The station commander met them. 'She's all right. Damned lucky to have got away with a few cuts and bruises. They've taken her to the local hospital. My driver will take you there now. Oh, and by the way, she's got a cool head on her.' He grinned. 'Even apologised for breaking the plane as they were pulling her out of the wreckage.'

'That's my girl,' Jack murmured as they strode to the waiting car. 'We can phone Jane from the hospital after we've seen her.'

They were shown into a room and found Ruth sitting on an examination table studying a rip in her slacks. She glanced up when they came in. 'Just look at this, I'll have to ask my mother if she can mend it for me. She's good at invisible darning.'

Jack bent down in front of her. 'You trying to get your own back, honey?'

One eye was fast closing, but the other gleamed in amusement. 'Frightened you, did I?'

'You sure did, and you're also going to have one hell of a black eye. Have you seen your face?'

She grimaced. 'I don't think I want to look.'

'Don't worry, there isn't any permanent damage done by the look of it. In a couple of weeks you'll be as beautiful as ever.'

'Flatterer.' She took hold of his hand.

Jack felt it shake and knew that she was putting on a show for them. She was more shaken than she was letting on. But so would he have been after a crash like that.

'What happened, Ruth?' Simon wanted to know.

'Everything was normal on approach. There wasn't anything to indicate problems. As I touched the field there was the almighty crash and the undercarriage collapsed. The plane skidded along on its belly before upending and flipping over. No warning sign came up to tell me it wasn't locked.'

'That's enough questions.' A doctor and nurse walked in. 'I must ask you to wait outside while we examine the patient.'

Jack leant against the wall in the corridor while Simon went to find a phone to let Jane know that Ruth was all right. That sure had been a close call. She could easily have been injured or even killed, and yet she was sitting in there complaining about a rip in her pants. But he knew only too well that there would be a delayed reaction. He had experienced it when he'd finally reached safety in France.

'I got through to Jane.' Simon stood beside Jack. 'She was very relieved.'

'Yeah, me too. We must have a look at that plane when we get back to the airfield.'

'Just what I was thinking.' Simon straightened up. 'Here's the doctor. How is she?'

'Bruised and shaken, but nothing's broken. However, we are going to keep her in overnight, just to make sure she isn't suffering from concussion. You can see her for a few minutes before they take her up to the ward.'

'I don't want to stay in,' were the first words she uttered when she saw them.

'But you're going to.' Simon spoke firmly. 'It's just a precaution, Ruth. Either Jack or myself will collect you in the morning and take you home.'

'All right.' She yawned, giving way easily. 'I do feel rather tired . . . Don't tell Mum and Dad, it will only worry them, and there's no real harm done.'

They agreed. Satisfied that Ruth was being taken good care of, they left, and once back at the airfield they made for the wrecked plane.

Jack removed his coat and tossed it down on the grass. 'I want to have a look in the cockpit.'

'You'll have a job getting in there, Jack. Let me have a go, I'm not as big as you.'

'I'll have a go first.' As the plane was upside down, Jack had to wriggle along and, after much struggling, managed to see inside the plane. He checked everything carefully, and then eased out again.

'What did you find?'

'As far as I could see everything looked normal.' He clambered up and examined the undercarriage, or what was left of it.

Simon joined him and whistled through his teeth. 'This is a real mess.'

'It sure is. I can't tell anything from this, so we'll have to wait for the investigators to find out what really went wrong.'

'Nothing more we can do at the moment, then.' Simon bent and picked up Jack's coat and handed it to him. 'You're the engineer, so what is your opinion? Mechanical failure?'

'I'd bet my last dollar on that. Ruth is too good, too careful and too experienced a pilot to have missed a warning sign. That would have been the kind of elementary mistake she would never make.'

'I agree.' Simon gazed up at the sky. 'The light's fading and we'd better get back. Lucy must be wondering where Ruth has got to.'

Lucy was looking out of the window when they arrived and she rushed out to meet them. 'Where's Ruth? Has she been stranded somewhere?'

'We've just seen her.' Jack urged his sister indoors. 'Make us some tea.'

'Not until you tell me why you're both here and she isn't.'

Simon made her sit down. 'She's all right, but when she landed, the undercarriage of her plane collapsed.'

'Oh, hell, but you say she's OK?'

'A few bumps and bruises. They're keeping her in hospital tonight. One of us will go and collect her in the morning.'

As it happened, Simon was the only one free the next day, and he was at the hospital by nine o'clock, knowing Ruth would want to get out of there as quickly as possible.

'Why don't you go and stay with your parents for a while?' Simon suggested. 'You're going to feel groggy for a couple of days.'

'That isn't a good idea.' Ruth touched her bruised face. 'I don't want them to see me like this.'

'Perhaps you're right, that's a real beauty of a black eye you've got there.'

She gave a worried sigh. 'Did you and Jack manage to get a look at the plane?'

'Jack squeezed himself in far enough to check everything in the cockpit, and then he examined the undercarriage. You know he's a genius with anything mechanical, but it was impossible to come to a definite conclusion on such a short examination. But, knowing you as he does, he's certain it wasn't your fault.'

'So am I, but it's a relief to know that.' She brightened up then.

By the time they reached the house it was pouring with rain, and they had only been there about ten minutes when Jack and Lucy arrived.

'Wow!' Lucy exclaimed when she saw Ruth. 'Are you sure you're OK?'

'Quite sure.' Jack kissed her and she smiled up at him. 'Has flying been rained off for the day?'

'Yep, according to the Met it's going to rain until tomorrow.'

Lucy was frowning at Simon. 'That's three of us who've had an accident. That leaves just you.'

'I'll pass on that.'

'You make sure you do, Simon.'

Chapter Thirty-Two

It was a week since Hitler had committed suicide, and everyone was waiting. The end of the war in Europe must be immanent. Ruth was back to ferrying, fully recovered from the crash.

'Good, you're here.' Andy caught up with her as she went to check in. 'I've received the results of the investigation. There was a serious mechanical failure and you've been cleared of all blame.'

She blew out a breath of relief. 'That is good news. Thank you, Andy.'

He was about to walk away when Sally rushed in. 'It's over! Germany has surrendered!'

People were now pouring into the Mess, appearing to come from nowhere. An Anson had just landed full of pilots, including Jack, Simon and Lucy. They were being told the news by excited ground staff, and then they all started to run.

'Is it true, Andy?' Simon asked as soon as they reached the Mess. The wireless was on but there was so much noise no one could hear it.

'Shush!' someone ordered.

There was immediate silence as they listened to the news they had waited over five years to hear. As soon as the broadcast ended, Lucy gave a yell of delight and began to rush around hugging anyone in sight.

'We did it! We beat the bastard!' She stopped and put her hand to her mouth. 'Oops, sorry, Jack tells me off if I swear.'

'I'll let you off this time,' he said, lifting up his sister and spinning her round. Then he handed her to Simon and caught hold of Ruth. 'We made it, sweetheart. We made it!'

There was so much noise in the room that Ruth wasn't sure she'd heard correctly. It sounded as if he'd called her sweetheart instead of the usual 'honey', but she couldn't be sure.

One thing she could be sure of: everyone was going wild with delight.

Andy and Jane shouted for quiet. It took a while to make themselves heard, but they finally managed to gain everyone's attention.

'Flying has finished for the day,' Andy told them. 'So go and celebrate.'

A loud cheer filled the room, and he held up his hand. 'But remember that the work of the ATA still goes on. I want to see you all back here in two days, sober and ready to fly. Now get out of here.'

The streets were full of people, all laughing and waving as the contingent of pilots from the ferry pool made their way through the crowds. The landlord of the pub had thrown open all the doors and windows, and people were pouring in.

'Everyone's welcome,' he shouted, waving to the pilots. 'Come and have a drink. I've got a couple of barrels I've been saving for just this celebration.'

The place was already heaving and Ruth laughed. 'We'll never get in there.'

'Yes, you will.' The landlord caught hold of Ruth and Lucy and began to push through the crowd, yelling at the top of his voice. 'Make way for my pilots, they get served first, and then the drinks are on the house until the barrels are dry.'

Amid much cheering, the crowd parted to let them through. The landlord slipped the men a small whisky with their beer, and the girls were given a clear liquid in a glass.

Ruth sniffed, then took a sip. 'Gin!'

The landlord winked. 'I've been saving that as well.'

There was a lot of pushing and shoving as everyone tried to get near the bar. 'Let's get out of here!' Simon shouted.

The garden at the back was just as crowded, but at least they were in the fresh air.

Jack tossed back his whisky and shuddered. 'My God, Simon, that's strong stuff.'

Simon did the same and then gazed at his empty glass. 'That wasn't watered down.'

Someone inside began to pound on the piano and with all the doors and windows open, it could be heard clearly.

After draining his beer glass, Jack caught hold of Ruth and began to jive with her. That was the signal for everyone to join in the dancing. The girls were passed from partner to partner until they were dizzy.

'Come on.' Jack appeared at Ruth's side again. 'We're going to London. They're having a hell of a time up there, so we've been told.'

They hurried back to the house where Simon had parked his car and piled in. Then they headed for London, wanting to be in the thick of the celebrations.

Trafalgar Square was a seething mass of people, singing, dancing and kissing everyone in sight. There were uniforms of every kind, and civilians, young and old. After the long years of war they were all determined to have a riotous time.

They joined in with a long line snaking its way round the square, until Simon gasped, 'Let's get a drink.'

Jack mopped his brow. 'Where on earth will we get in anywhere today?'

'Let's try the Savoy,' Lucy suggested. 'We had a great time there when we arrived. Do you know, I'm the only one of that first group who's stayed until the end?'

'Hey, this isn't the end.' Jack cleared the way through the crowds. 'We won't be able to say that until Japan has also surrendered, but this sure is a huge step in the right direction.'

It took some time to walk the short distance to the Savoy as everyone wanted to shake their hands, and Ruth couldn't help wondering how many people knew what they were, or what they had been doing during this long war. But they were in uniform and that seemed to be enough as they were all kissed over and over again.

'Wowee!' Lucy gasped. 'What's happened to that good old English reserve?'

'It'll soon be back,' Simon remarked dryly. 'But for now it looks as if anything goes.'

'Hey, Ruth,' Lucy said. 'Gussie can have her baby now.'

'It's due any day so we'll check on her tomorrow.'

When they reached the Savoy it was also packed, but it was much more comfortable than milling around in the crowds they'd just left. Jack asked if they had any rooms available, but there wasn't a chance, so by midnight they decided to drive back.

It was three in the morning before any of them managed to get some sleep.

'What a night!' Lucy was holding on to the sink as she waited for the kettle to boil. 'What's the time, Ruth?'

'Two o'clock. I wonder if the men are awake yet.'

'Doubt it.' Lucy poured from the teapot and stared at the cup in disbelief. 'Whoops, I forgot to put in the tea! I don't think I'm awake yet. I'd better start again.'

They had just made a fresh pot when Jack and Simon arrived. Without saying a word, Simon took two mugs from the dresser and pushed them towards Ruth. She filled them and watched them drink thirstily. They seemed to be able to talk after that.

'That's better.' Simon had a glint in his eyes. 'While Jack was still asleep I went to the ferry pool just in case we were needed.'

'I hope not,' Lucy groaned

'No, but there was a message from Harry. Gussie had a healthy boy at six last night. Eight pounds, one ounce.'

'She had it on the day the war ended!' Ruth laughed in delight. 'That's just the sort of thing you would expect from Gussie.'

Lucy was jumping with excitement, not a sign of her tiredness now. 'We've got to go and see her. They're in Scampton, Lincolnshire now, but how can we get there?'

Simon glanced at his watch. 'Jane was asking for a volunteer to collect Captain Anders. He's been visiting his family in Lincoln. I'll have to leave in an hour.'

The girls looked at each other, and then back at Simon.

'Are you taking the Anson?' Ruth asked, well knowing Simon's quiet sense of humour. When he nodded, she said, 'And what if three passengers stowed away before you took off?'

'I wouldn't even notice.'

Lucy gurgled and pulled Ruth to her feet. 'Come on, let's get going before Simon gets his eyesight back in focus!'

The men were laughing as the girls made a stampede for the stairs to collect the presents they had been saving for Gussie and the baby.

They were back in no time at all and Lucy grinned at Simon. 'I ought to call you Mr Fix-It.'

'I do my best, but remember: the flight is officially ATA business, so we'll go straight to the hospital. There will only be about an hour before we have to return.'

'That's plenty,' Lucy said. 'Thanks, Simon, you're a darling.'

There wasn't much activity at the airfield so they were able to take off at once, and were soon walking into the ward.

Gussie saw them at once and began waving frantically. 'Over here! How did you get here? I thought everyone would be sleeping off the celebrations.'

'We just had to come and see our godson.' Ruth gazed at the baby sleeping peacefully in a cot beside the bed. 'Oh, congratulations, Gussie! He's beautiful.'

Lucy wiped away a tear. 'I'll say! Clever you, Gussie, giving birth on such a special day! What better way to celebrate a new beginning? We've brought some presents for you.'

The parcels were all over the bed as Gussie tore them open, going into raptures as each gift was opened. There was an exquisite christening gown made by Ruth's mother, a complete set of knitted clothes from Lucy – she had turned out to be surprisingly expert with knitting needles, which was something Gussie had never mastered. There were also various baby plates and mugs. Simon produced a silver egg cup and spoon in a leather case.

Gussie was quite overcome, and when Jack handed her another small leather box, she had tears in her eyes when she opened it.

'It's to bring the little guy good luck,' Jack explained. 'It's served me well.'

Ruth was surprised. She had no idea Jack was superstitious. 'What is it?' she asked.

Gussie carefully removed the disk from the box and examined it. 'It's a silver dollar. But Jack, this is quite old.'

'Yeah, an old stunt pilot gave it to me when I was sixteen, but I don't need it now. I've had more luck than any man deserves.'

Lucy was studying her brother in amazement, but said nothing.

'Thank you, all of you.' Gussie held the silver dollar over

the cot. 'I'll be sure James knows what a fine man gave him this.'

'Is that his name?' Simon asked.

'Yes, we're naming him after Harry's dad. When we told him I swear there were tears in his eyes.'

'I'm sure there were.' Simon glanced at his watch. 'I hate to rush you all, but we mustn't keep Captain Anders waiting.'

'Thanks for coming, and for the wonderful gifts.' Gussie tapped the cot. 'Say cheerio to your godparents, James. We'll let them know when the christening has been arranged, won't we?'

The baby took absolutely no notice, and his mother smiled indulgently. 'His manners will improve. He's only interested in food and sleep at the moment.'

'That's what I call a sensible little man.' Jack leant over the cot and ran his fingers gently over the little face. 'You grow up like your ma and pa, and you'll do OK in life.'

When they were outside, Lucy caught hold of her brother's arm. 'I didn't know you had that silver dollar.'

'Old Buzz gave it to me. He said it had seen him through the First World War. I've written down the history of the coin and tucked it in the bottom of the box. I thought the little guy might appreciate it when he gets older.'

Ruth was touched by this gesture. That coin must have been a treasured possession, but he'd given it away to a new life. She was constantly finding unknown depths to this strong man's character, and each time her love grew. 'Did you have it with you in France?' she asked gently.

'Sure.' He placed an arm around her shoulder. 'Lucky,

huh? That's a fine boy they've got there. Let's hope he never has to face a war in his lifetime.'

They all heartily agreed with that sentiment.

When they arrived back at the airfield, Captain Anders was just getting out of a car. He studied his reception committee with amusement. 'Did it need four pilots to come for me?'

Lucy, open as usual, said, 'Simon's the pilot, but we came for the ride. Gussie's had a baby boy and we nipped in to see her.'

'Ah, that is good news. Are mother and baby doing well?'

'They're fine. Hope you don't mind us hitching a lift?'

'I'd have done the same thing, Lucy.' He glanced at Simon. 'Ready to leave? The war in Europe might be over, but we've still got work to do.'

'Do you know how much longer they're going to need the ATA, Andy?' Jack asked as they piled into the Anson.

'I haven't a date, but this will probably be our last year. I expect you're both looking forward to going home?'

'Mom will be pleased to see us again, won't she, Jack?'

He merely nodded, and Ruth gazed out of the window as they gained height. Soon this would all come to an end, and there was more than a twinge of sadness at the prospect.

Chapter Thirty-Three

15th August was the day of the christening. It was to be held in Harry's home town of Twickenham. Once again Gussie had chosen a momentous day for the occasion. It was VJ day. Two atomic bombs had been dropped on Japan, and they were such horrific weapons that Japan had had no choice but to give up.

Celebrations were in full swing, but in the beautiful old church there was peace, except for baby James complaining about the indignity of having water dripped on his head. Harry's parents were beaming with pride. Not only had their son survived, when so many bomber crews hadn't, but they had a delightful daughter-in-law, and the precious gift of a grandson. Not every family had been so blessed, and amid the joy there would also be sadness.

Ruth held the fretful baby in her arms. This was a new life in a world where so many had died. She was well aware that the return to normality wasn't going to be easy, but this child, and many more like him, was the future. She smiled down at him and found a curious pair of bright blue eyes gazing up at her. Then he caught sight of the wings on her jacket and a little hand reached out to touch, the colour obviously catching his attention.

Harry grinned and took his son from her. 'Want wings like that, do you, James? Well, you'll have to wait until you're older, but your mum and dad are both pilots, and so are all your godparents. Not many boys will be able to boast about that, will they?'

They went back to the house with Harry's parents and drank to the baby and the end of the war. Then they returned to Maidenhead and danced the night away.

There was still ferrying to do, but they all knew it wouldn't be for much longer. Jack and Simon were doing mostly cargo trips across the Channel in the Ansons, while the girls flew anything that came their way. There was a more relaxed atmosphere now, and they just enjoyed the flying without the pressure of the past few years.

Two weeks after the christening, Ruth and Lucy were in the Mess waiting to see if they could pick up another job, when Jack strode in.

Ruth glanced up from the book she was reading. 'Had a good trip?'

He nodded and sat with them. 'It was a bit bumpy over the Channel and the Met have just told me there's some bad weather coming.'

'Oh.' Lucy pulled a face. 'That means we might be grounded tomorrow. Is Simon with you?'

'Should be in any minute now. He's bringing a Spit back for an overhaul.'

Suddenly there was the sound of running feet and orders being shouted. Jack shot up and ran outside. Ruth and Lucy were slower to respond, but they caught up with him, and all three of them watched as a plane approached with smoke pouring from the engine.

'Is that Simon?' Lucy shook her brother's arm, agitated. 'Is it?'

He shaded his eyes. 'Yeah, that's him. Stay here,' he ordered, and moved towards the edge of the field.

'I saw flames, Ruth,' Lucy gasped. 'Oh, God, there's fire!'

Ruth had seen it as well and her chest was tight with fear, but she managed to grab hold of Lucy to stop her running forward. 'Leave it to the men. They'll get him out as soon as he's down.'

Jack was on the wing before the plane had even stopped. The war was finally over and there was no way he was going to let his friend die in peacetime.

The canopy was already open and Jack hauled Simon out, dragging him free of the plane with sheer brute force, and almost dragging him out of danger.

'She's going up,' Simon gasped as his feet touched the ground.

The explosion knocked them both off their feet and Jack shielded Simon from the blast.

'Get off me, Jack, you're bloody heavy!'

'Sorry.' He rolled to one side, grinning. 'Just protecting my investment in the flying school.'

'You're staying?'

'Yep. I've worked out a solution. All we've got to do now is make my sister realise she's in love with you, and we're in business.'

'I know she likes me, but I'm not sure her feelings are that deep.'

Jack stood up, dragging Simon with him, and then he laughed and slapped him on the back. 'I know my sister, and believe me; she's in love with you. She just hasn't realised it yet.'

'What are they doing?' Lucy was standing open-mouthed, unable to believe her eyes. 'They're laughing! What the hell's so funny? The pair of them nearly got themselves killed!'

'Let's go and find out.' Ruth was just as curious. They marched towards the men, who were dusting themselves down, looking rather pleased with things.

'What the hell do you think you're doing?' Lucy was livid. 'You've just frightened us out of our wits, and you look as if you're having a relaxing day in the country!'

'Now don't get so upset, Lucy.'

She shook off her brother's hand and stormed up to Simon. 'I told you not to have a crash just because the rest of us did, but you didn't listen, did you? Oh, no, you had to go one better and blow the damned thing up!' Tears of fright were streaming down her face.

Simon wrapped his arms around her and rocked her while she wept. 'Does this mean you care about me?'

'Care? Of course I care! I'm in love with you.'

'Will you marry me, Lucy?' he asked quietly.

The tears dried up and she gazed at him. 'Do you mean that?'

'I most certainly do. I fell in love with you the first time I set eyes on you. So, what's your answer?'

'Yes, yes, please!'

Jack winked at Ruth. 'About time she admitted that. Now we can sort everything out at last.'

'What do you mean by that?' she asked as they made their way back to the Mess.

'You'll see,' was all he said. Then he left her to take hold of his sister's arm and guide her away so they could talk in private.

Ruth stood beside Simon and smiled up at him, so relieved he had survived unscathed, and that he and Lucy were going to marry. 'Congratulations, Simon.'

'Thanks.' He chuckled. 'I had to nearly blow myself up before she admitted how she felt about me. I had to take advantage of the situation and ask her to marry me.'

'It certainly did the job.' Ruth turned her attention back to brother and sister. Jack was obviously explaining something to Lucy and she was nodding and laughing. 'What are they up to?' she asked Simon, puzzled.

'Sorting out some family business, I expect.'

The implications of Simon and Lucy marrying then hit Ruth hard. 'Will you be going to America to open your flying school there?'

'My plans are unchanged.'

She chewed her lip anxiously. Lucy might not want to live here, but it sounded as if Simon had no intention of leaving. 'It's complicated, isn't it?'

'Not at all.' Simon sounded quite confident. 'Jack's got everything in hand.'

'What do you mean?'

'You'll see.'

Ruth grimaced. 'Not you as well, Simon. Jack's just told me the same thing. I seem to be the only one who doesn't know what's going on.'

'I know you're worried Jack's going to leave, Ruth, but whatever he's planning, it will include you. The man's crazy about you and he just wants everything tied up neatly before he says anything.'

'I just wish he'd talk to me. We could sort out any problems together. You say he loves me, but not knowing for sure is making my imagination run riot. I'm being silly, I know that, but I do love him so much.'

'He's a man of few words, Ruth, we both know that, and it's only natural you feel unsettled, but you can take it from me that you have nothing to be concerned about.'

She nodded. 'I'll only relax when I hear that from Jack.'

This was the longest letter Bet had ever received from her son. She had read it through at least a dozen times, and then sent a reply straight away. What he was suggesting frightened her, but they were her children and their happiness was all that mattered to her. She couldn't be more pleased that Lucy was going to marry Simon, and she was excited about Jack's plans. She prayed it would all work out for him. She rubbed a hand over her middle as it churned in apprehension. But they were asking a great deal of her.

'Bet!' Kathy, her neighbour, rushed in. 'My boy's on his way home and will be here within the next couple of weeks!'

'That's wonderful news.'

Kathy was so excited she couldn't sit still. 'What about your two? When will they be home?'

'They want to stay in England until the ATA is disbanded.' Bet sighed and picked up the letter, already becoming dog-eared from constant handling. 'They've been there a long time, especially Jack, and they've made new lives for themselves and many friends. There are big changes ahead for the Nelson family.'

'But the war's over.' Kathy looked puzzled. 'Don't they want to come home?'

Bet smiled brightly, hiding her apprehension, not prepared to discuss this with anyone just yet. 'There's a couple of romances going on there, so they have a lot to sort out first. Lucy is going to marry Simon, and I'm hoping Jack and Ruth will marry.'

'How exciting! That will be worth waiting a bit longer for, won't it?'

'Yes, it will, and I'll be seeing them before the end of the year for sure. Now, tell me what your letter says.'

A week later, Ruth was no wiser about Jack's plans. Even Lucy wouldn't tell her, but how she was managing to keep her mouth shut was a mystery. She was bubbling with happiness.

'Won't it be great to be part of Simon's flying school, Ruth? As soon as the ATA don't want us any more we can concentrate on getting it up and running.'

This was a good opening for Ruth as Lucy was talking freely. 'How do you feel about living here permanently? Won't you miss your home, your mother and Jack?'

'This is my home now, Ruth.' Lucy hesitated, obviously censoring her words before she spoke. 'And of course I want to see Mom again . . . Ah, here's Simon and Jack.' Lucy rushed out to meet them.

Ruth fumed. She could strangle the three of them. They were keeping secrets from her, but she was damned if she'd ask Jack what he thought he was up to in case his plans didn't include her. That would be too embarrassing. But there was hope in her heart now. Lucy was staying here so there was a chance that Jack would stay too. Jack had given no indication that he intended to leave her and return to America for good. In fact, quite the opposite: he was even more affectionate and attentive, but still he said nothing about their future. If they did both make their home here then what would they do about their mother? Ruth recognised that this was a real dilemma for them.

She heard Lucy ask Jack if he'd heard from their mother, as she opened the front door to them. Then Jack's deep voice saying something Ruth couldn't hear.

When they walked into the kitchen they were all looking pleased with themselves. This was too much for Ruth and she couldn't stop herself saying, 'I think it's about time you told me what's going on. And don't stand there looking innocent. If you're planning something that doesn't include me, then all right!' She glared at Jack. 'We've been together a long time and I have a right to know if you're going to stay, Jack.'

'I haven't treated you right, have I, honey?' He placed a hand on her shoulder. 'It's all sorted out at last, so will you give me one more day and I'll explain everything?'

'One more day?'

'Yep, be on the airfield at eight tomorrow morning. I've got a surprise for you.'

'Why can't you tell me now?' She couldn't understand this delay. Why the continued secrecy?

'This isn't the time or the place for what I want to do. Will you let me do this the way I've planned?'

'Knowing you, Jack, I don't suppose I have any choice. I hope it's a nice surprise.'

'So do I.'

It was a strange answer, but she had to be satisfied with that. He would tell her what was on his mind when he was ready, and not a moment before. It was her own fault for falling in love with such a complex man, but she wouldn't change him for the world.

Chapter Thirty-Four

'Lucy!' Ruth searched the little house, but there was no sign of her friend so she assumed she'd left early to go out with Simon. They had a couple of days off and the weather was good; they were probably taking advantage of the free time. Jack had asked her to go to the airfield this morning and she was curious to find out what he was being so secretive about. She couldn't imagine why they had to be at the airfield before he could tell her about his future plans. But there was only one way to find out . . .

When she arrived he was standing by an Anson, and she walked towards him. 'Are you working today?'

He shook his head, looking rather nervous. He took hold of her hands and pulled her towards him. 'It was aircraft that brought us together, so I thought this would be the appropriate place.'

She frowned, wondering what on earth he was on

about. This was the first time she had ever seen him looking anything but confident.

'When we first met I promised to take you to Paris and buy you a new frock for the one I ruined. That's where we're going today . . .' He paused. 'But you'll have to buy one that you can wear at our wedding.'

At first, the words she had longed to hear from him didn't register properly. Then she gasped. '*Our* wedding?'

Now he looked worried. 'You do want us to be married, don't you? I hope you do, honey, because I'm staying and I'm never going to let you go.'

She laughed and threw her arms around him. 'Of course I do, you idiot, but I've never been sure that's what you wanted. I do love you so much, Jack Nelson!'

'Great!' He was relaxed and smiling now. 'Get in the plane, honey, we've got some shopping to do.'

She climbed in, still laughing. It hadn't been much of a proposal, but that was Jack, and she loved him just the way he was.

'He's finally got around to it then?'

'Lucy! I wondered where you'd got to this morning.'

'Oh, I just had to get out of your way or else I'd have spilt everything. Jack was determined to propose at the airfield.' Lucy wiggled in delight. 'I didn't know my brother had such a romantic streak in him.'

'Neither did I,' Ruth agreed, as she strapped herself in, then she reached out and took hold of Lucy's hand. 'I was so afraid he would go home and I'd never see him again.'

'Not a chance! That brother of mine is crazy about you,

and has been from the moment he saw you. He's never told you that, huh?'

'Never.' The plane began to taxi and Ruth looked at the front seats. Simon and Jack were in uniform, making this an official flight. There was also some cargo on the plane, but as this was a day off, Lucy and Ruth were wearing ordinary clothes. 'What's your mother going to say about both her children marrying and staying in this country?'

'She's over the moon.'

'What?' This was certainly turning out to be a morning of surprises. 'You mean she already knows?'

'She doesn't know you've accepted Jack's proposal yet, but we knew you would.' Lucy looked smug.

Ruth sat back. 'All right, you'd better tell me all about it.'

'Well, Jack loves being here, and he loves you, Ruth. He might not say it in words, but I know my brother, and he can't leave you. He knew I loved Simon even before I did, so he then had the dilemma of what to do about our mom. We both want to stay here because this is where our future is, but that wouldn't be fair on Mom. It would break her heart if we were so far away. Jack came up with a plan, but didn't know if she would even consider it.' Lucy beamed. 'But she has. Our mom sure has guts.'

'What's she going to do?'

'Come and live here, of course.'

Ruth was stunned. 'You mean she will leave her home and come and live in a strange country?'

Lucy shrieked. 'It isn't so strange . . . well, not much, and she'll soon get used to it. We did.'

'Suppose she hates it here?' Ruth considered this a tremendous step for Bet to take.

'She won't, but if by any chance she gets too homesick, Jack will take her back and see she's OK. Mom's only going to rent out her house until she's settled, and then consider selling it, if she's happy here.'

Ruth nodded. 'That's wise. When is she coming? I can't wait to meet her.'

'It might take a couple of months to deal with everything, so we thought it would be wise if we left the weddings until December. She'll be here by then.'

Even the weddings had been arranged, Ruth thought wryly, but she didn't care. It wouldn't be right to go ahead until Bet arrived, and December was just fine with her. 'Are we having a double wedding?'

'Not likely!' Lucy was horrified. 'You can marry after us.'

'Oh, thanks.'

'Think nothing of it.' Lucy peered out of the window. 'Do you think we'll be able to buy clothes in Paris yet?'

'I doubt it, but it will be fun trying.'

The plane banked as Simon made his approach to the airfield, and they were soon on the ground.

After seeing that the cargo was unloaded, they headed for the city in a Jeep that Jack had managed to borrow.

The place was full of servicemen, all enjoying the late summer sun, and it was surprising to see how quickly things were returning to normal. They had a drink in a cafe by the Seine and then set off to have a good look around.

Ruth walked beside Jack and looked up at him. 'Lucy tells me we're getting married in December.'

The corners of Jack's mouth twitched. 'I've made a lousy job of this, haven't I, honey?'

'I'm not complaining. I was afraid I was going to lose you as soon as the war was over.'

He stopped walking and stared at her in amazement. 'Not a chance! There is no way I would risk losing you. I've been in love with you ever since you snarled at me for spoiling your frock.'

'Do you know, that's the first time you've ever said you love me.'

'Is it?' He shook his head, puzzled. 'But I've shown you all the time how I feel about you. Actions speak louder than words.' He kissed her nose, eyes glowing. 'And I'll show you again tonight. We're booked into a cosy little hotel.'

'Are we staying the night?'

'Sure, this is going to be a romantic two days for all of us.' He took hold of her hands. 'I know you've been wondering what the hell I intended to do, but I couldn't say anything until I knew if Ma would come over here.'

'And if she hadn't agreed?' Ruth asked quietly.

'Then I would have had to return to America, but I'd have come back for you, hopefully bringing Ma with me. I can't live the rest of my life without you, honey.'

'You've had quite a lot to work out, haven't you?'

He nodded and took a deep breath. 'But it's all turned out fine, thank the Lord.'

'Come on, you two,' Lucy called. 'Don't stand on the sidewalk blocking everyone's way.'

'We're coming.' Jack took hold of Ruth's arm as they strode towards the others. 'About a December wedding, honey: you can choose a different time if you like, but we want Ma here first. She'd never forgive us if we married before she got here.'

'Of course she must be here. I wouldn't have it any other way.' Ruth nestled close to him as they walked along. 'December will be perfect.'

As Bet gazed around her home, emotion welled up in her. Her husband, John, had died suddenly when the children were so young. They'd moved into this house only a few months earlier, and she had been determined to make it the home they'd dreamt of. It had been a struggle, but she'd managed it by working two jobs, one while the children had been in school, and another three evenings a week. Kathy had been a good friend all through those years, and still was. Once Jack and Lucy were earning, they'd pitched in, and five years ago the house had been paid for. Leaving it was going to be tough, but she wouldn't sell it. And leaving her friends was going to be just as hard, but her children weren't coming back, and she had to be near them. With both of them marrying she might soon be a grandmother. How could she not be close enough to visit?

A tear trickled down her cheek and she brushed it away in disgust. Don't be so stupid, she told herself. It's just a house.

Kathy rushed into the kitchen. 'Bet, you remember Paula?'

'Sure, she's the little girl Al was dating before he went in the army.'

'He's just told me she's waited for him and they're going to get married. Isn't that wonderful?'

'Oh, Kathy, I'm so pleased.' Al had only been home for

a couple of weeks and was already back working with his beloved horses. She was so happy for her friend. Then an idea came to her. 'Where are they going to live?'

'That's a problem. As they both work at the stud they'll have to find somewhere in this area, but there doesn't seem to be much around to rent at the moment.'

'Would they like to rent this house from me?' Bet saw the surprise on her friend's face, as they hadn't discussed Bet's plans yet. 'Jack and Lucy aren't coming home, Kathy. They've asked me to join them in England.'

'What?' Kathy sat down with a thump, lost for words.

For the next hour Bet told her friend all the news.

'Oh, my, I'm sure going to miss you, but if I were in your place, I'd do the same. You make sure you write every week.'

'I promise. Now, do you think Al and Paula would like to live here?'

'I'm sure they'd love it. When are you leaving?'

'I've got to let Jack know when everything's settled here, and then he's going to book me a passage on a boat.'

'What an adventure you'll have! You must be pleased Ruth and Simon are marrying your two.'

'I am, and it will be lovely to meet them at last. Although I already feel as if I know them.'

'I'm sure you'll all be very happy.' Kathy tugged at Bet's arm. 'Come on, let's go and tell Al about the house. They'll take good care of it for you, Bet.'

'I know they will.' She was relieved. It was an ideal solution. She hadn't liked the idea of strangers living in her house.

* * *

It was late October before Bet was on her way. Not the best time to make the crossing, but she discovered that she was a good sailor and didn't suffer from seasickness like many other passengers. She was excited about seeing her children again, and to meet Ruth and Simon at last, but there was also a gnawing worry.

Bet leant on the rail and watched the grey, churning sea. It mirrored her anxiety perfectly. She had never been out of America before, and here she was, on her way to make her home in a new country. It was a country her children loved, but would she feel the same? Was she doing the right thing? Jack had been enthusiastic about the life they were planning for themselves, but he'd assured her that if she really hated it in England he would see she got back to America and was all right. She knew she could trust him. For all his restlessness as he'd been growing up, if he said he would do something then he did. He would always go out of his way to be sure he never went back on his word. Her children couldn't be more different. Lucy poured out her hopes and fears, but Jack kept everything to himself until whatever was troubling him was resolved, and only then would he talk about it.

They would be docking in Southampton in about two hours, so Bet stayed at the rail, waiting for her first glimpse of England.

Passengers were now coming up on deck, wrapped up against the cold wind. There were a few youngsters on board, coming home after spending the war in America. Bet wondered how they were going to adjust to life in a country drained by a long, hard fight for survival. They would have to get to know their families all over again. After such a long separation they would feel like strangers in their own country. Her heart ached for them. There would no doubt be difficult times ahead for both parents and children.

As the ship came into dock, Bet rushed to the other side so she could scan the waiting crowds. It didn't take her long to spot her tall son, and she fought to stop tears clouding her vision. It was so many years since he'd walked out the door to come and fly for the ATA. Lucy had told her he'd changed and she could sense this. There was a mature man on the quay, relaxed and at peace with himself. And there was Lucy standing beside him, as she had always done since she was a young child. They had both found what they had been looking for, and she would as well. At that moment her doubts melted away and she waved frantically.

It seemed to take an age before she could walk off the ship and be swept off her feet by Jack, and kissed and cried over by Lucy.

Another hour went by before they could retrieve her luggage. This was then loaded into the car belonging to Simon, they told her.

'Where are Ruth and Simon?' she asked, as soon as they were on their way.

'They're waiting at Ruth's house for you. Her folks have insisted that you stay with them until we can get you settled in a place of your own.' Jack cast his mother an affectionate glance. 'You'll like it there, Ma. They've been real good to us.'

'I know, Jack, but are you sure it's OK? I could stay in a hotel for a while.'

'Mom!' Lucy exclaimed. 'We wouldn't hear of it, and neither would Ruth's folks. They said you must stay with them for as long as you like. They've got a huge house. Simon's folks are also there waiting to meet you.'

'Oh dear.' Bet patted her hair. 'I look such a mess.'

Jack and Lucy laughed. 'You look fine,' they assured her.

'Ruth's mom is a great gardener,' Lucy explained. 'You wait until you see it in the spring. It's a glorious place.'

Jack relaxed as he listened to them chatting. He had known early on that he wanted to make his home here, and when he'd fallen for Ruth, there was no way he could imagine his future without her. The offer to be a part of Simon's flying school had made him even more determined to find a way to stay, but he'd needed to do the right thing by Ma and Lucy as well. It had been a dilemma that had caused him quite a few sleepless nights, but it had finally come right.

Chapter Thirty-Five

'They're here!' Ruth saw the car stop outside the house and she ran for the door. She was so looking forward to meeting Bet at last.

It was chaos as the introductions were made, and seeing that Bet was looking quite overcome by the welcome, Ruth took her upstairs to show her the room Alice had prepared for her.

Bet stood just inside the door and gazed around, stunned. 'This is beautiful. I've never slept in a four-poster bed before.'

'It's very comfortable.'

Bet sat on the edge of the bed and blew her nose. 'I didn't realise you had such a grand home. This is like a palace.'

'It's been in the Aspinall family for several generations, but it's a home, Bet, and you can treat it as such. Jack and Lucy have always loved to stay here.'

'That's right, Ma.' Jack came into the room. 'It's a great place to relax.'

'I've got a four-poster bed!' Bet looked up at her son and grinned.

'So I see. I must have a word with Alice. She never offered me that.'

Ruth's mother appeared at that moment and stood beside Jack, looking highly amused. 'You're too big for it. Your feet would have stuck out of the end, but it's just the right size for Bet.' Alice smiled. 'I've made tea, or would you prefer coffee? I've still got some left you sent me.'

'You've got to have tea, Ma. It's grand stuff, and got this country through the war. They drink gallons of it.'

'So do you,' Ruth teased.

'I needed it to keep me flying. The ATA never give us time to eat.'

They were all laughing as they made their way down to the sitting room. It was a cosy sight with a log fire burning in the grate and tea laid out ready for everyone. Bet seemed to relax immediately, but this lovely old house did that to everyone who entered it.

Bet had to tell them about her journey over, and when the mothers began to talk about arrangements for the weddings, Jack winked at Ruth. 'Time we left,' he said quietly.

They all said cheerio and got in the car to make their way back to the airfield.

Now Bet had arrived, plans for the future went ahead at full speed. Simon and Jack took a trip to Cornwall to check over the planes and make sure they were in good flying order. Ruth and Lucy toured around Heston looking for houses to rent. Simon had already obtained permission to reopen his flying school, so they needed to live as near as possible to the airfield. Then they went to see Bet.

They found her in the kitchen showing Alice how to make American pancakes.

'Lovely,' Lucy said as she greeted them. 'Have we got any maple syrup?'

Alice held up a bottle. 'This was in one of the parcels your mother sent me, but I wasn't sure what to do with it.'

'We'll show you,' Lucy said, as they all sat down to enjoy the feast. 'Mom, our flying school will be at Heston, as Simon has already explained to you, and we've been looking for houses in that area, but you need to tell us where you'd like to live.'

'Do you think it would be possible for me to find a small house in this area?' She gave the girls a fond smile. 'I don't want to get under your feet, and I'd like to stay near Alice and George, if possible.'

'I've told Bet she can make her home with us,' Alice said, 'but she wants her own place, and I can understand that.'

'I'm sure we can find something.' Ruth was delighted to see that Bet and her mother had become firm friends.

They went on to discuss the weddings and agreed that Lucy and Simon should marry the first Saturday in December, then Jack and Ruth the following week. That would give both couples a chance to have a short honeymoon and then they could all spend Christmas together.

'Gosh, that doesn't give us much time.' Lucy pulled a comical face at Ruth. 'We never did find suitable dresses in Paris, did we? What are we going to wear?'

'We could marry in uniform, I suppose.'

They all looked at Ruth in horror at that suggestion.

'You most certainly will not!' Alice exclaimed. 'I still have my wedding dress, and I'm sure it will fit you, Ruth.'

'And I've brought mine with me for Lucy. I'd heard all about the rationing and knew it might be difficult to get hold of wedding dresses.'

'Some girls have been getting round the rationing by having them made of parachute silk, but we haven't got time for that.' Lucy kissed her mother. 'Thanks, Mom, I'll be proud to wear your beautiful dress.'

'Me too, Mum.' The dress was exquisite, but Ruth had had no idea her mother still had it. 'That solves that problem.'

'What problem is that?' Simon asked as he and Jack arrived.

'Mind your own business,' Lucy teased. 'This is women's business.'

'Ah, in that case we'd better stay out of it, Jack.'

'Too right.' He stared at the empty plates. 'You been making pancakes, Ma?'

Bet stood up. 'Sit down and I'll make you a fresh batch. The farmer down the road gave us a few eggs. I can't get on with this dried egg stuff.'

'I'll give you a hand.' Alice disappeared into the kitchen with Bet.

'How are the planes?' Ruth asked Simon.

'Working perfectly after Jack got his hands on them. We can start bringing them back early next year, and we can have the school up and flying by the spring.' His face was alight with anticipation. 'Pupils are already coming forward for lessons.'

'That's wonderful.' Ruth caught Simon's excitement. The flying school had always been his pride and joy. Now he could start again, but on a much larger scale this time. They were anticipating a lot of youngsters wanting to learn to fly, and with four of them teaching they could take on a lot of pupils.

'There's one sad note.' Jack looked serious. 'There's going to be a closing ceremony at White Waltham on the 30th of November when the ATA flag will be lowered for the last time.'

There was silence around the table. They'd known this was being planned. Now they had the date.

As the Air Transport Auxiliary flag was lowered, Ruth knew that each pilot there had his or her own memories of the war years. Jack, Lucy, Simon and herself were lucky; they would continue flying with the school, but many were wondering if their flying careers were coming to an end.

Their families and various dignitaries were there to see the end of the ATA. Ruth glanced around, delighted to see that Gussie and Harry had been able to come. Bet was bursting with pride at the role her children had played in this unique organisation. They had come a long way to help a country in desperate need, and had been welcomed, respected and loved. The ATA had quickly built into an efficient force, consisting of many different nationalities, all individuals in their own right, but with a common passion for flying.

Ruth's thoughts turned to those who had become good friends, and those who had been killed doing the job, Tricia and Rob being just two of those to lose their lives.

Jack touched her hand as the flag was folded, and they shared the poignant moment. Words were unnecessary. They knew what a vital job they had done, and were proud to have been a part of it.

Now the future was ahead of them, but the memory of the golden wings they had worn with pride would always be with them.